1 MONTH
FREE
READING

at
www.ForgottenBooks.com

By purchasing this book you are eligible for one month membership to ForgottenBooks.com, giving you unlimited access to our entire collection of over 1,000,000 titles via our web site and mobile apps.

To claim your free month visit:
www.forgottenbooks.com/free816693

* Offer is valid for 45 days from date of purchase. Terms and conditions apply.

English
Français
Deutsche
Italiano
Español
Português

www.forgottenbooks.com

Mythology Photography **Fiction**
Fishing Christianity **Art** Cooking
Essays Buddhism Freemasonry
Medicine **Biology** Music **Ancient Egypt** Evolution Carpentry Physics
Dance Geology **Mathematics** Fitness
Shakespeare **Folklore** Yoga Marketing
Confidence Immortality Biographies
Poetry **Psychology** Witchcraft
Electronics Chemistry History **Law**
Accounting **Philosophy** Anthropology
Alchemy Drama Quantum Mechanics
Atheism Sexual Health **Ancient History**
Entrepreneurship Languages Sport
Paleontology Needlework Islam
Metaphysics Investment Archaeology
Parenting Statistics Criminology
Motivational

SOUTHENNAN.

By JOHN GALT, Esq.,

AUTHOR OF

"LAWRIE TODD," "THE ANNALS OF THE PARISH," &c.

> When royal Mary, blithe of mood,
> Kept holyday in Holyrood.
> — Hogg.

IN TWO VOLUMES.

VOL. I.

NEW-YORK:
PRINTED BY J. & J. HARPER, 82 CLIFF-STREET.

SOLD BY COLLINS AND HANNAY, COLLINS AND CO., G. AND C. AND H. CARVILL, O. A. ROORBACH, WHITE, GALLAHER, AND WHITE, A. T. GOODRICH, W. B. GILLEY, E. BLISS, C. S. FRANCIS, G. C. MORGAN, M. BANCROFT, W. BURGESS, N. B. HOLMES, M'ELRATH AND BANGS, E. B. CLAYTON, AND J. P. HAVEN;—ALBANY, O. STEELE, AND LITTLE AND CUMMINGS.

1830.

THE NEW YORK
PUBLIC LIBRARY
944608
ASTOR, LENOX AND
TILDEN FOUNDATIONS
R   1940   L

SOUTHENNAN.

CHAPTER I.

*Athens? pray why to Athens? you intend not
To kick against the world, turn cynic, stoic,
Or read the logic lecture, or become
An Areopagite, and judge in cases
Touching the Commonwealth? for, as I take it,
The budding of your chin cannot prognosticate
So grave an honour.*   THE BROKEN HEART.

When it was known in Scotland that Queen Mary had left Paris to embark for her ancient kingdom, the nobility and gentry, in great numbers, resorted to Edinburgh. Among others who hastened to welcome their beautiful sovereign was the young laird of Southennan, a gallant who for his knightly presence had then no parallel in all the west, and for the courtesy of his manners he was not less eminently distinguished among the most accomplished of the Scottish youth.

When the Lord Fleming went to France with the deputation from the three estates of the kingdom, appointed to witness the nuptials of Mary with the French king, young Walter of Southennan, then entering his sixteenth year, attended him as his page, and after the celebration of the marriage returned to England, where he completed his education, under the auspices of his maternal relations; for his mother was an English lady of high rank, the daughter of the Lord Derwent, to whom his father surrendered himself a prisoner in the mutinous field of the Solway moss, and by whom he was entertained more as a guest than a prisoner. During the period of that captivity the fair Isabel was wooed and won.

Soon after the marriage she was conveyed to Scotland; but before she was yet a mother, her husband was killed while hunting among the moors of Renfrewshire. His horse bounded in the chase, close to the edge of the precipice of Kempoch, and, startled by the danger, suddenly recoiled, and threw him over the rock. A large stone still marks the spot where the accident happened.

From the death of her husband the gentle widow spent her lonely days in the sequestered house of Southennan. A retreat more suitable for mournfulness could not easily have been found. The ruins of it are still standing. About five-and-twenty years ago they were picturesque and pathetical. Often have we contemplated them, wondering what could have come to pass there in the olden time, and indulged the romantic fancies which their lone condition and melancholy aspect inspired.

It was a quadrangular building, with an embattled gateway in the wall, which connected the two wings. The orchard and garden lay along the south side of the green hills of Fairlie, at the bottom of which it stood, and on which a computable number of the beech and sycamore shook their heads, few and far between. About a score of the meagre and naked ash marked out where an avenue might have been; and in them, time out of mind, certain magpies had been allowed an unmolested domicile. On the northern side of the mansion a little sparkling brook ran, whispering from its rimples peace and felicity to the genius of the place. In truth it was a pleasant and a shady solitude, such as if only graceful forms and gentle spirits could ever there have been inhabitants.

When the preparations for Southennan's journey had been completed, Abigail Cuninghame his mother's housekeeper, on the eve of his departure, on being summoned to bring lights as usual into her lady's bower chamber, said,

"I doubt mem we ha'e but one fair candle this night in the house. The night work wi' which we have been so thrang, wi' the making up o' the laird's needcessities, has caused a sore consumption of light. But as soon as he is aff the morn's morning I positively will ha'e another melting."

"Thou canst not think, Abigail," replied the lady, "that I am able to work at this lace stitching with only one candle."

"Gude forbid, mem, that I should be sae fantastical. It would pingle out your eyne; but I had a notion you wouldna, on sic an occasion, be inclined for any sort o' thrift, far less the particularity o' flowering cambric. I was thinking ye would rather ha'e been in a disposition to gi'e the laird a few words of motherly counsel, for if a' tales be true he'll no be out o' the need o't at yon place the Court, and to do so ye lack na the light o' wicks, the light o' wisdom's far better."

"Well, Abigail, let it be as thou sayest, send Southennan to me."

The message did not require to be carried far. At that moment the young laird entered the room, and Abigail, who at the same time had gone out, returned presently with the solitary candle, remarking to him with her old familiarity, that she trowed he would see worse lights before he got to the end of his journey, and that it was wholesome to use bairns betimes to hardship.

Southennan, who had been riding all day over the rough environs, being both tired and hungry, replied that he was in want of something more substantial than light, and requested her to bring him some refreshment.

"Now that's a moving calamity," said Abigail, "for ha'e not I packed up in Hughoc's basket every *dividual dressed bit o' eatable matter that's this night within the four walls of the house o' Southennan. Couldna ye laird thole till ye ha'e taken the first ride o' your journey in the morning."

Southennan laughed at the old woman's economical expedient, but his importunate appetite would not allow him to adopt it, so that in the end she was obliged to comply with his expostulation, and to open the basket. While so engaged, his lady mother, after some preliminary conversation touching the matters and things of his visit to Edinburgh, began to remind him that he was still but a very young man, and of small experience in the devices and crooked policy of the world.

"Thou art," said she, "of an easy nature, thinking too well of all men, by which thou wilt assuredly find detriment. Not that thou lackest discernment, for in that thou hast few superiors, but thou dost not act by what thou seest, nor hast thou suspicion enough to be watchful of thyself. Wert thou as true to Southennan, as I doubt not thou wilt ever prove thyself to be to his friends, thou shouldst not receive admonishment from me; but believe thy mother, who lovest thee with all a mother's imaginable affection for an only child, it would be better with thee if thou couldst account all the world knaves, until thou hast discovered the honest. I would not, however, have thee evade companionship. On the contrary, treat every one with courtesy, but let there be always dignity in thy familiarity, and more of freedom than of condescension in thy deportment, for such begets regard—condescension alone but cold esteem; beware of strangers, but I would not thou shouldst stand aloof from them, nor avoid their fellowship. I only counsel thee not to give them thy confidence, until thou hast noted well to what likings their habitudes incline. The spendthrift shun,' whether his prodigality come of dissipation or of negligence; there is ever danger in being in reciprocity with such. Be chary of thy words, even towards those whom thou mayest love best. Tell no man all thy opinion of another, and remember that the least thou sayest of any man it will be safest with thee; not that I would have this virtue of prudence shrivelled up into pusillanimity, but only drawn around thee as soldiers contract their camps for security. And remember also that thine ancestors on both sides have ever been renowned for their valour. In all thy deportment I beseech thee to study, that thou mayest be esteemed gentle, for who can be a gentleman that hath not gentleness for the supreme quality of his manners. In the fashion of thy dress observe propriety, in the style and colour look to those who are well spoken of, but to the button be no man's follower. As thou art of the world be like the world, and ever bear in thy appearance something of that which without apparent purpose shall mark thee out as one, that, free from conceit, hath yet some knowledge of his own worth. I would descant to thee, Walter, long on these topics, but if thou needest thy mother's counsel when thou art among thy companions, what I might say would avail thee little. In all things be thy reliance on God and thyself, and take care not to be often in the way of putting thy mettle to the test."

While she was thus speaking, Abigail Cuninghame having set out the refreshment, the admonition was interrupted by the young laird's rising to partake.

CHAPTER II.

"He called down his merry men all,
By one, by two, by three;
William would fain have been the first,
But now the last is he."

THE PILGRIM.

The retinue with which Southennan set out for the capital was rather more important than exactly accorded with the condition of his circumstances. It betokened that he carried with him high hopes and aspirations.

He was well mounted and gallantly attired, wearing in his black velvet bonnet the eye of a peacock's feather, fastened in a silver buckle studded with garnets and chrystals. His body-servant, Balby Stobs, was an elderly staid person, who had many years held the same office with his father; and it was evident at the first glance that he was a character not unworthy of his master's esteem, and in full possession of his own.

He wore a broad, flat, household-made blue bonnet, the brim of which overshadowed his face, unlike the smart erect cap of the Highlanders, which, by not protecting the cheeks from the shower, nor the eyes from the sunshine, is the cause of the distended lips and contracted eyes of that warlike and irascible race. It was without ornament, save a huge bushy tuft on the top instead of the nipple that surmounts the apex of the Highland bonnet. His jerkin was of homespun gray, over which he wore a blue and white checkered plaid crossing the back and breast from the right shoulder, and tied on the left over the hilt of his rapier. His gumashins were of dark gray worsted, fastened with red garters somewhat sprucely knotted in bows under the knee.

If we consider him as the squire, we must look to Hughoc Birkie as the page. A bold, round faced, thick set boy, with an open, blithe, careless countenance; a reckless heartbreak on account of his thoughtlessness to his aunt, the sagacious and thrifty Abigail Cuninghame, who much wondered for what he was so well regarded by the other servants; for she did not, as she often said, believe there was a single seed of any good in his whole body. Hughoc, in the general cut and colour of his dress and appearance was not unlike his superior Stobs; but over his right eye he wore a cockade with a brisk feather stuck in it, and besides the roses at his knees, his garters had long fringed ends twirling in the wind. The maidens of the household had often assisted in his decoration. He was not quite so handsomely mounted as his elder compeer; but his horse was good, a short bodied cob, in shape and humour as much like himself as a quadruped could be to a shapely sturdy boy.

The squire carried with him in saddle bags the garniture of his master, and Hughoc was placed in the midst of an aggregate of their common luggage and two baskets of provisions, like a cadger bound to a fair.

Besides the two servants, Southennan was accompanied by Father Jerome, a Catholic priest; for the family was papistical.

This consecrated person was a most commendable character. He had come from England with the lady, and had, previous to the young laird's visit to France, been his tutor, and had performed his duties with exemplary intelligence. He was now an old man, heavy and corpulent, but withal of such a quiet self-sustained temper, that neither the pranks nor the occasional neglect of Hughoc Birkie could disturb his equanimity. He rode a mule, an animal not rare in Scotland in those days; like himself, it was old and somewhat abated of its vigour; it was also, like himself, sedate and of a quiet tortoise-like nature, making seemingly small speed on the road, and as it never once deviated to the right or to the left, but went perseveringly forward, if it travelled slower in the day's journey than his companions, it never was the last that reached the stable-door in the evening.

The special business which took the old man at that time to Edinburgh, was known only to himself; perhaps his lady knew something of it; but if she did she concealed her knowledge by affecting to marvel at what could possibly entice him in his age to return into the world.

Southennan would have been pleased had Father Jerome staid at home; for he thought there was already enough of age in his cortegé, in the person of Stobs, to whom, however, he was much attached. Hughoc was deemed indispensable; but it was not so obvious to the mother of the young laird, that a raw country boy, who had never seen a nobler city than the village of Largs was in those days, could be of much service to a gallant in the capital. Hughoc indeed might have been well spared, had not his master privately resolved in his own mind to make some figure at Court, and thought he could do it better by the attendance of a brisk and handsome page, than by the admonitory presence of his graver squire; for Baldy had, among other distinguished virtues, innumerable good advices to give on all occasions; but his master, with the lightheadedness of a young mind, did not much relish the idea of riding the streets with Wisdom at his elbow.

Father Jerome was the first who mounted; he was out at the gate, and a good half hour on his journey, before Southennan was disentangled from the advices and benedictions of his mother. Hughoc also was timeously on horseback, but did not venture to advance before his master; he only curvetted his horse round the court for the amusement of the maids, and replied to their jeers and laughter as if he had been already a victor among them. The sedate Baldy had, with his characteristic circumspection, fastened his own horse by the bridle to the ring at the hall door, and walked his master's noble and well caparisoned gelding, as proud as the horse itself—a little troubled in mind that the laird should let so much of the cool of the morning slip away.

At last Southennan made his appearance; the mirth of Hughoc was instantly hushed, and, winking to the women, he retired to the opposite side of the court, to allow room for his master to pass first through the gate. The laird bounded into the saddle, and soon made his exit, followed by Baldy, who, albeit his years, sprung upon his horse with an air that would have done credit to the agility of a younger man. Hughoc followed him out of the court-yard, waving his bonnet in silence, with a look of expressive drollery, to the household and corners as he passed.

CHAPTER III.

"How sweet these solitary places are!
How wantonly the wind blows through the leaves,
And courts and plays with 'em.
————Hark! how yon purling stream
Dances and murmurs; the birds sing softly too."
THE PILGRIM.

The progress of Southennan and his men over the moors was slow. All traces of the road they took have long since been obliterated by the heath, if even then road it could be called, though it had been used from time immemorial, being the track of communication between the eastern and western parts of the kingdom and the Hebrides. It led from Portincross Castle, which stands under the promontory, beyond West Kilbride, not only to Edinburgh but to the Queen's-ferry. Some antiquaries say it was the road by which many of the ancient Scottish Kings were conveyed from Scone to the "store-house" of their ancestors in Iona.

On leaving his own gate, Southennan, following the route which Father Jerome had taken, passed southward to Kilbride, where, turning to the left inland, he proceeded over the hills and moors towards Paisley. His intention was to halt there the first night.

Had there been any choice in his option, he could not have chosen a more dreary course. After having ascended the hills, and so far declined behind them as to lose sight of Arran, and the dark mountains of Argyle, he came upon a wide, silent, and sullen heath, pathless in every direction save that in which the road lay. The road itself was more like the stony channel of a dried up brook than a highway. The hand of man had nothing to do in its formation; it was made by the hoofs and feet of the travellers.

Yet is that sullen solitude, in the sportsman's season, not without beauty or interest. The heath presented one rich and splendid carpet of purple; and Hughoc, for lack of cross-bow, snapped with his fingers at the grouse and other game, which rose on the right and left of their path, as they rode easily along.

When the cavalcade started the morning was bright and beautiful; a few thin feathery vapours, more like sun-gilded snowflakes than clouds, floated at rest in the azure, so high aloft that they had the effect of making the welkin appear as if it had been expanded into unusual spaciousness. The winds were asleep in the hollows of the moorland, but a soft western breeze rippled the distant sea, and made it flicker in the sunshine, while the gentle waves, as they spread in placid undulations on the sunny sands of Ardrossan bay, heard afar off, were musical in their murmurs.

To Southennan, whose mind was apt in delicate fancies, the sound, as it rose, softened by the distance, seemed like the churm of the mermaid, when she sits on the rock combing her green tresses, and wiling the young adventurer with the flatteries of the summer sea. He did not, it is true, confidently believe in the existence of these fallacious syrens; he only cherished the fancy of it, because it served as it were to people the void between the beings of the airy element and the unknown creatures which inhabit the depths of the deep; for Father Jerome had explained to him, that the mythology of the mermaids was but a pleasant impersonation of rocks and shallows in a murmuring calm, when the emotion of the softly rolling swell causes the tangle which hangs on them to oscillate to and fro, like the ringlets of a maiden when she combs her hair.

But as he proceeded over the dismal heath, these gay fables, which took their being in his imagination from the influence of the sunshine on the water, and the foreheads of the hills, gladdened by the morning light, were darkened with reflections of a duller hue.

Without being superstitious, beyond the ordinary credulity of the age, the mind of Southennan was delicately susceptible of impressions from the aspect and colouring of surrounding objects. His spirits often received their tone more from external circumstances than from any innate buoyancy or consttutional thoughtfulness.

As he ascended the height above Kilbride, when all the gorgeous assemblage of mountains and headlands, and the bright waters of the extensive firth, lay in the glory of the morning, he not only indulged his fancy in cheerful hopes and radiant anticipations, but encouraged the boy to sing, who had, unconsciously, commenced a ditty of the olden time. But as they rode farther into the desert of the heath, Hughoc obeyed the saddening genius of the solitude, and of his own accord suspended his song, while Baldy, symphonious to the wilderness, soon after began to lift up his lonely voice with an ancient ballad, describing a battle field in the moonlight, with widows wailing among the slain, seeking for those they had loved —and lost. As the day advanced, the soft and breathing air freshened into a breeze, which swept the heath with a sound like that of rushing water.

The road happened to turn suddenly into a shallow hollow, in which this sound was not heard, nor the breeze felt, and every thing was still. The travellers halted, for their plunge into this silence threw a momentary awe upon their spirits. Baldy forgot his ballad, and his master, clapping spurs to his horse, rode on as if excited by some prompting of resolution to escape from that dumb and dreary place.

They had not, however, proceeded far, when they again were all induced to halt ; the sound of a deep solemn voice chanting one of the canticles of the mass rose before them. Baldy crossed himself, and took off his bonnet, making a sign to the boy to do the same : the Laird looked back to them and said :

" It is Father Jerome, he is resting and waiting for us."

The old man had dismounted near a spring, by the side of which two large stones had been rolled by some benevolent traveller, for seats to those who might come after him. It was in a sylvan nook of the little valley ; for miles, on all sides, only the brown and barren heather was to be seen ; but here a margin of grass, bright and green, surrounded the well, and a few hazel and brambles hung over it.

Father Jerome invited Southennan to alight, as they could hardly expect to meet within the moors a fitter place for refreshing themselves and their horses. The laird acceded to the invitation, and Baldy and Hughoc also dismounted, and the store basket of Abigail was placed on the ground.

While Father Jerome and Southennan were enjoying their breakfast, the boy led his own horse down along the little rill which flowed from the spring, on the edge of which a fringe of verdure meandered through the heath, until it was lost in a strip of meadow,—the border of the Shaws water, a considerable stream which there crosses the moor. Baldy peevishly complained of the boy's thoughtlessness in not taking the mule, or another of the horses with him ; but he had not long indulged this humour, when Hughoc, who had disappeared behind a knoll, was seen re-mounted coming back at the gallop, in evident alarm and consternation.

CHAPTER IV.

"A frame of adamant, a soul of fire,
No dangers fright him, and no labours tire."
JOHNSON.

In the mean time Southennan and Father Jerome, taking no heed of their attendants, were making such incisions as blunt knives could accomplish on the dried beef, and teeth could inflict on the oatmeal bannocks with which Abigail Cuninghame had plentifully supplied their basket. Hughoc, however, as soon as he came up to Baldy, began to relate to him something very wonderful. His expanded eyes and distended nostrils indicating, as much as the vehemence of his gestures and earnest voice, that he had made some important discovery, at least that he deemed it such.

The young laird, who had observed his gesticulations, directed the chaplain's attention to the expressive pregnant looks of the boy. In the same instant that the holy father turned his head to regard him, Hughoc uttered a cry, and Baldy started, turning his eyes eagerly towards the bushes which overhung the spring where Southennan and the priest were taking their refreshment.

Southennan sprang hastily to his feet, but the old man, being much heavier, moved slowly round, and, laying his hands upon the stone on which he had sat, raised himself leisurely.

On the top of the bank, behind the bushes, a tall, swarthy, shaggy, and gaunt figure, with a cross-bow in his hand and a quiver of arrows on his shoulder, appeared. He was also armed with a staff in his grasp, almost as tall as a spear. It had a sharp, dirk-like point, fastened by a rude mass of iron, rayed with iron spikes, and a hook attached to it, a dreadful weapon, either for stroke or pull.

This rough, weather-beaten outlaw wore his vest and collar open. His neck was bare, of a bronze colour, and his breast was as shaggy as the bosom of a wolf; his locks were matted and knotty, and he wore an iron scull-cap, which seemed, above the tufty mass of his dark and grissled hair like the shaven scalp of an uncouth anchorite. His vest, which had originally been crimson, wear and the weather had changed into a dingy-purple: it had once possessed three rows of innumerable small brass bell-buttons, but many of them were then gone, and the gold-lace with which it had been trimmed was tattered and tarnished. His short trowsers scarcely reached his knees, which were bare ; his legs were also without hosen, and pieces of untanned ox-skin were tied about his feet, and came up like moccasins about his ancles—a primitive protection for the feet, partaking, in some degree, of all the qualities of the buskin, the shoe, and the sandal. From his belt he wore a broadsword, with a rusty basketed hilt, and a dagger, which by its glittering handle, contrasted with his robber-like appearance, suggested an apprehension that it had been the spoil of a foeman of some consideration.

Southennan looked at him with a smile, admiring his wild and stalwart form and demeanour, as he stood on the brow of the rising ground, like an oak which had been scathed by the tempest, or a tower which, though in ruins, was yet capable, with the freebooters it harboured, to make a stern resistance.

" What would ye, Knockwhinnie," said Southennan, for he knew the outlaw.

" Leave to go with you to Edinburgh," was the reply.

" How can you think of going to Edinburgh ?—you told me a price is set upon your head : you will be seized before we reach Paisley : but what would you in Edinburgh ?"

" Petition the Queen's Highness for pardon. I am not a guilty man, but an avenger. I but attempted to execute justice on the criminal who quenched the joy of my hearth."

" I have pitied you," replied the young Laird, " and will do so still, even to the hazard of my own undoing. I will try what may be done to procure a remission of the sentence proclaimed against you, but it is not meet that you should travel publicly in that garb on the highway."

" If that be all it is soon doffed," replied Knockwhinnie ; and, turning round, he blew a small ivory whistle which hung from his neck by a light silver chain, and descending to the spot where the provisions were set out, on the invitation of Southennan, largely partook of them.

As he was eating, Father Jerome frequently turned his eyes heavenward and crossed himself. Baldy gave his attendance with an unvarying visage, but Hughoc every now and then stooped and turned up the corner of his eye with a degree of shrewdness and awe, evidently wondering wherefore it was that such an outcast was treated with so much courtesy. Before

Knockwhinnie had finished his repast, a young man, bravely appareled as a groom, came to the top of the rising ground, leading by the bridle a splendid horse, and mounted on another scarcely less superbly caparisoned. The outlaw, waving to him with his hand, immediately arose, and followed his servant to that knoll on the heath, from behind which Hughoc had so hastily returned.

Southennan stood for some time silent and perplexed. At last, bidding his servants partake of the refreshments, he touched Father Jerome slightly on the arm, and led him off to a short distance from them.

"What shall we do?" said Southennan: "this desperate man will assuredly come with us."

"The presentation of his petition," replied the chaplain, "is plainly not all the intent which takes him to Edinburgh; he has, I am persuaded, some other purpose; for, were it not so, it had been better for him to have trusted you. What is his story? I have sometimes heard of his name, but I knew not that he was so near a neighbour."

"Nor did I," said the young Laird: "his usual haunt is beyond the Gryfe, and about the pad of Neilston. Of his story I know but little: it was however from himself I heard it, and it was tragical. I will, however, ask him to tell me more of it."

"Surely," cried the alarmed priest, "you will not permit an outlaw, and such an outcast-looking trooper to travel in our company."

"He has said he will come," replied Southennan, "and I fancy he intends to do so, for I apprehend he is one that will have his own way. I have remarked, however, that he hath such breeding, that were I to refuse him, he would not mix with us, but follow. Indeed, to acknowledge the truth, Father, but for the risk he runs himself, I should not be displeased with his company—the weather and a bed on the heath, with but the heavens for a tester, have done more damage to the man than to the knight."

"Is he of that degree?"

"That you ask, makes me doubt, but only because I never heard. I have, however, observed that, short as our acquaintanceship has been, much of his roughness is put on, and when unguardedly he talked of a courtly pastime, he spoke as one that had flourished in the eye-light of fair ladies, with gallants of knightly urbanity."

While they were thus conversing, Knockwhinnie reappeared, mounted, and in costly apparel. He was now equipped like a prosperous gentleman, wearing a lofty plume in his cap, and though his embrowned complexion could not be so speedily changed, he bore a proud and warlike port, confirming to Father Jerome the opinion which Southennan had expressed.

"For a time, Southennan," said Knockwhinnie, as he drew near, "I have cast my slough—think you the outlaw will be recognised in this garb?"

"No, not the outlaw," replied the young Laird, eyeing him thoughtfully, "but one that made him so may."

"Allons!" cried Knockwhinnie, gently pricking his horse, and adding, "the Queen, I have heard, brings a noble company with her from Paris, and I may see among them some of my French friends."

Father Jerome, at these words, exchanged looks with Southennan, who said briskly,

"Then it is not for your pardon only that you seek the Queen's presence, and undertake this hazardous expedition."

"No," was the answer; and with a dark and searching look, he muttered deeply and hoarsely into the ear of Southennan, "I seek revenge."

CHAPTER V.

——"Here's a rich devouring cormorant,
Comes up to town with his leathern budget stuffed
Till it crack again."
THE FAITHFUL FRIEND.

FATHER Jerome, having again mounted, was the first who left the spring where the party had refreshed themselves, steering his mule at her sober accustomed pace across the heath. Southennan and Knockwhinnie rode together, and at some distance behind, Stayns, the servant of the outlaw, with Baldy and the boy followed.

By this time the wind had risen and blew gustily over the moor, and the skies overcast threatened rain; but owing to the interest which Southennan took in the conversation of his companion, the pace of the travellers was not mended, and their servants in consequence had leisure for a chat in their way.

Baldy had not much faith in Stayns on several accounts; first, because he was an English lad, and rather more familiar, as he thought, than became the rank of his servitude; and secondly, he belonged to a master who for some other cause than the " biggin o' kirks" was then not on very intimate terms with any sort of household society; but the greatest cause of Baldy's dislike was his irreligion, as he scarcely seemed to know the difference between the old and the new faith. He, as well as all the house of Southennan, was of the Roman Church; but with the exception of himself and Abigail Cuninghame, none of the servants were very inveterate in their attachment to the worship of their fathers; few, indeed, of the common people were as yet well acquainted with the special doctrines of the heresy. Even Father Jerome was not deeply versed in that matter; he took more pains to preserve the old piety alive on the household altar, though it sometimes flamed but feebly, than to heap it with the billets and coals of bigotry.

Thus though it happened that Baldy was civil to the servant of his master's companion, he yet manifested no particular inclination to cultivate his acquaintance, but behaved towards him with a degree of taciturnity that might not have been ill described a sulkiness.

Stayns was a lively, shrewd youth, and not being altogether satisfied with the uncompanionable humour of Baldy, after some time dropped behind, and threw himself into discourse with Hughoc, who was then whistling aloud to cheer his courage up; for he was somewhat disconcerted at the idea of visiting the Royal Court in the company of a banished man. Whether Stayns had any pranks to play upon Southennan's squire and page, or was only stirred by curiosity, time will determine; but after some light and jocular remarks to the boy, he said,

" This affair of going to see the Queen will cost your master something."

" Is'e warrant it," replied Hughoc—" twal pennies and a boddle—they say it is dreadfu' dear to live in Embro."

" Yes," rejoined Stayns; " and fair cost is not the worst of it. I hope you have not only a purse well filled, but a snug pocket to keep it in."

" As to the filling," said Hughoc, " the less said on that

2*

head the better ; but it would tak the supplest finger on Clootie's claw to find the pouch that I keep my purse in."

" And doubtless the old priest there has been equally provident," said Stayns.

" Whisht—whisht!" cried the boy, " Lord sake gin you speak o' his purse ye'll hae cauld iron in your kyte like a flash o' lightning."

" Indeed!" replied Stayns : " has he then such a treasure ?"

" Ye shouldna' speer at me, for I'm a' but sworn no' to say a word about what he has or what he has na' ; but the likes o' his valise is no to be found at every dyke side, as ye may guess without speering."

" Why ! I have not travelled with such a well-furnished company this many a day," said Stayns, with an emphatic laugh. " And your master, what may he have taken with him ?"

" Lord! man, ye're awfu' curious! What ken I what the Laird has ? Ye should ask himsel', if ye're greenin 'to ken." And with these words, Hughoc, giving his cob a hearty cut with his whip on the flank, was alongside of Baldy, leaving Stayns to follow by himself.

" Man Baldy, that Knockwhinnie's man is an unca' queer fish ; he has been wiseing by a' manner o' means to learn what siller we ha'e about us and amang us."

" Has he ?" cried Baldy, with a look of alarm.

" 'Deed he has, and to let you intil a secret, Baldy, I'm no' sure that I like it. Didna' ye say that his master was a rank ringing robber ? Gude safe's ! I wish we hadna' foregathered wi' him."

" I hope," said Baldy, not quite content with the news, " ye gave him no satisfaction as to what we ha'e ?"

" Just as little as I could in decency," replied Hughoc ; " but it wasna' possible to pretend that we were gaun to Embro' to link and gallant wi' the Queen, an' de'il-be-licket in our pouch : though the lad's only an Englisher, he's no' sae saft as to believe that spade shafts will bear plums ; but I hope we'll be in the town of Paisley before dark, for a' that."

" I hope we shall," replied Baldy; " but what said he to you, Hughoc ?"

" Na, that's no' an easy remembrance ; but it was a' to the purpose o' what I had, and what ye might have ; and he counted in his ain mind the Laird at mair merks' worth than was gude manners."

"I'll tak' an occasion to tell Southennan," said Baldy, thoughtfully: "we must ha'e a' our eyne gleg about us."

"Oh! Baldy," cried Hughoc, "surely ye're no feart that they'll do us an injustice, are ye? What if, when we're asleep in the night, they should ——"

"Whisht!" cried Baldy, softly; Stayns being by this time close behind them.

"This Scotch wind is confoundedly cold," said he, as he came up.

"Ay, it's a geyan' droll wind," replied Baldy, constraining himself into more affability than he had hitherto shown to the stranger.

"Droll!" exclaimed Stayns, "I think it devilish sulky."

"Is the deevil a sulky thing, think ye?" interposed Hughoc, attempting to imitate the sandy suavity of his superior.

At that moment, the Laird and Knockwhinnie having reached the top of a rising ground, which overlooked the vale of the Gryfe, and the wide-spread heath, patched with a few fields in crop, between it and the Cathkin hills, halted and called to Baldy to bring him his cloak; for the clouds, which had been thickening in the west for some time, were breaking in the valley, and the shower, careering along the plain, warned the Laird to provide against it. Baldy rode up with the cloak, and while assisting to put it on, Knockwhinnie rode forward.

"Ye'll ha'e a deal of auld acquaintance wi' that gentleman," said Baldy to his master.

"No," replied the Laird, carelessly, neither particularly heeding the remark, nor the significant manner in which it was expressed; and he added, "I have heard more than I have seen of him."

"That's very satisfactory—very," rejoined Baldy, "for I wouldna' ha'e just been content to tak' so lang a journey wi' an utter stranger; nor would I let wot to him, or any other body, what money I had wi' me."

Southennan turned quickly round, and, looking Baldy steadily in the face for a moment, said, with a smile, "So, you don't like him?"

"I'll no' say that," was the reply, "for he is certainly a very well faur't and discreetly mannered gentleman; but's no' every gude master that has a servant worthy o' him."

"What know you of his servant?"

"'Deed, Laird, I may easily answer that question; for I ne'er saw him atween the eyne till he brought up the horses at yon uncanny whistle; but there's a kennawhat about him that's no' just in our ain auld honest country fashion; but maybe the lad canna help it, for the Englishers in general, especially them that's born and bred amang horses, never demean themselves like our sober and weel-behaved farm lads; they ha'e an unco' turn for latherons and revellings, which canna' be upheld without money, and where they get the power o' money that many o' them wastes, is a wonder to industrious folk. Hech! but yon's a heavy shower that's coming o'er the knowes; hows'ever, I'm blithe ye ha'e gotten sic an excellent character o' the master."

"Nay, as to that, Baldy, whether he dirked one or ten, he has not confessed to me."

"Jesu Maria!" exclaimed Baldy, "that's bad enough; it might, hows'ever, ha'e been waur, if it wasna' dune in a righteous cause. But the rain's coming on, and yonder he's waiting for you. I redde you, master, to tak' care o' yoursel'."

The Laird rode forward. Baldy, with the other servants followed, his confidence neither in the integrity of master nor man much increased by his colloquy with Southennan.

CHAPTER VI.

The day is lowering—stilly black
Sleeps the grim wave; while heaven's crack,
Dispers'd and wild, 'twixt earth and sky,
Hangs like a shatter'd canopy.

MOORE.

THE rain continued to increase; but the wind subsided as the travellers descended to the lower part of the moors, and a thick mist gradually settled around them, insomuch that they were often perplexed to recover their path when they happened to step aside from it. This made their progress slower than they had calculated, and the journey to Paisley, which was expected to be concluded early in the afternoon, appeared likely to occupy the whole day. In the mean time, Knockwhinnie had disclosed so much of his history to Southennan that the Laird's opinion of him had very much improved. Greatly to the astonishment both of Baldy and Hughoc, they observed that their master addressed the outlaw with a degree of deference, inconsistent with what they conceived to be the odds between their respective degrees of consideration.

With the wonted caprice of the moorland weather, after the lazy mist had for upwards of two hours crawled in its palpable obscurity over the ground, the wind suddenly changed, and it was immediately resolved into a thorough soaking rain, which obliged the travellers to mend their pace, the road appearing more distinctly before them, and to ride for shelter towards a house which they saw at some distance standing a little off the road.

This house had something more considerable in its appearance than an ordinary farm-steading; it was two stories, the lower windows were grated, indicating a consciousness on the part of the inmates of danger; those on the upper floor were also gloomy enough, for only a small strip of the upper part was glazed, the rest having shutters, or more properly doors, to keep out the wind: these were unpainted, and the boards were darkly tinged by the weather; yet altogether it was not a desolate place; on the contrary, considering the age and situation, it was entitled to the epithet of respectable.

Southennan, who was acquainted with Kinlochie, the possessor, rode at once to the door, and sought shelter from the shower for himself and his party: this was readily, and even jovially granted; for Kinlochie was one of those hearty free characters, of a rough and wild time, who do not stand much on etiquette, but gladly receive their friends, without sufficiently considering how far it may be suitable to the circumstances of their own household and domestic economy. He therefore made Southennan and Knockwhinnie sincerely welcome, and the house rang with imprecations on all concerned, for their tardiness in not getting fires lighted, and what change of apparel the chests could afford for the dripping travellers.

At first his civilities were chiefly directed towards Southennan, whom he regarded as his chiefest guest; but when the fire blazed up (for the windows being closed, the apartment was obscure), a strong light brightened on the face of Knockwhinnie, and made him suddenly pause, and look eagerly for a moment at the outlaw. It was evident he was moved by some recollection of his features, and Southennan observed his emotion, but took no notice of it to him then. By a significant glance, however, at Knockwhinnie, he apprised him that their host seemed to have some knowledge of him.

The embrowned visage of Knockwhinnie underwent no change at this intelligence; but he undoubtedly felt some degree of alarm, although, on looking at Kinlochie, he could recall no remembrance of ever having seen him; for he said in a whisper to his young companion, when their host left the room for a moment, "He knows me, you think—what is it that he knows?"

"I shall soon ascertain," replied Southennan, and instantly followed Kinlochie, whom, much to his surprise, he found standing near the door in a state of hesitation.

The apartment into which the guests had been shown to dry themselves was a sort of domestic parlour, which opened from a more considerable chamber, that served for all the uses of the hall in greater houses, in those days of feudal hospitality; a large chimney blazed high at one side, near to which the servants were seated, together with two of Kinlochie's own men, and whose presence was the cause of his hesitation.

"I am glad you have come out, Southennan," said he, as the young Laird appeared; and drawing him aside, he added, "Were you acquainted before with your companion? for I understand he joined you with his man on the moor."

"Why, Kinlochie, you surprise me; for that is the very question I am come to ask yourself, as you appeared to have some recollection of him."

"Then he is but a way-side acquaintance," rejoined Kinlochie, with a degree of gravity and earnestness which Southennan could not but remark, especially when his host said, in a warm friendly tone, "Are ye sure of being safe, in these wild times, in travelling with a stranger?"

"Knockwhinnie is not altogether a stranger to me," was the reply.

"Knockwhinnie!" cried Kinlochie; "is that the name he goes by?"

"Has he any other? By what you say, it would seem you know him, or his right name—what know you of him?"

"Nothing, in the way of acquaintance; but I have seen him before, and under circumstances that cannot be soon forgotten: I would rather, for the friendship I bear you and all your kin, that I had seen you in less questionable company."

"But tell me why you say so; in what circumstances have you seen him?"

"It is a tale that will take time to tell; but I wish he were well out of my house, for while he is in it, I must needs protect him."

"I beseech you to let me know something of what you allude to; it would seem there is hazard in his company, and you cannot better show your friendship than by putting me on my guard."

"You know I was at the siege of Leith; the kingdom was then in an unsettled state, and men righted themselves with their own hands: the law was too tedious. Sometimes, in the intervals of the siege, I went, with others of the camp, to Edinburgh; and there, one evening, at the cross, we saw one of the queen dowager's French gentlemen, whose name we knew, standing there with others, when a belted knight came suddenly up to them, and, without saying a word, plunged his dirk into the French gentleman: that knight was he whom you call Knockwhinnie: he instantly fled down one of the closes which lead to the Grass Market, and escaped: I would know him again among ten thousand men; you call him Knockwhinnie?"

"I know him by no other name: what cause was assigned for the assassination?"

"None; he had but the night before, it was said, arrived from France, and, for some dishonour done to him by Dufroy —so the French officer was called—inflicted that vengeance."

"Dufroy! said you? the gentleman still lives!"

"That may be; he was not then killed, though grievously wounded."

"Good heavens! Dufroy!" exclaimed Southennan, unconsciously to himself.

"Then you know him?" replied Kinlochie; "how may that be? for this event took place when you were but a stripling, and it was rumoured at the time, that Dufroy returned with the French troops to France."

"But I have been at Paris, as you know; and there I met with the Count Dufroy, who had been in Scotland: I became his debtor for many courtesies."

"He is reported to be coming over again in the Queen's retinue," said Kinlochie.

"You say the cause of the attempt on his life was not known; what could it be?"

But Kinlochie could give no farther information. The business of the siege had, on the night of the attempted assassination, so engrossed the attention of every one in the camp, that even those who had witnessed it were wholly interested by their own duties, and had not leisure even to think of other concerns.

CHAPTER VII.

> " I'm like a wretched debtor,
> That has a sum to tender on the forfeit
> Of all his worth, yet dare not offer it."
>
> A WIFE FOR A MONTH.

WHEN Southennan returned into the chamber where the Outlaw was sitting, his countenance was so clouded that Knockwhinnie said to him—

" Well, what have you learned ; what does he know of me ?"

" Not much : but he was present when you attempted the life of a gentleman at the Cross of Edinburgh."

" Many more were there," replied the Outlaw, dryly and thoughtfully. " It is strange he should have recollected me so well, for it is not likely that he knew me before. I had been many years in the Guards of France, and I came to Edinburgh but the night before that unfortunate affair, nor has he seen me since : but it is often said, that a glance of a man, in certain circumstances, is sufficient to enable you to recollect him ever after."

" It gives me pleasure," said Southennan, " to hear you speak with regret of that affair ; I trust the wrong by which you were instigated has been remedied ?"

" It cannot be," said Knockwhinnie, with a sigh.

" I thought it might," replied the young Laird, " because you called it unfortunate."

" It was so," cried Knockwhinnie, sternly, " for the blow failed."

" The wrong must be deep that time cannot mitigate."

" It was, Southennan ! it crushed my heart : my wife was his victim. His life alone can appease my vengeance."

" But are you well assured of the guilt of Dufroy ?"

Knochwhinie started from his seat at the name ; but mastering his emotion, he immediately resumed it, saying, with resolute calmness, " You have heard his name ?"

" Even so ; and I have known the Count. He treated me with much kindness when I was in France. I have not since seen a worthier gentleman."

" Oh, yes,—he is not without virtues. Had he been

less worthy he never could have done me such irremediable wrong."

At this crisis of their conversation Kinlochie hastily entered, and addressed himself abruptly to Southennan.

"A man on horseback has just come in, who says, that early to-morrow the Sheriff will be here with a troop of horses, having received information that an Outlaw is somewhere lurking among these moors."

"I am here; and you know it!" cried the Outlaw, springing from his seat, and in the same moment standing over him with his drawn dagger.

"Put up your weapon, sir," said Kinlochie, coolly, for he was a brave soldier; "I respect the protection which my roof affords, but it were safer to evade the search than to hazard being taken here. Does your man know you?"

"I believe not; he may guess; but he is trustworthy.—Do yours, Southennan, know?"

"No; but the circumstances in which we joined will make them probably guess."

"Then," replied Kinlochie, "it were as well you were all off together, and that you made some change in your route. I would advise, that, instead of proceeding to Paisley, you cross the Clyde at the Renfrew ferry, and take the road by Glasgow, to Linlithgow. The clouds are breaking, and promise a fine evening; some repast for you will soon be ready; when you have taken it I would urge you to depart."

The reason in this advice Southennan was not altogether inclined to follow: he was averse to be mixed farther up with Knockwhinnie's ravelled fortunes. He, however, said nothing; leaving it to his own sense of propriety, considering the manner in which he had obtruded his company, to adopt the course which his danger so obviously pointed out. Knockwhinnie, indeed, was sensible of this, and observing the silence of Southennan, said—

"Let not this affair, Southennan, have any influence on you. I should have been happy to have passed with you, but it may not be. With you, I should have been less noticed than in travelling alone."

Finally, it was agreed that the Outlaw should proceed by the way of Glasgow, and Southennan pursue the course he had originally intended to take. In the meantime Father Jerome, whom they had left behind, following, despite of the rain, at the wonted precise pace of his mule, came up to the house where he conjectured they had taken shelter. From him they

Vol. I.—3

learned that there were several other horsemen on the moor, by one of whom he had been informed that the Sheriff was already out, and that some of those whom he had seen were men of his party, nor was it improbable they would come to Kinlochie's that night.

This information disturbed the whole party. The risk of Knockwhinnie in going before the evening was evident; nor was his safety very certain even by remaining in the house, as it was not improbable that the wetness of the weather would drive in those who were in pursuit of him.—Some time was in consequence spent in idle debate as to what should be done, when Southennan proposed to depart at once.

"We must risk something, whether we go or stay," said he, "and I would rather risk it at once."

Kinlochie approved of this, but urged them to separate as soon as practicable; his regard for Southennan made him anxious that he should incur no farther hazard with the Outlaw, who was equally anxious that they should not continue together, now that he saw the difficulty into which Southennan was likely to be brought on his account. But the danger of the Outlaw acted differently on the feelings of Southennan. Desirous as he was a few minutes before to escape from the entanglement into which he had been so innocently drawn, he felt for his condition; he thought there was something like pusillanimity in quitting him at his utmost need, and, for some time, an honourable controversy arose between them, the one being eager to separate, and the other averse to permit it. Kinlochie, however, was too eager on his own account to be rid of the whole party, to leave the contest to themselves. He reminded them, that while they were debating, the enemy was drawing nearer, and urged them to settle the question rather on the road, than by delaying their departure; at last he succeeded, and after making a hearty meal, they prepared to set out.

It happened, however, that Father Jerome had been so thoroughly wetted that he was obliged to undress, and hang his clothes at the fire to dry. Southennan, who observed Knockwhinnie once or twice throw his eye wistfully towards them, said—

"If they would fit—there have been worse stratagems, in situations similar to yours, than taking possession of them."

"I have been thinking so," replied the Outlaw; "but what would the chaplain himself say?"

"We must not wait for his consent, if they will serve."

While thus speaking, Father Jerome, who, for lack of other garments, had gone to bed, sent a message by Baldy, requesting to speak with Southennan; who immediately obeyed the summons.

As soon as he had left the room, Baldy said, in a suppressed voice, to Knockwhinnie, "I doubt, sir, that the man in the ha' has mair business to do here than to dry himsel' at the fire; and may be it were better if ye could get to the other side of the knowe before he sees you; for I ha'e gathered frae him that the Shirra's men are already out, though he said they were no expected afore the morn: and that he himsel' is one of them."

CHAPTER VIII.

" He must break thro' three doors and cut the throats of ten tall fellows, if that he escape us."
THE LOVER'S PROGRESS.

THE departure from Kinlochie's house was managed with some address. The Outlaw went out alone, and his horse was taken to him by Stayns. Soon after, Southennan and his servants mounted at the door, and followed; but it was thought as well to leave Friar Jerome and Hughoc, to bring up the rear.

As they approached the more settled country, Baldy was sent forward, and directed to conduct himself like an ordinary traveller, and to have his eyes and ears open to all sorts of information: instead of going to Paisley, he was, however, directed to proceed towards Renfrew, and wait for them at the ferry.

Baldy was not altogether pleased with this arrangement. There was something which he could not penetrate about his master's companion; moreover he was a stranger, and that of itself was objectionable, for Baldy was in no way or degree partial to what was unknown. But his fidelity overcame all his scruples, and he rode on as directed, without offering the slightest scruple.

He had not parted half an hour from his master, when he met a number of the Sheriff's men, who had been obliged to take shelter, during the rain, in a farm-house, and he was stopped and strictly questioned by them concerning any report he might have heard about the haunts of Knockwhinnie. To all which he freely answered, in such a manner, that without giving them any information, satisfied his own conscience that he had told them nothing but the truth. He was, however, perplexed at the description they gave of the Outlaw, which corresponded exactly to the first appearance of Knockwhinnie, and left him in no doubt that the stranger was one and the same individual; but true to the confidence placed in him, he afforded them no hint by which they might have guessed that the Outlaw had left his lair in the moor.

When the Sheriff's men parted from Baldy, they pursued their course straight toward Kinlochie, where they intended to stop that night; for although the rain was over, the sky was still doubtful, and in such a time a couch on the open heath was not particularly desirable. But they had not proceeded far, when they fell in with Friar Jerome and Hughoc, coming leisurely along, talking much, and the boy bearing his full share of the conversation.

The leader of the Sheriff's party appeared inclined to pass on without speaking to them; but one of his men knew both the chaplain and the boy, and hailed them in passing, inquiring their news; meaning thereby what they could tell of the Outlaw, for what else could in those days be heard of in that part of the country?

Friar Jerome not being disposed to enter into conversation with them, pursued his way onward at his slow and wonted pace, while Hughoc lingered behind, and was not tardy in his answers.

"Oh! 'deed," said he, to the first interrogatory concerning Knockwhinnie, after they had given him the description; "I'm sure he has been lurking about our quarters, for I saw a man this morning that kens him very well, and he foregathered wi' him nae farther gane than the day before yesterday. Didna' ye say he had an iron skullcap and a red waistcoat?"

"In what direction was he then?"

"Na, sir, that's mair than I can tell; but he's flechtering about the moor like a black-cock, and where he was seen the day, ye canna' count on finding him the morn. What has he done that ye're making such a foray to find him?"

"The Shirra kens," replied Aaron Henderson, the man with whom Hughoc was holding his colloquy; "for it's no more our business to meddle with such matters, than for soldiers to reason of the causes of the battles they're to fight."

"Weel! catch him if ye can," said Hughoc; "but I would na' be in your line for something, riding with swords and rungs to catch or fell an honest man, and no' to ken for what. It's an awfu' business!"

Hughoc, on saying thus, rode on, and soon again came up with the chaplain and his mule; but instead of addressing him with his usual familiarity, he dropped behind, and appeared thoughtful, often looking behind and around with wary eyes, in apprehension of some expected danger.

When they came to the spot where the road to Paisley diverges to the right, and that to Renfrew to the left, the party was halting there for them. Southennan, as they approached, rode back to the chaplain, and held a short conversation with him apart in an under voice, and in leaving him directed him aloud to proceed to Paisley. In the mean time, Knockwhinnie walked his gallant gelding onward as cautiously as if it had been a mule, and he accustomed to ride no other sort of animal.

Before this time the sun had set, and the rosy twilight was fading into gray, giving the assurance of a sunny morrow. In parting from the friar, Southennan, noticing the promise, desired Hughoc to go with the chaplain.

They had not, however, proceeded far, when they fell in with another of the Sheriff's beagles, whom they attempted to pass without speaking; but the man addressed himself to the chaplain. The old man, however, rode on without halting; and Hughoc cried to the officer, "Ye need na' speak to our Mess John, for he's as deaf as an image in the kirk: say what's your will, and I'll answer if I can."

The man then repeated to him what had been heard from so many others before, and inquired if they had fallen in with any body answering to the description of the Outlaw.

"Lord! man," replied Hughoc, "if ye think o' getting him by that account, I doubt ye'll be in a mistake; for that's the very effigy o' a neighbour o' ours, a desperate soldier, who was out in the auld Queen's wars. He wears an iron cowl and a red waistcoat, and the heft of his spear's like a weaver's beam. 'Od sake! I would advise you, if ye fa' in wi' him, to speak him kindly, for he has a neive like a beer mell. A cuff from our lucky Lennox's yarn beetle would be but a pat compared with the power o' his arm. Therefore I redde ye, if ye hae any reverence for your head, no' to make a touzle wi' him until ye hae found that he's no' your man. But Father Jerome's looking back for me, and I maun wish you gude night, for he's a cankery body, and winna stop lang. Gude night—look to your hernpan if ye come within the reach of our neighbour's staff."

So saying, Hughoc rode on to the chaplain, and when he came up to him, related the substance of what had passed. The old man made no reply, but spurred his mule in a manner unusual both to himself and the beast; which, instead of mending its pace, on being pricked, stood stock still.

In the meantime, Southennan and his party pursued their course towards the Renfrew ferry at a round trot, exchanging but few words with one another. Just as they reached the confluence of the two Carts at Inchinnan, and were about to take the ford, several of the Sheriff's men on horseback were seen coming up to them at full speed; and almost at the same moment two more appeared on the other side of the river. Neither Southennan, nor his companion, nor the servants, evinced any emotion on the occasion, but leisurely examined the ford before attempting to cross; the recent rains having swelled and troubled the stream. At last they entered the water, Baldy leading the van; by the time they reached the bank, the Sheriff's men were also in the river, and escape, had it been intended, was impracticable. Such, however, was the coolness of Southennan and all his party, that it was not apparent they had the slightest intention to avoid their pursuers; on the contrary, immediately on quitting the water, they proceeded on at the same brisk unhurried rate at which they were riding when the Sheriff's hounds first came in sight.

CHAPTER IX.

" Hair-breadth 'scapes."
OTHELLO.

OUR travellers having proceeded at a constant and brisk pace towards the ferry across the Clyde at Renfrew, reached it before their pursuers came up with them, and the boat being ready, Southennan requested Knockwhinnie and his man Stayns to embark and push over, while he would wait and see what it was the men wanted. This was no sooner said than done.

Before the boat had reached the middle of the stream the Sheriff's men arrived, and the leader of them, with the usual suavity of such dignitaries, requested to know who it was that had just crossed the river? Southennan replied, "A gentleman who joined me on the road."

"His name?"

"Knockwhinnie," replied Southennan, with a slight perceptible hesitation—"I have heard him so called, but I have only spoken to him for the first time this morning."

The men looked at one another, and the leader said, "The boy spoke of Knockwhinnie as if he were in the west; and then, turning to the young Laird, he inquired "if he knew what business Knockwhinnie had in Edinburgh?"

"I think," replied Southennan, a little proudly, "that you caanot expect me to answer that question. He joined me on the moor almost an entire stranger. I knew him by sight, but how could I question him concerning his affairs on such an imperfect knowledge?"

At this juncture Knockwhinnie and his servant landed on the opposite bank, where they left the boat unfastened, for they had embarked without the ferryman, and immediately remounted, having swam their horses. The boat soon receded from the bank, and the tide being then ebbing, was taken by the stream down the river.

For this incident Southennan was unprepared, and appeared unaffectedly disconcerted. The Sheriff's men at once exclaimed that the fugitive could be no other than the Outlaw, and broke out into vehement imprecations against him for having so tricked them of the boat. Southennan did not exchange many words with them, but remounted, and desiring Baldy to do the same, said he would ride to Paisley for the night, and accordingly immediately set off, leaving the disappointed beagles growling on the shore.

He had not, however, left them long, when the ferryman joined them, and, indignant at the loss of his boat, stood mingling his maledictions with theirs, in the expectation of one of the passage boats from Glasgow making her appearance. They waited in the hope of being conveyed across by her, and he, that she would endeavour to pick up the boat.

At last she appeared, and when she had landed her passengers, the Sheriff's men embarked, and were speedily in pursuit of the fugitives. They came up to them within a mile of the city. It seemed by the appearance of the horses, that Knockwhinnie and Stayns had ridden hard, although at the time when their pursuers came up, they were walking at a leisurely rate. The leader of the pursuers observed this, and concluding from it that all was right in the way he wanted, directed his men at once to surround them, as well as to prepare themselves for resistance, as it was not to be expected the Outlaw would surrender without a struggle. At the same time he was not very firm in his purpose, being conscious that in his zeal he was exceeding his authority, by transgressing the jurisdiction of the Sheriff of Lanark. However, his men did as he directed, and in the course of a few minutes the fugitives were surrounded.

Stayns being an Englishman, and not very clearly understanding the Renfrewshire dialect, evaded the first question which Henderson, the Sheriff's man, put to him. This might have been really owing, as he said, to his not exactly comprehending the language, or perhaps with the intent to gain time ; for it was evident, by what had taken place, how much it was an object to do so. The man, becoming impatient at the equivocation, addressed himself to Knockwhinnie, who was sitting quietly on his horse, with a lethargic appearance.

"Your name, sir?" said Henderson, addressing him abruptly.

"What occasion is there that you should inquire my name?" was the answer.

"I must know it ; I am empowered by the Sheriff of Renfrewshire to arrest you wherever I should find you."

To this no reply was given ; for seeing there could be no longer any equivocation, Father Jerome, lifting the cap of Knockwhinnie, showed the shaven crown which was beneath. The Outlaw and he had changed clothes at Kinlochie, and Knockwhinnie with Hughoc were long before this time at rest in a hostel in Paisley.

Henderson was for a moment confounded at discovering the chaplain in the warlike garb of a French officer, for he was not unacquainted with him ; but in some degree amused at being so well deceived, he began to laugh, and all present joined, and enjoyed the joke.

It was now too far in the evening for the Sheriff's men to think of returning across the ferry that night, with the slightest chance of overtaking the fugitives, for they could not doubt that Southennan, having gone to Paisley, would there apprize Knockwhinnie of what was likely to take place, and that he would be very far from their grasp, before they could reach him.

Accordingly they proceeded all in one band to Glasgow, which they reached just as the candles were beginning to be lighted, and stopped at an hostel in the Gallowgate, which in latter days became improved into the respectable inn of the Saracen's Head.

Father Jerome was not, however, much satisfied with his masquerade apparel; and soon after alighting, desired Stayns, who was a shrewd and sharp fellow, to go to the Blackfriars' convent in the High-street, and request a friar, with whom he was acquainted, to come to him, and to bring with him the garb of his order, to enable him to resume his proper ecclesiastical appearance. Stayns, however, thought that the message afforded him an opportunity of rendering his master more essential service, and, in consequence, instead of proceeding on foot to the convent, he re-saddled his horse, and riding to the ferry at the foot of the Saltmarket, was taken across, and proceeded to Paisley, leaving Father Jerome to the protection of Providence.

CHAPTER X.

"I could wish
That the first pillow, whereon I was cradled,
Had proved to me a grave."

FORD.

In the mean time the Queen, after leaving the Straits of Dover, had met with a fair wind, and arrived sooner than was expected at Leith. The preparations making for her reception were not completed, and she disembarked with her attendants, under circumstances but little calculated to reconcile her to the change in her fortunes. None of the dignitaries or great officers of the kingdom were in attendance to receive her; the day was bleak, and all the landscape saddened with a lowering and inclement sky.

It is said, that when she stepped on the shore and contrasted its cold and lonely aspect with the splendour from which she had come, that she burst into tears; and in passing over the links of Leith to the palace of Holyrood, she frequently sighed as she cast her eyes on the furze and rude soil around, and the naked and frowning cliffs of Arthur's Seat, and the rocks of the Salisbury Craigs.

Among her train was Adelaide, the adopted daughter of the Count Dufroy who had incurred the animosity of Knockwhinnie, and Chatelard, one of her secretaries, a young gentleman of the French court, distinguished by his personal accomplishments, and particularly for his taste and skill in music.

The beautiful Adelaide had not become acquainted with the accomplishments of Chatelard with impunity; but, with maidenly propriety, she endeavoured to repress every outward indication of her affection, while she fondly cherished it in her heart; still she was not always so guarded as not occasionally to evince the interest which Chatelard had excited, and her royal mistress more than once playfully expressed her suspicion of the secret attachment.

But on Chatelard her charms and her gentleness were ineffectual: he, in common with the other gallants of the court, admired her beauty and acknowledged the grace and sweetness of her manners, but when she was not present he had no recollection that so lovely and soft a being was in existence, for his bosom was filled with the image of another—a passion more hopeless than her's.

Like all who approached his royal mistress, he had felt the influence of that beauty which had no parallel, and the enchantment of that gracefulness which was, according to historians, never beheld without admiration or love. Mary was then in the bloom of youth and in the pride of her surprising charms. The blight had not then tainted the blossom; the early dew-drop still sparkled on its leaf as it glowed in the sunshine, caressed by the gales of prosperity.

The devotion of Chatelard to the Queen was not unknown among her Majesty's immediate attendants. The fond eyes of the mild and retiring Adelaide—

" Who never told her love,
But let Concealment, like a worm i' the bud,
Prey on the damask roses of her cheek,"

were, perhaps, the first that detected his ambitious passion; but the Queen herself never appeared to perceive the flame which her own radiance had kindled; on the contrary, she regarded the unfortunate Chatelard with a degree of intellectual compassion, more withering than scorn to the hopes of love, and Chatelard felt it as such. Even before the departure from Paris he was sensible, by the behaviour of Mary, that she had discovered his secret, and had chosen a demeanour of mingled dignity and pity to apprize him of the vain folly which had taken possession of his heart; nor could he equivocate to himself by any fallacy of self-flattery, that the condescension with which she advised him not to think of coming to the rude climate of Scotland had any other object than to intimate, with the delicacy peculiar to her own exquisite discernment, that he was incurring the hazard of presumption by yielding to his infatuation.

But on that night—the night of her arrival in the habitation of her royal ancestors, she bestowed upon him a mark of attention which his vanity, not discerning the causes from which it flowed, interpreted to signify some yielding regard awakening in the bosom of the Queen. When the nobles and gentry of the realm who were then in Edinburgh had offered their congratulations, Mary withdrew to her private apartment with Adelaide and certain other of her ladies, and, being affected with irrepressible presentiments of sorrow, she ordered her musicians to play during their joyless supper, and in compliment to her Scottish subjects, directed that only the minstrels belonging to the palace should attend.

Whatever power they might have possessed over the pathetic melodies of their native land, they, unfortunately, did not perceive the pensive mood of the Queen, and in consequence, yielding to the suggestions of their own loyalty, they jarred her dejected feelings with brisk and enlivening airs, in unison with the pleasure which they felt themselves. Mary saw the spring which prompted these expressions of joy, and endured, for a considerable time, the music that was so discordant to the mood of her spirit. Had she then dismissed the minstrels, they would have exulted in the honour of having been heard so long by their royal mistress; but their envy was awakened, when it was understood that the musicians who had come with her from France were summoned, after they quitted the presence, to supply that solace which they had failed to produce. But the foreign musicians also failed: the shadow of coming Fate was on the spirit of the Queen, and something more than the spell of sounds was required to change her ruminations.

She sat amid her ladies, with her cheek leaning on her hand, and her eyes moistened with the tears of remembrance. Nor were the ladies more cheerful, for they already felt the mournful difference between the chill climate and rude aspect of

Scotland, and the luxuriant hills and sparkling valleys they had left.

" I wish," after a long pause, said the Queen, " that some one would sing to me the woes of a dismayed heart, or any ditty that deplores past joys and breathes of hopelessness :"— and she added, in the thought of the moment, " Send for Chatelard, and let him bring his lute with him."

Adelaide started at this request ; her love was alarmed ; but apprehensive lest her emotion should be discovered, she rose, and delivered the message to the page in the antechamber, and it was soon obeyed. Chatelard, on entering the room, at once perceived, by the pale and dejected countenance of the Queen, that she was not tuned to the joyous harmony that rung in other parts of the palace, and he composed his voice and lute to strains of a melancholy cast: he chose for his theme a song of the Troubadours, a true-bred knight, in Palestine, lamenting his rejected love. This tale of fictitious passion reflected the truth of his own feelings, but not more of his than of those of the fair and disconsolate Adelaïde, whose emotion became, as he proceeded with the romantic ballad, so strong, that she could no longer suppress her tears, and to conceal them was obliged to leave the room.

CHAPTER XI.

" In short, my lord,
He saw her—loved her."
LOVE'S SACRIFICE.

IT was on the evening of the Queen's arrival that Southennan reached Edinburgh with Knockwhinnie. Their adventures, after escaping the beagles of the Sheriff of Renfrewshire, as already described, possessed no particular interest ; but on reaching the city, which it was so contrived should take place in the evening, just before the shutting of the gates, Knockwhinnie deemed it expedient to separate himself from the young Laird. Perhaps his own safety was not his sole motive ; he might have some purpose connected with his vowed vengeance against the Count Dufroy, for by this time he had acknowledged that he did not intend to present any petition to the

Queen, but was actuated, in coming to the metropolis, by his revenge.

In the course of the journey, Southennan had several times attempted to draw the Outlaw into some relation of the particular circumstances regarding the alleged seduction of his lady by Dufroy; but his thoughts were wild on the subject, and he was ever rendered incapable by the vehemence of his feelings to proceed with the narrative.

Southennan gathered from the several abortive attempts, that there was something equivocal in the imputed guilt, and he intimated his doubt to Knockwhinnie. It was only once, however, that he did so, for the surmise, instead of suggesting pleasure or hope, only excited violent bursts and vows of passion. It was therefore not unpleasant to Southennan that Knockwhinnie, on entering the town, had so separated himself.

But to do the young Laird justice, it must not be supposed, when the Outlaw quitted him, that he was resolved to take no farther interest in his fate. On the contrary, the satisfaction he derived from the incident was in consequence of the opportunity it afforded him to inquire more exactly into the real circumstances of the story, than he could possibly do if they remained associated. The unhappy Outlaw had in the course of the journey inspired him with sentiments of much regard, and awakened a sympathy for his distress of mind, that would in any case have moved the generous nature of Southennan to mitigate his suffering by all the means in his power.

Accordingly, having given directions to Baldy, his confidential servant, to provide lodgings, he proceeded from the hostel where he intended to stop for that night, to Holyrood House, in quest of some of his friends whom he expected to meet there, or to gather news concerning them. Thus it happened, that when Adelaide came from the Queen's chamber, he was standing in the gallery through which she passed to her own apartment, waiting for the return of one of the domestics of the palace, that he had sent in quest of Chatelard, whom he had previously known at Paris, but of whose engagement at that time with her Majesty the servant had not known.

The beautiful and buoyant figure of Adelaide, as she came towards the spot where Southennan was standing in the obscurely lighted gallery, seemed to possess something more airy and graceful that he had ever beheld in woman; and when, as she passed, he saw that she was in tears, his admiration of her elegance was immediately blended with sentiments of pity and tenderness. But he was alone—no one was in the gallery

Vol. I.—4

to inform him who she was, or to what cause her distress at such a time could be owing, especially as she had come out of the royal apartments.

The servant whom he had sent in quest of Chatelard was long in returning, which gave Southennan time to ruminate concerning what he had seen, and of the elegant creature who so awakened his sympathy, until her image took possession of his thoughts, and he could not conceal from himself that he had never beheld so delightful a vision.

At last the domestic came back, with the intelligence that Chatelard was with her Majesty. He was followed by a gentleman, whom Southennan at once recognized as the Count Dufroy, who on hearing his name mentioned in the room where it was expected that Chatelard was at play with others of the French gentlemen, had recollected his gallant appearance as the page of the Lord Fleming, and came to renew his acquaintance.

Southennan, on seeing the Count, and reflecting on the peril in which he stood with respect to Knockwhinnie, was for a moment disturbed; but after their respective felicitations were exchanged, he could not but deem the meeting, so early, fortunate, and resolved at once to come to some explanation on the subject with the Count. He accordingly proposed that they should adjourn from the gallery to the gardens, the night being sultry, and the moon high and bright.

"Nothing can be more fortunate than this meeting," said Southennan; "and I trust, when I explain what it is that makes me say so, you will not regard me as intrusive, in asking a question or two concerning a subject in which you may think I can have no possible reason to be interested. When you were last in Scotland, it is said that an attempt was made on your life, in the midst of many gentlemen then assembled at the cross of Edinburgh."

"It is true," replied the Count, thoughtfully; "and my enemy was Knockwhinnie, son-in-law of my friend, the Lord Kilburnie."

"By what motive was he actuated?" inquired Southennan; "for I have heard that he had but just returned from France, and was personally unknown to you.

Dufroy made no immediate answer, but looked steadily, almost sternly, for a short time at Southennan: he then said, with an impressive emphasis,

"There must be some special cause which moves you,

Southennan, to ask that question. Are you related to Knockwhinnie?"

"No," replied the young Laird, guardedly, for he perceived that he had touched some long dormant feeling; "I have but lately heard his story, and that he is, I am grieved to say, fired against you with inextinguishable revenge."

A slight glow passed over the visage of the Count, his eyes flashed for a moment, and with a sudden shudder, as if touched with electricity, he exclaimed,

"Is it possible that he is in that humour still?"

"And I fear will always be, if what I have heard be true," replied the young Laird, with firmness and dignity.

"What have you heard?" said the Count, a little proudly, evidently, however, more astonished than offended: but, before Southennan could make any reply, one of the pages summoned Dufroy to attend the Queen, and our hero returned with him to the gallery, where he found Chatelard.

CHAPTER XII.

"Who's there?
Nay, answer me, stand and unfold yourself."
HAMLET.

SOUTHENNAN, having no other opportunity that night of resuming his conversation with the Count Dufroy, left the palace to return to the house where his horses were stabled.

He walked warily through the narrow lanes and dark streets, with that obscure dread which strangers ever experience in cities. Perhaps his apprehension was increased by the number of unknown persons whom the arrival of the queen had attracted, many of whom, notwithstanding the lateness of the hour, were still abroad. But the dreadful predilection of the age, to avenge in person private wrongs* sufficiently justified his wariness; for, although he had not an enemy, he was yet

* The causes which gave rise to the frequent assassinations of the period to which our story relates, require to be noticed, that the lax justice of the time may not seem incredible: we shall therefore abridge Dr. Robertson's account of the matter.

aware that mistakes were sometimes committed, and that the victim was not always the object of the revenge.

In passing through the gate which separated, in those days, the palace of Holyrood from the city, he observed a man closely muffled in his cloak, notwithstanding the sultriness of the weather, walking up towards the Cross, within the shadow of the houses, which the moonlight at the time threw black

"Resentment," says he, " is one of the strongest passions of man: it prompts the injured to inflict himself the vengeance due for what he has suffered; but to permit this would be destructive to society, and, therefore, private revenge was early disarmed, and the sword of justice committed to the magistrate. At first, the punishment of crimes was retaliation, the offender forfeited limb for limb, and life for life: a compensation in money succeeded to the rigour of this institution. The law in these but ministered to the gratification of resentments. He who suffered the wrong was the only person who had a right to pursue, to exact, and to remit punishment. But while the law allowed such scope to the revenge of one party, the interests of the other were not neglected. If the evidence of his guilt did not amount to full proof, or if he reckoned himself unjustly accused, he had a right to challenge his adversary to single combat, and, on obtaining the victory, vindicated his honour. This practice became so common, that justice had seldom to use her balance; the sword decided the contest, and revenge was publicly nourished with blood, until society could no longer endure the ferocity. The trial by combat was then discouraged, the payment of compensation was abolished, and the punishment for crimes became more severe: but Police was young, her hands were infantine, her jurisdiction undetermined, the evasion of offenders easy, and the administration of justice feeble and dilatory. To the haughty and irascible nobles, among whom the causes of discord were many and inevitable, who were quick in discerning injury, and impatient to revenge it—who deemed it infamous to submit to any enemy, and cowardly to forgive him—the slow proceedings of the judicature were unsatisfactory, and that vengeance which the impotent hand of the magistrate could not, or durst not inflict, their own could easily execute. Thus, in the weakness of the law and deficiencies of police, men assumed, as in a state of nature, the right of redressing their own wrongs, and thus assassination, a crime the most destructive to society, came not only to be frequently perpetrated with impunity, but to be accounted not even dishonourable.

" The authors of those days have perfectly imbibed the sentiments of their contemporaries with respect to assassination, and they who had leisure to reflect and to judge appear to be no more shocked at this crime than the persons who committed it during the heat and impetuosity of passion. Buchanan describes the murder of Cardinal Beaton and of Rizzio, without expressing those feelings which are natural to a man, or that indignation which becomes a historian. Knox, whose mind was fiercer and more unpolished, relates the death of Beaton and of the Duke of Guise, not only without censure, but with the utmost exultation. On the other hand, the Bishop of Ross mentions the assassina-

upon the street. There was nothing so particular in this circumstance as to excite his attention, and he probably would have continued his course without casting a second glance at the stranger, but for an incident which, in those perilous days, was calculated to increase his vigilance.

In passing a lamp under a niche, at the corner of a dark wynd, where an image of a saint had a short time before stood, the stranger stepped on before him, and suddenly turning round as he came within the light, eyed him with an eager and sharp look.

The spirit of Southennan was roused by this rudeness; but before he had time to demand an explanation, the obtruder had hastily moved forward.

A short way before them, higher up the street, was a bonfire, around which a crowd of boys and artisans were displaying their loyalty by riotously throwing about brands snatched from the burning, to the great annoyance of the more debonair lieges who happened to pass. In approaching towards it, Southennan observed that the stranger placed himself in the entrance of a close by which he was obliged to pass, he had no doubt for the purpose of renewing his unmannerly inspection. Quickened to resentment by this notion, the young Laird resolved not to let the rudeness be repeated with impunity; but a moment's reflection, and the remembrance of his mother's counsel, convinced him that he ought not to brave the insolence of one, whom it might be no honour to treat so much as an equal, or to seek a quarrel with; and accordingly, he passed over to the other side of the street.

The stranger, regardless of consequences, and determined to satisfy his curiosity, also crossed the street a little above the bonfire, and met Southennan exactly opposite to it. There was something so like defiance in this new impertinence, that our hero felt himself constrained to abandon his prudence, and to inquire why he was thus dodged and waylaid. Accordingly,

---

tion of the Earl of Murray with some degree of applause. Lord Ruthven, the principal actor in the conspiracy against Rizzio, wrote an account of it a short time before his own death, and, in all his long narrative, there is not one expression of regret, or one symptom of compunction, for a crime no less dishonourable than barbarous. Morton, equally guilty of the same crime, entertains the same sentiments concerning it, and in his last moments, neither he himself, nor the ministers who attended him, seem to have considered it as an action which called for repentance. Even then he talks of David's slaughter, as coolly as if it had been an innocent or commendable deed."

he walked proudly towards the stranger; but, before he could address him, the other, who had by this time obtained from the light of the fire a full view of his person, respectfully came forward, and apologised for his indecorum.

" It is due, sir," said he, " for the rudeness of which I have been guilty, that I should frankly explain to you the reason of my conduct. I was informed that a gentleman whom I have great cause to seek, had this evening arrived in Edinburgh from the west country. He was described to me dressed as you are, and that he was in the Abbey. I followed him thither just as you were coming out; and when you appeared, answering to the description, I was only prevented by your more youthful mien from then addressing you as him. It is many years since we have met, and I made allowance for some alteration upon him; but it was not until I had a full view of your person, that I was satisfied you were not the man."

Something in the expression of " the man," struck Southennan discordantly; and he could not for an instant doubt that the person whom the stranger sought was Knockwhinnie, for whom he had been himself described, nor was it without pain that he heard the unfortunate Outlaw was so soon suspected of being in Edinburgh. Without entering, however, into any explanation, he accepted the stranger's apology, and parting from him, pursued his way homeward.

This simple casualty was augmented in interest to him by the demeanour and physiognomy of the stranger, as seen by the strong red glare of the bonfire; and his remarkable appearance took possession of his imagination, the natural affinity of which to whatever was wild and strange, had never before been so powerfully called into action.

The general contour of the stranger's figure was martial and athletic; his features were bold and handsome; but there was a sinister cast in his eyes, which gave a disagreeable expression to his dark countenance. He was so wrapped up in his cloak, that the style of his dress could not be seen, except a part of his vest, which was richly embroidered, and he wore buff gauntlets; all which indicated a personage above the common ranks. His years were, perhaps, not so many as the lines of his face seemed by the light of the fire to show; but he was at least more than double the age of Southennan. In his speech he was evidently a Scotchman, but his accent had a foreign sound in it—not, however, exactly like that which his countrymen who went to France commonly brought home with them, nor was it altogether an imitation of the English. In a word, it was evident that he had been some time abroad, and that he was a man of military habits, as well as of an intrepid spirit: his self-possession clearly showed this.

As the young Laird reflected on the rencounter, it seemed to grow in his imagination to an adventure, and he reasoned about it until he had fairly persuaded himself that the stranger was some one whom the pride of Knockwhinnie had provoked into an adversary, and who had come in search of him to make good their quarrel. With this train of thought passing through his mind, he reached the door of his inn, where he found Baldy and Hughoc standing together, anxiously wearying for his return. On observing him, Hughoc immediately ran for a light, and Baldy, with a familiarity which he rarely ever ventured upon, begged him to speak softly as he entered the house, and taking the light from the boy, conducted him to an upper room, which had been prepared for his reception.

CHAPTER XIII.

"Boy thou art quick and trusty;
Be withal close and silent; and thy pains
Shall meet a liberal addition."
THE FANCIES CHASTE AND NOBLE.

WHEN Baldy had set the lights upon the table, instead of retiring he lingered in the room, seemingly in expectation of being questioned. But the mind of his master was so busy with conjectures about the stranger, that he was not in any humour for conversation. Baldy, however, had evidently something to communicate; and after waiting a reasonable time, he began, of his own accord, to tell what had happened during the absence of Southennan at the palace.

"Laird," said he, "it's extraordinar' what has come o'er Father Jerome this night; he has surely a dreadfu' heap o' friends in this town. How they came to ken that he was come, and that we were come, and that Knockwhinnie and his man had come wi' us, is a miracle to me! You hadna' left the house five minutes, at the very utmost, when a man that had since been a friar, as by the length o' his beard was plainly to be seen, came inquiring for Father Jerome; and when I showed him in where the auld man was sitting, it was wonderfu' to hear the phrases of lang syne acquaintanceship that passed between them, and how they rejoiced that the Queen was such a beautiful Christian, hoping the end o' a' hersey was nigh at hand. As it wouldna' hae been discreet in me to hearken to their conversation, I left them to themselves, and went to the door; and when I went there, wha should I meet wi,' but a kind o' an outlandish captain, of a stern visage, in his peremptors asking anent Knockwhinnie; and then came others and others. What can it be that has brought Father Jerome so far afield? For at the Place we a' thought he had but a light errand."

Southennan had attended only to the latter part of this speech; and though he said nothing, he could not but agree that there was something mysterious in the chaplain's visit to Edinburgh at that particular period. He was the more persuaded of this, by the manner in which the old man had always evaded a direct answer, as often as he was spoken to on the subject. But the inquiry which had been made for Knockwhinnie interested him deeper : the description of the person who had inquired for the Outlaw, answered to that of the stranger whom he had met in the street; and he apprehended that the notoriety which already attached to his party, augured no good to Knockwhinnie, while it threatened trouble to himsel; although he was unable to discern any cause from which it could arise, beyond the innocent circumstance of his having travelled in companionship with the Outlaw.

Not, however, choosing to make his servant a party to his thoughts, he said to Baldy, " It is natural that Father Jerome's old friends should be eager to see him, and that some of Knockwhinnie's acquaintance should also, if they heard he was in town, be of the same mind."

"Na," replied Baldy, " that's no' the fair daylight of the concern. That Father Jerome has a purpose to perform, is as certain as any other true visibility : and that the stark and stern Johnnie-Armstrong-looking sodger officer had mair in his mind about Knockwhinnie than he said to me, is no' a misdoubt. I wish the auld chaplain, doited body, was weel at hame, and that we had never foregathered wi' the other!"

This opinion, so much in accordance with his own thoughts, awakened the attention of Southennan, and he looked sharply at Baldy, as he said,

" What do you know, or what have you heard, about either

the one or the other? Tell me at once, and don't summer and winter about it in that manner?"

"Weel, Laird, if ye'll just hae patience I'll tell you a'. Depend upon't there's some cotrivance between Father Jerome and others o' the auld true religion here in Embro'; and there's some dule pactioned and convenanted against Knockwhinnie, puir man! It would be weel for him, or I'm mista'en if he were again out o' this nest of conspirators, and on the free moors o' the west."

Southennan was too well acquainted with the tedious roundabout ways of Baldy, to expect he would come earlier to a satisfactory explanation by increasing the impatience of his tone; so, instead of sharpening it with more direct questions, he simply said,

"Whatever may be Father Jerome's business, it does not concern me; he is a worthy honest man, and I have no reason to fear scaith, either at his hands or those of any other; but I confess it would grieve me exceedingly, were any accident to befal Knockwhinnie, before I have learned more of his misfortunes; for he is a brave man and has endured more than he has inflicted."

"There can be nae doubt o' that," said Baldy; "but it was a terrible thing to stab an honest man blindfolded, wha had never done him any wrang; and a' this at the instigation o' his ain sworn enemy."

It was plain from this that Baldy had learned something more about Knockwhinnie, and the attempted assassination of Count Dufroy, than his master was yet acquainted with.

"Who was his enemy? and what know you of his unfortunate attack on the Count Dufroy?"

"If ye mean," replied Baldy, "the truth o' the matter, I canna say its meikle; but it's currently reported, for mair than ae person has spoken o't in my presence, that it wasna' the French Count that wranged Knockwhinnie, but the rampageous Laird o' Auchenbrae, wha is the kinsman o' the Shirra o' Renfrew; and there's nae want o' tongues that can tell the purpose which took Knockwhinnie out o' his wilder howfs, was to wreak his vengeance on that wrongous offender. Indeed, I jalous that by a somehow the outlandish man is nae other than that reprobate cousin to the Shirra."

This seemed not unplausible, as it accounted in some degree for that zeal and rigour of pursuit from which Knockwhinnie had so adroitly escaped on the moors of Renfrewshire.

"But have you heard, Baldy, what the wrong was which provoked Knockwhinnie to attempt the life of the French gentlemen?"

"I canna' just say preceesely that I hae heard that; but it was either or neither something about a lady o' a light character. It's terrible to think what a stramash thae kittle-cattle hae made in the world since the apple-stealing o' grannie Eve."

His master perceiving, by this remark, that the stock of Baldy's news or facts was nearly exhausted, desired him to see if the house could supply him with supper. Before, however, Baldy could leave the room, Hughoc burst in, evidently in great consternation.

"Oh! Laird," cried the boy, "here's an awfu' thing! Father Jerome has been sitting a' the while wi' three unco men; and just as they were ganging awa,' the Provost's halberdiers cam and took ane o' them up for an ill-doer. But what he has done, and what they will do wi' him, is a world's wonder."

Southennan, on hearing this, turned somewhat sternly towards Baldy, and said,

"You suspected, sir, that something not right was going on; be explicit with me, and tell what you suspected! Why was it that you, in a clandestine manner, as it were, lighted me up into this chamber? You knew that Father Jerome and his confederates were engaged in a business which I must consider, from what has now taken place, as at least equivocal." And turning to Hughoc, he added, "I think thou hast knavery enough from instinct to execute a sly errand; follow those men of the Provost, and when thou hast learned the cause of the arrest, come back and let me know."

Here Baldy, a little diffidently, said, "Though the callant is as gleg as a goshawk at hame in the country, I doubt, as he has na experience, he may want the sagacity to wend himself in safety through the crooked closses of the town."

"Art thou afraid, boy, to do my bidding?" said Southennan, evidently angered by the interposition of Baldy.

Hughoc briskly replied, "By night or by day, Laird, by fire or by water, Laird, I'se warrant ye'll see I'll try to do what behooves me!"

With that he hastily left the room, and was sullenly followed by Baldy.

CHAPTER XIV.

"I would we were removed from this town, Anthony,
That we might taste some quiet: for mine own part,
I am almost melted with continual trotting
After inquiries."

THE CHANCES.

BALDY, on going down stairs, went into the kitchen, and, in rather a surly manner, directed the hostess to get ready something for his master's supper. Without inquiring what she had to give, he retired into the chamber where Father Jerome was sitting alone, a good deal disconcerted at the untoward dispersion of his friends.

It was soon obvious that a better understanding existed between the chaplain and the Laird's body servant, than was previously supposed by many, who thought they knew them both well. Baldy, unbidden, seated himself at the table on which the old Priest was leaning, and without any particular preface, inquired what had happened.

"I doubt," said Father Jerome, shaking his head, "the friends of our cause here are too sanguine. They boast of this man and of that; of the faithfulness of one lord, and of the wavering state of others, who have been most froward in the mutiny against the Church; but it is only of individual men they speak. I fear, good Archibald, that the spirit of the times runs strong against us in the current of the people's thoughts."

"But what has caused the incoming of the Provost's men, and the arrest o' —— which was it they took?"

"Brother Michael, of Kilwinning, a zealous and fervent son of the Church; but lacking a little of that discretion which is needful, before either zeal or fervour can be turned to good account. What offence he may have committed was not explained; they took him as he sat where you are now sitting, and he himself, as if conscious that he was responsible to them, rose at once, pale and much agitated, and submissively walked away."

"Hadna' your other friends," rejoined Baldy, "a guess o'

the cause? It's really a hard thing that a man shoud be seized like a malefactor, without kenning for what, and a churchman too."

"Ay, my friend," replied the venerable chaplain thoughtfully, "times are changed with my brethren; but though the Provost's men said nothing, 1 could see that Friar Michael well knew the reason of his arrest."

"Then you think," said Baldy, after a pause, " that ours is a gane cause; and that this coming o' the Queen is to be o' nae benefit to the soul's health o' puir Scotland."

The worthy ecclesiastic made no immediate reply; he sat in evident perplexity, and sighed deeply. When at last he did resume the conversation, it was in a tone of solemnity and regret.

"I am an old man," said he, "infirm of limb, and too heavy to move lightly in the troubles of this time: so I told you, Archibald, when ye brought the message to me from the Master of Grossreguel, but I was willing to do my duty. I thought, however, that the men who were sent from the country to meet here on the Queen's arrival, were of another sort than the specimens I have seen this night. Alas, for our cause! it bodes ill to any undertaking, when those who are entrusted with it are moved by private interests, or by the impulses of passion. Of the seventeen brothers who have been with me already, there has not appeared one among them whom a wary and judicious man would trust with the wool of a dog; they can see nothing in the service which the Church requires of them, but extirpation and a sordid rescue of their revenues. I, therefore, greatly grieve, Archibald, to find our cause in such a plight. We have been traduced and slandered for the irregularities of our morals, but how are we ever to recover the good opinion of the world, if we seek only to regain the means that led us into temptation."

Baldy was not altogether prepared, notwithstanding his long acquaintance with the speaker, for the moderation and charity of these sentiments, and he looked not a little surprised at the acknowledgment on the part of so good man, that there was some truth in the alleged enormities of the clergy.

"Do ye then think," said he, "that the evil cloud which has broken in sic a storm on kirk and cloister, is the fruit of a judgment and sentence?"

"I can never think, Archibald," replied Father Jerome, with sedate emphasis; "that the Spirit of the Church is the cause of the evils which have come to pass."

"It is, it is," cried Hughoc, bursting in, almost out of breath; and who, seeing his master was not there, shut the door and ran up stairs.

"It is what?" cried Southennan, as the boy rushed into the room.

"It is himself," replied the breathless boy; "its the gley'd gruesome man that came speering for Knockwhinnie. Gude preserve us from witches and warlocks, and a' lang-nebbit-things! to think a sodger officer, wi' a gowden waistcoat and a sword by his side, was hidden in a friar's cloak. Weel I wot, it's no the cloak that maks the friar, nor the sword that proves the sodger! It's Friar Michael o' Kilwinning, the pawkie deevil! he just came whisking in before you, master, and Baldy shoved him into the room where Father Jerome and the other twa shavelings have been cawing like rooks a' the night. Baldy, the loon, I'm sure, kent him; but I saw nae mair o' him than if he had been the glint o' a flash o' lightning. Safe 's, master, this Embro's no an honest town!"

Southennan, who had not been altogether satisfied with the equivocal explanations of his man, was indignant at this intelligence, even while the dictates of his own confidence in the superior sanctity of the Roman faith led him to view with indulgence any effort that the chaplain might make in that cause. But he suppressed the emotion with which he regarded the conduct of Baldy, and inquired of the boy what more he had learned concerning Friar Michael and the cause of his arrest.

"Oh," replied Hughoc, "you couldna expect me to bide and hear the Provost's paternoster, when I saw wha it was he had gotten in his clutches; for Friar Michael is —— I'll no say what; but if ye'll speer at my auntie Abigail, she'll gar the hair on your head stand on end wi' the stories of his ne-plus-ultras wi' women and wine! He is a ——"

At this crisis the door opened with the hostess and her handmaiden bringing in the supper, and Hughoc, patting the side of his nose with his right fore-finger, indicated that silence was in their presence expedient.

While the supper was in the process of being set out, Southennan, as if nothing particular had occurred, said, in a careless manner to the boy, "Have you seen nothing of Knockwhinnie, since I went to the palace?"

"That's a hard question," replied Hughoc. "I hae seen him, Laird, if I can believe my eyne; but it was another man, if I can trust my understanding. For just as I was coming

Vol. I.—5

out o' the clerk's chamber, where the Provost sits in a muckle arm-chair for the benefit o' ill doers, I saw the glimpses o' Knockwhinnie's kindled eyne in the shadow o' the trance: but then the body o' the man was that o' an auld carle drooping o'er his staff. A dreadfu' hoast he had; so that I couldna' bide till it was o'er, or I would hae spoken to him. What a place this Embro' is for guisarts and turncoats!"

This information thickened the cogitations of Southennan. " What a fool am I!" thought he to himself, " to be thus troubled about these vagabonds. I am now rid of them—I'll have nothing more to say to them—I have come here to enjoy myself, and to push my fortune at court; any connexion with such delinquents can only mar it."

And he turned to the hostess, sitting down at the same time to the table, and bade her bring him a stoup of wine.

" We hae Malvesey; we hae Rhenish; we hae Sherries; and if your honour would be pleased, I hae spice in the house, and can cook you a flaggon o' Hippocras," replied the hostess, with her hands daintily placed on her apron string, and giving a beck, a sort of courtesy staccato, if short motions may be designated by terms descriptive of abrupt sounds.

Southennan preferred the Rhenish, on account of the sultriness of the evening, and the hostess speedily returned with a flask, wickered with bent, and set it before him with a tall green glass.

CHAPTER XV.

——————— " A princess!
A princess of the royal blood of Scotland,
In the full spring of youth, and fresh in beauty!"
PERKIN WARBECK.

THE arrival of Mary in her ancient kingdom was to all her people an auspicious event. Her known attachment to the Roman faith inspired the professors of that religion with new life. The Reformers, by the leading members of their order being in possession of the government, in almost all its departments and faculties, dreaded no overthrow; but they knew that their adversaries were quickened in their enmity by the confidence which they reposed in the personal influence of the Queen, and in consequence were jealous and vigilant. In every thing there was spring and promise; but the buds and blossoms were premature. It is, however, not required in our agreeable task to describe the blight which so early fell upon them: the events within the scope of our story are, in general, light and gay; and we have to speak of the ill-fated Mary when she was in the plenitude of her charms, and never seen without inspiring delight and admiration.

When we reflect that she was then in the bloom and buoyancy of only eighteen, history, in treating of her early reign, seems not only ungracious but morose. She was still too young to have learned the devices of guilt, and her fame was untainted with the breath of any slander. Her talents were superior, and felt to be such, beyond even the adulation that is offered to royalty; her manners were as fascinating as the loveliness of her person; and when imagination paints her amid the stern elders and probationers of Presbytery, it seems doubtful, while the light of her beauty brightens their dark and rugged countenances, whether the complacency with which they regard her arises from contemplating the gracefulness of her deportment, or from the intelligence of an eloquence, wonderful in one so young. In the glorious Aurora of womanhood, it is astonishing that any pen was found iron enough in the hand of man, even in that rude age, to impute to her those faults and sins which are only found connected with luxurious maturity long matriculated in the records of public shame.

But even in that fair dawn of her stormy day, the demon of her fate was ever by her side. The elegant endowments which were bestowed to command the hearts of the world, were, to poor Mary, the most baneful gifts; that which was splendour when seen from a distance, was felt to be flame within the sphere of her domestic influence.

We have already adverted to the daring admiration of the accomplished Chatelard: in describing the hopeless passion of the gentle Adelaide for him, we must relate the affecting consequences of his attachment to Mary—the most romantic incident in the history of queens.

Adelaide, after quitting the presence of the Queen as already mentioned, hastened to her chamber. She could not but acknowledge to herself the superior graces of her royal mistress, she could not condemn Chatelard for preferring such superiority to her own meeker charms, and she felt, with a pang unspeakable, how easy it was for the Queen to plunge her irrevocably in the depths of sorrow and despair.

That evening was the first in which Chatclard, with his pathetic lute, was permitted to entertain the privacy of the Queen. It is true, that in the voyage from France he had frequently been called to the exercise of his exquisite taste and skill; but then it was on the open deck, and when Mary was surrounded by the nobles and courtiers that accompanied her in the voyage. To command the attendance of Chatelard on the very first night of their arrival, and when access was denied to all the court, save only the ladies in immediate attendance, appeared to the dejected Adelaide as ominous of the death of her feeble hope. She wept with despondency, and repined that she was ever placed as a foil, for so she modestly deemed herself, beside the incomparable Mary.

The same unpremeditated incident, which fell like a snow-flake, cold and softly on her gentle heart, kindled in the breast of the aspiring Chatelard, an ardour as bold as his presumptuous love. He flattered himself that in the condescension with which he had been treated, Mary sought his presence for some fonder purpose than the melody of his delicious airs, and he interpreted the pensive languor which the music produced to the influence of a secret and dearer spell. But with all the boundless rapture in which his ambitious imagination expatiated in that moment, he was aware of the dangerous brink on which he stood. He had heard too much of the irascible temper of the Scottish nation, how riveted they were in their purposes, how proud in their characters, and how jealous in their national honour, to hope that the Queen would ever bestow on him her hand. This was discarded as an impossible imagination. But the warmth and impetuosity of his passion suggested anticipations of an intercourse that would ensure to him the power and the enjoyment of a king. Still, notwithstanding the bold fantasy of his ill-measured attachment, a fear of the obstacles which the haughty nobility and a rigid people would oppose to the consummation of his wishes, taught him that it was necessary to be cautious in expressing the enthusiasm which lifted him in hope so far above the lowly level of his birth.

Chatelard had not been, during the voyage, an unobservant spectator of the timid and maidenly glances with which Adelaide had sometimes regarded him. His vanity was at no loss to interpret their import; but it was a cruel and a heartless resolution, to determine that night to make the modest love of so mild and gracious a creature, an instrument to further the daring schemes of his own audacious passion.

It would be unjust to the discernment of the Queen, to conceal that she had noticed the unconscious workings of his fond presumption, but they gave her no disturbance. Her dignity, she conceived, raised her beyond the reach of his aspirations, and with a playfulness becoming her temper and her years, she resolved to punish, while she trifled with his imprudence. She saw, that in inviting him that evening into her presence she had exposed herself to the tattle and gossip of the Court, and she had something like a suspicion, that in preferring his music to that of the Scottish minstrels, she had, perhaps, offended the pride of some of them; and the resolution which followed these her reflections, was, alas! one of her earliest errors. She saw not, that in resolving to change her deportment towards him into cold and retired dignity, she would tacitly convey to him that she had discovered his sentiments, and thus encourage him to persevere by saving him from the hazardous adventure of any declaration.

Such was the state of those bosoms within the walls of Holyrood-House, in the tranquillity of which we are most interested. It will be seen that there was sufficient cause among them, to raise fearful apprehensions as to the honour and happiness of the different parties. Nor can the sympathy of the reader be withheld from the innocent feminine resolution of the Queen. It was justified, if the expression may be allowed, by the simplicity of youth; and, moreover, she was altogether unacquainted with the remorseless determination of Chatelard, to affect a passion for Adelaide, to mask the insolence of his arrogant affection for herself.

CHAPTER XVI.

"His easy, vacant face, proclaimed a heart."
CHURCHILL.

KNOCKWHINNIE, from the time he parted with Southennan, had not been idle. After giving Stayns his horse, he went to the Unicorn, a tavern in the then fashionable Canongate, kept by one Thomas Balwham.

This tavern was much frequented by the courtiers and persons of note, who had occasion to visit Edinburgh. At this particular time it was the resort of the French gentlemen who came over with the Queen; and the object of Knockwhinnie in going there, was to obtain what information he could respecting Dufroy.

On entering the house, he went straight to the host's private apartment, for he had known him in other times, and no sooner did Balwham see him, than he exclaimed,

"Eh! Knockwhinnie, where hae ye been this mony a-day. Oh! but I'm blythe to see you; and nae doubt ye hae heard the news, or ye wouldna' been so venturesome as to come in fair day-light to Embro."

Knockwhinnie shook his old familiar host warmly by the hand, without speaking. He then sat down in an obscure corner of the room, and appeared a good deal affected by recollections which seemed suddenly to break upon him. Balwham, seeing his emotion, resumed—

"Its nae marvel, Knockwhinnie, that the news troubles you, for although as unfortunate mischances hae fallen out o' as gude hands, it would ha'e been an awfu' thing had ye slain the French gentlemen, instead o' that ringen deevil Montgomerie o' Auchenbrae."

"What do ye mean?" exclaimed Knockwhinnie, starting in consternation from his seat, "of what news do you speak? —why of Auchenbrae?—to what do you allude?—and what mistake was there in the vengeance I would have inflicted on Dufroy?"

"It's no possible," replied his host, "that ye canna' hae

heard the tidings that hae come wi' the gentlemen in the Queen's train. You, that the truth o' them maist concerns!"

"I have heard nothing," replied the outlaw, gloomily returning into his seat; "I am but just come in. I have been for some weeks living a solitary and a savage life in the moors of the West. What is it you have heard? I beseech you to sit down, and calmly tell me, and I will endeavour to control the feelings which your strange words have inflamed."

Balwham was surprised at hearing this; and, taking a chair near to Knockwhinnie, said,

"Hech! but ye ha'e suffered a great deal since ye were put to the horn, but I hope it's a' o'er now, especially as the Count looks weel and brawly. And then he has been sic a father to your daughter, as I ha'e heard some o' the gentlemen, that's now in the house, this very day tell :—they say he has 'dopted her for his own, and that she gangs by his name, and that nae Christian man could, for tenderness, be a truer parent."

In all this there was so much strange matter, that Knockwhinnie sat in a state of confusion, as if he had been stunned by a blow. Dufroy had adopted his daughter, his attack on the Count's life was in error, the profligate Auchenbrae was the one who deserved the dagger!—these thoughts passed wildly through his mind. Unable to collect himself sufficiently to ask for an explanation, he sat with his countenance pale and vacant, and his eyes almost void of speculation, while the garrulous host continued:

"And it maun be sic a gratification to you to see the young leddy, whom every body says is a perfect pearlet o' beauty, and had she been a princess, would ha'e been as bonny as the Queen hersel'. She is by a' accounts mair a minion wi' the Queen's Majesty, than her wee curly white dog; a wonderfu' creature, the likes o' which was ne'er seen in the bounds o' Scottish land, till the Queen stept out the boat wi't in her ain royal arms. Sic a love and pet, they say——"

Knockwhinnie impatiently interrupted him, and said, "For Heaven's sake, Balwham, be merciful, and have more method. Tell me what you have heard that concerns me. All the world seems to know that which I am most interested in knowing, and cannot learn!"

"'Deed, Knockwhinnie," replied his host, "ye're really in an unco condition o' ignorance. Ha'e ye no heard that your leddy died in a convent in Caen, in Normandy?"

"No."

"Ha'e ye no heard that the Count has since been a father to your daughter?"

"You have said so."

"Ha'e ye no heard that the Count is your compassionate friend?"

"Tell me how—tell me how!"

"Now, Knockwhinnie, if ye'll no hear me patiently, I'll ne'er be able to make you understand the rights o' the case."

"What is said of Auchenbrae, how comes his tarnished name to be mixed with my misfortunes?"

"Ye ken they say that it was wi' him your leddy spouse jumped the castle wall, and was galloping off ahint him; when by an accident the Count, wi' the politesse o' a French cavalier, came up in the moonlight, and rescued her out o' his clutches; but before your servants that were in the pursuit reached the spot, Auchenbrae was aff and out-o'-sight; and so they thought the Count was the malefactor. That's ae version o' the tale, which a' the tongues o' the town, that ha'e any time to spare frae speaking o' the Queen's Majesty, are this night telling."

"Who can prove the truth of this story?" exclaimed the outlaw, starting from his seat.

"Bide a-wee—bide a-wee!" said Balwham; "dinna ye think, Knockwhinnie, that the Count himsel' is the probable man rightly to tell you the story?"

At this crisis a noise and bustle was heard in the house, and the honest host was loudly called for by name. It was occasioned by the Provost's halberdiers coming in search of Knockwhinnie, against whom they had a warrant. It happened that in going out to see the occasion of the noise, Balwham left the door open, by which Knockwhinnie heard his name repeated, and in consequence leaped out of the window and concealed himself in an out-house. His host, desirous to befriend him, and yet being responsible to the magistrates for his own conduct, was perplexed when he heard the purpose upon which the halberdiers had come. He, however, affecting not to understand whom it was they were in search of, spoke louder than was necessary, in order that Knockwhinnie might be apprized of his danger; and when he heard the rustle of his escape by the window, knowing by it that the bird was flown, he confidently assured the officers that the outlaw was not in the house. Upon this one of the halberdiers remarked to his companions, that his information they would still find was right, and that it would have been as well had they taken his advice, and gone straight to Widow Hutchie's, where Southennan had put up; for the man with the embroidered vest beneath a friar's cloak, who was hanging about the door of that house, was assuredly no other than Knockwhinnie.

Balwham told them that they were, as respected that man, in error, for he knew him very well.

" He has been," said he, " in this house a' the afternoon, and is a friar belonging to the abbacy of Kilwinning, wha came in this morning frae the west, to meet some ither shavelings about their idols and their trumpery;" for the Maister Balwham was of the new light of the Reformation, especially when he had occasion to speak with the armed servants of that great pillar of the Protestant cause, Provost Maccalzean. " And I can tell you," added the host, " that maybe he's a tod worth the hunting; for he's nae other than Auchenbrae, the rampageous laird that used to keep the shire o' Renfrew in het water frae Yule to Yule, and is the even down adversary o' puir Knockwhinnie, because he has done that afflicted man an injury that canna' be repaired."

" Auchenbrae!" exclaimed one of the halberdiers: " that's the other honourable outlaw that we're to take up, *in vindictam publicam.*"

" Hech, man Johnnie," cried our worthy friend, Vintner Balwham, " but ye ha'e become learned in the law."

" It's a duty incumbent," replied Johnnie, " for a provost's halberdier to know something: I have ta'en the oath to be *fidly in offeeshy.*"

" Whar' did ye learn that fishy? Was't frae Maggy Scate o' Fisheraw, or Jenny Partans o' Prestonpans, or Peggy Cockles o' Musselburgh?"

" Nane o' your blethers, Maister Balwham! It would be mair to the purpose, since we haena' found a dishonester man than the host o' the Unicorn, yoursel', in the house, that ye should be mulcted a tass o' Lodovie."

The Maister Balwham, glad to get rid of them on these conditions, summoned his handmaid, Dorothea, with the gardevine, to serve the solacium.

CHAPTER XVII.

> "Give me a case to put my visage in,
> A visor for a visor; what care I
> What curious eye doth quote deformities?
> Here are the beetle-brows shall blush for me."
> ROMEO AND JULIET.

As soon as Knockwhinnie heard the Unicorn again quiet, he left his hiding-place and went back into the house, where having learned from Balwham what had taken place with the Provost's men, and that they had gone in quest of Auchenbrae, he expressed great impatience to follow them; but his host strongly dissuaded him from attempting it.

"First learn," said he, "if the news be true that the French gallants and others were rehearsing here anent your auld adversary, as ye supposed him, the Count; for, until some remeid o' law is gotten upon it, ye may be brought to trouble, if ye happen to be ta'en up for the auld affair."

Knockwhinnie thought there was good reason in this; but he was wilful, and had so long led a life regardless of the wonted customs of society, that, while he admitted the justness of Balwham's observations, he only thought of evading his advice, and accordingly replied—

"What you say deserves attention; but it too deeply concerns, not only my interests but my peace of mind, to ascertain as quickly as possible the exact circumstances in which I am now placed: in short, Balwham, I must claim your help in this matter. There were occasions in other times, when for mere pranks and ploys, you could find the means of maskings; can you not lend or borrow for me some of those old disguises that you were wont to supply in the plays before Lent? I remember that you had the garb of an old carle with a long beard is it still forthcoming?"

"Ah! Knockwhinnie, yon days o' pranks and ploys are a' reformed awa'! Instead o' maskings and mummings, we maun now tune our pipes to psalms and springs o' worship. But now that I think on't, the garb for Elijah in the Desert, which is the one ye speak o', is in the press; and if it's no eaten into remnants by the moths, ye shall ha'e it, and the beard likewise."

The host accordingly opened the wardrobe, and beneath a plentiful assortment of blankets and napery, the prophet's gown and beard were found, in very tolerable condition.

"Ah!" said the host, as he assisted Knockwhinnie to put them on, "we'll ne'er see sic days and nights o' jollity again. This Reformation, as it's called, is a dreadfu' dauntoner to mirth and gude custom. I weel recollect that the last man wha wore this gown was the auld Yerl o' Mar! A cantie bodie it was, for though he was then weel wan through three score and ten, he was yet a birkie sparrow ; and put on this dress, to scog him in some killfuddoching that he had wi' Madame La Mode, the old Queen's millinder, a cockletopt French leddy, that was soon after sent out o' the kingdom, by order o' the Queen Regent, for——"

"Make haste," interrupted Knockwhinnie; "make haste!" and his toilet being made, Balwham surveyed him for a moment at some little distance, saying, "They'll hae clear eyne and bent brows that can discover the stout Laird o' Knockwhinnie in thae garments o' eild. But ye maun stoop your head, and take a sore hoast; for there ne'er was either anchorite or prophet wi' sic square shouthers, and sae stalwart a mien."

Being thus disguised, the Outlaw proceeded after the Provost's men to Widow Hutchie's; but before he reached the door, he met them coming from it, with Friar Michael, alias Auchenbrae, in custody, followed by a crowd. He could not, however, with all the artifice of his disguise, entirely conceal himself; for the boy Hughoc, as already related, discovered him. But he was not detected by any other, and passed on with the crowd after the prisoner, into the council-chamber.

The Provost was seated, as befitted his dignity, at the head of the council-table, with the bailies and counsellors around it ; for although it was now a late hour, yet such was the riotous state of the city, on account of the people flocking in from all parts of the country to greet the Queen's Majesty, and many of them not of the best of characters, it was necessary that all in authority should be vigilant and at their posts.

When the halberdiers presented Auchenbrae to his Lordship, one of the Bailies said in a whisper to his neighbour, glancing at the prisoner, "Isna' he a dure-looking sinner?"

The learned Johnnie Gaff, in the mean time, handing the warrant to the Provost, said—

"Nae doubt, my Lord, your Lordship kens that the first thing ye hae to do in the precognition, is to speer *in presentia dominorum*, if the panel has a *person standing judeeshy* ?"

"Johnnie!" said the Provost, looking at him with proper magisterial solemnity, and adding, with a dignified inflexion of voice, "I know my duty!" And, turning to the prisoner, he said, "Hugh Montgomerie, of Auchenbrae, what is your name?"

"I think," replied the delinquent, "your Lordship has no need to ask that question."

"He cònfesses to the fact," said the Lord Dean of Guild.

"Yes," observed the Provost, and, looking towards the clerk, dictated—"Hugh Montgomerie, of Auchenbrae, being convened before us, declares that he is Hugh Montgomerie, of Auchenbrae."

"I beg your Lordship's pardon," interposed the accused; "I have made no such declaration."

"Hold your peace," exclaimed one of the Bailies, "and don't interrupt the procedure!"

"Clerk, have ye written down what I told you?" said the Provost; and, addressing himself to the prisoner, inquired, "Hugh Montgomerie, of Auchenbrae, have not you been guilty of haimsucken?"

"Oh!" cried Johnnie Gaff, "my Lord, ye hae forgotten to caution the panel no' to say anything that'll hurt himself; for it's laid down in the law, that every man is bound to be innocent, for his own sake, until he be found guilty."

"Clerk," said one of the counsellors across the table, "is that really the law?"

"I canna' speak positively," replied the Clerk; "but I rather think that it is the new law. At least, I hae heard the like used in pleadings afore the Lords."

"Well, but we must stick to the matter in hand," said the Provost. "Clerk, write down declares——what did ye delare, prisoner?"

"Declare! nothing," replied Auchenbrae.

"Don't be contumacious," said one of the Bailies, advisingly.

"When did this take place?" inquired the Provost.

"What?" rejoined the prisoner.

"He's dure, indeed," said the Bailie who first remarked his ungainly countenance.

"I'm thinking, my Lord," interposed Johnnie Gaff, "that

the proceedings, *quoties toties*, should be *quam primum*, that is as soon as possible"—

"Be silent, sir!" said the Provost.

At this moment the whole Council, who had been somewhat astonished at the Latin and loquacity of Johnnie Gaff, and his compeers being no less so, looked marvelling at one another, while Auchenbrae nimbly leaped from between the officers, and made his escape by the door, which, on account of the warmth of the weather, had been left open.

"Stop him! stop him!" cried provost, bailies, counsellors, clerk, and officers, all at once.

"He's a most audacious varlet!" cried the Provost, while the officers hurried in pursuit.

"Johnnie Gaff! Johnnie Gaff!" cried the physiognomical Bailie; "hadna' ye better take a fugæ warrant wi' you?"

Johnnie turned round, and, with a look of ineffable contempt at the ignorance of the magistrate, in talking of a fugæ warrant on such an occasion, exclaimed, "There's nae warrant wanted but a gude pair o' heels and hands!" and then stately strode out at the door, saying to himself, but loud enough to be heard by all present, "Hech, sirs! it's a fine time when bailies hae gotten Latin tongues!"

CHAPTER XVIII.

"I'll bless that hand
Whose honourable pity seals the passport
For my incessant turmoils to their rest."
THE LADY'S TRIAL.

SOUTHENNAN had, in the mean time, been so interested by the news that Hughoc had brought of the disguise in which he had detected Knockwhinnie, that he could not repress his anxiety to learn what had happened to him. Accordingly, notwithstanding the lateness of the hour, before he had half finished supper, he rose from table, and ordered the boy to show him the way to the council-chamber in the Tolbooth, where the magistrates were sitting. But he had not occasion to proceed far: scarcely had he left the door, when the Outlaw in the prophet's garb made his appearance. Southennan would have passed him without notice but for the boy, who at once recognised him.

"Well met!" exclaimed Knockwhinnie, in a hollow, undertoned, agitated voice; "I have been in quest of you."

Southennan immediately turned round to go back into the house with him; but the Outlaw laid his hand upon his arm, and said, "Not there; let us rather walk, I am not safe in any house. It is known I am in the town; warrants are out against me; I am hunted every where. Merciful Heaven! spare me but until I shall have executed thy justice!"

Southennan waved with his hand to the boy to leave them, and go home to bed; but Hughoc had heard as much, in these few words, as an ordinary dose of mandragora could not have lulled; and, prompted by curiosity to hear more, he followed them with stealthy steps in the shadow of the houses, heedless of the consequences he might incur by so attempting to play the eaves-dropper on his master.

"What has befallen you, Knockwhinnie;" said the young Laird, as they moved from Widow Hutchie's door; "What has so shaken you?"

The Outlaw, with considerable emotion, related what the host of the Unicorn had told him, and how he had, in consequence, been incited to disguise himself, and to follow Auchenbrae to the presence of the magistrates; "where," said he, "I discovered, among the halberdiers, an old servant of my own, who was in the house of Knockwhinnie when it was dishonoured; a trustworthy fellow, though fantastically affecting law and learning. If he discover me, he may perhaps shut his eyes; but I doubt if his integrity will allow him to have so much compassion. He was one of those who saw my wife with Dufroy; or, as Balwham has it, who found her with him after Auchenbrae had escaped."

Southennan remained for some time thoughtful, and then said, "Surely, now you will suspend the execution of your purpose against Dufroy, until the truth of Balwham's story is ascertained."

"To-morrow," replied the Outlaw, with feeling, "to morow my fate must be decided : I cannot longer live in this coninual whirlwind."

"But your misfortune has taken a new form. It seems doubtful if the Count is the seducer; it is even doubtful, I think, if your lady may have been guilty."

"Say not so, say not so!" cried the unhappy Knockwhinnie : "tell me not that I have been so rash as to use my dagger without just cause; so inhuman as to abandon my beloved Margaret, and she innocent!"

"At least," resumed Southennan, "you cannot but pause. I will in the morning see Dufroy; I will give myself up to the investigation of this strange business. In the mean time conceal yourself. If Dufroy is guiltless of the ruin you ascribe to him, I know he is so noble minded and so worthy a gentlemen, that but little persuasion will be wanted to induce him to stay the warrants out against you; and then you will have freedom to sift the truth."

She was too gentle and too pure," exclaimed Knockwhinnie, "ever to have been won by such a tavern royster as Auchenbrae. I shall want no other proof of her innocence, than that she was rescued from him. But why came she not to me? Why did she so shun me, and give my child to Dufroy?"

"Have you not already told me," replied the young Laird, calmly, "that, on first hearing the news of your lady having fled with Dufroy, you instantly started from Paris, and suffered no hinderance in your haste until you had wreaked your vengeance, as you supposed, here in Edinburgh on him. Since that time, until the rumour rose of the Queen's intended return, you have lived the wild life of a fugitive. It is time, Knockwhinnie! that you should bridle your impetuosity, and before again taking council of revenge, know what has been the wrong, and who is the offender.

"You would almost persuade me that I am the guiltiest—"

"Not so : I would but urge you to be surer in your cause before you strike again. Those Frenchmen, from whom Balwham has drawn his information, doubtless know something of the truth : I will see them before going to the court. Moreover, Auchenbrae could not be alone in the abduction of your lady; some servant or companion he undoubtedly had, by whose testimony her fame may be vindicated."

"Alas!" replied Knockwhinnie, "she is dead! What will her vindication now avail; the world's pity and her husband's love cannot affect her more!" and he suddenly burst into tears.

At this moment a noise of tumult and hallooing was heard approaching, and they turned into a dark wynd to avoid the crowd, while Hughoc, who was close behind unseen, ran up the steps of an outside stair for the same purpose. Southennan and his companion were, however, obliged to return from their retreat, in consequence of the inhabitants coming out of their houses with candles and croozies to see the occasion of the uproar, and they took refuge within the staircase, which the boy had ascended, thus affording him an opportunity of being gratified to the full extent of the desire which had prompted him to follow them.

"I shall not be surprised," said Knockwhinnie, "if this mob is with the Provost's men who went in pursuit of Auchenbrae. If so, I will go with them."

"Be not so wilful," replied Southennan: "if they have taken him, he now will be kept in safe custody till the morning; and you have many questions that must be answered before you can demand atonement from Auchenbrae, supposing Balwham's information correct."

"My long estrangement from the restraints and usages of society," said the Outlaw, with a sigh, "have made me too apt to obey the impulse of the moment. I shall submit to your advice. In one so young I have seldom met with so much discretion."

By this time the crowd was passing the foot of the stair, and by the numerous lights in the open windows, it proved, as Knockwhinnie expected, that the tumult was occasioned by the halberdiers having seized Auchenbrae, whom they were conducting back to the Tolbooth.

"It is him!" said Knockwhinnie, as they passed, and Hughoc, forgetting himself and his concealment, stooped his head close down to his master's ear, and subjoined,

"It's Friar Michael, o' Kilwinning."

Southennan turned round upon the boy, astonished at finding him there, but Hughoc soon extricated himself by saying, in consequence of what he had overheard,

"Werena' ye wishing to hear, Laird, where some o' Auchenbrae's rampageous men or friends could be heard o'?"

"What do you know o' them?" interposed Knockwhinnie, somewhat severely.

"Oh, naething," replied the boy; "but only if the Laird be minded to see ony o' them, I, maybe, could gie a guess where some were to be found."

"How came you," cried Southennan, angrily, "to know whether I had any such wish?"

"Just by an instinct, and because every body in Widow Hutchie's has gotten an unco tale about Auchenbrae and Knockwhinnie."

"And where may this follower of Auchenbrae be met with?"

"He was reested," replied Hughoc, "when ye were down

looking at the Queen, in the Abbey, and carried awa' to the Ward House in the Canongate, there to be riddled and sifted anent a transgression."

"Then is he, I doubt not," said Southennan, addressing himself to Knockwhinnie as they descended from where they were standing, into the street,—" arrested on account of something connected with your business; but the night is far spent, and we can do nothing before the morning. In the mean time, I can only repeat, keep yourself out of sight until we have learned something that may be trusted. I shall not ask you to come with me; the boy, however, will remain with you till you have found an asylum for the night, when he will return to let me know where I shall find you in the morning."

CHAPTER XIV.

"Hark! the game is roused!"

CYMBELINE.

AUCHENBRAE had been arrested on a warrant for the crime of haimsucken, committed on the person of Kinlochie, in his own house. When he found, after scouring the moors of Renfrewshire, that Knockwhinnie had been there during the rain, as we have described, and was allowed to depart unmolested, sharp words arose between them, a quarrel ensued, in which Kinlochie was wounded, and he being a resolute character followed him to Edinburgh for satisfaction, and was the cause of his arrest. There had, indeed, been an old grudge between them; for Auchenbrae, presuming on the sheriff being his kinsman, held in little respect the rights of his neighbours, while in the pursuit of his own profligate courses.

During the re-examination of Auchenbrae, when he was again brought before the magistrates, touching this alleged offence, several questions were put to him, which, in contempt of consequences, he had the hardihood to answer to his own crimination. He confessed the fact of the wound he had given, but refused to explain the motives by which he had been actuated, acknowledging however, that it was at his instance the Sheriff's men had been sent out in quest of Knockwhinnie, whom he was resolved to bring to punishment.

When questioned as the particular reasons which at that time moved him to proceed with such rigour against the Outlaw, he doggedly declined to reply. The magistrates, however deficient in the formalities of juridical procedure, were yet, in the plain substantial business of justice and investigation, shrewd and intelligent, and would not endure this contumacy. A controversy, in consequence, arose, which, though irrelevant to the offence with which the prisoner was charged, tended to the ends of justice ; for the story of Knockwhinnie's attempt on the life of Dufroy was brought to mind, by which it appeared that Auchenbrae had in some measure been concerned in it.

Johnnie Gaff, who was a deeply-interested spectator of these irregular discussions, on hearing this, interposed, and requested that he might be examined as to what he knew of that affair, and was accordingly permitted to declare—

"*Nitialibuz*," said Johnnie, "that's in the first place, *primo loco*, I, John Gaff, umquhile a servitor in the ha' of Knockwhinnie, and now a messenger-at-arms, and in the train o' my Lord Provost o' the Burgh of Embro', hae been cogneezant"—

"Stop!" cried the Provost ; "we havena' time to be particular anent the niceties o' law ; just tell us the right truth, and we'll dispense for this sederunt with the use of Latin words."

Johnnie, not altogether pleased at being so interrupted in the display of his legal knowledge and erudition, then related with a commendable brevity, partly arising from the ill humour of the moment, the flight, as he called it, of the Lady Knockwhinnie.

"She was sitting by hersel'," said he, "at her bower window, looking out at the moon, or counting the stars, when her waiting-woman, Jenny Tawpie, saw twa men on horseback passing under the window. Jenny was at the time on the leads o' the castle; and, being on the leads, she lookit down like a doo wi' the tail o' her e'e, and speered what they wanted ; and ane o' them, she said, answered wi' the voice o' Auchenbrae, that she had kent o' the auld for nae gude. Weel, down she cam' rinnin', and alarmed us, the men that were sitting at the ha' fire ; and we rose, and girded on our swords, and went out to see wha it was, and what they wanted. But afore we could get the castle yett opened, and the draw-brigg down, the ne'er-do-weels, be they wha they may, had gotten the leddy out o' the window, and were aff and awa' wi' her in tha grips o' ane o' them. I trow it was then fye-gae-rin and fye-gae-ride wi' us a'. We did na' wait to saddle or bridle, but just wi' the halter we mounted, and rade after; but they had sae far the heels o' us, that we didna come up wi' them till we had crossed the ford, where we found our leddy lying on the grass, and the Count Dufroy pityfully bending o'er her, his man and twa horses standing beside them; which made it plain and manifest that it wasna' Auchenbrae, but the Frenchman, that had won her by his parleproos. That, ye see, was the why and the wherefore that my past maister, Knockwhinnie, gied the Count a bit deg in the side: every honest man wha heard the tale was sorrowfu' that it wasna' effeckwal."

"What say you to this, Auchenbrae?" said the Provost.

"Just that I am sorrowful, too," was the reply.

"What for are ye sorrowful?" inquired one of the Counsellors who was nearest to him.

"Look at my haffit!" cried the prisoner, impatiently.

"The Gude preserve us!" cried the Counsellor, glancing at it; "as sure 's death, it's as plain as my loof: his lug's awa'!"

"Yes, he struck it off with his sword, in tearing the lady from my arms."

"Oh!" cried the whole of the Magistrates and Counsellors, raising their hands, "it's you then that was the guilty man;" and subjained Johnnie Gaff, "our Jenny Tawpie was right after a', and it was Auchenbrae that the leddy ran awa' wi'!"

Here the Provost, after consulting the Dean of Guild, proposed to adjourn until next morning.

"This business," said he, "thickens, and must be thinned. We'll send this very night a request to the Count Dufroy in the palace, to come to us in the morning, that we may sift the business to the sediment. Johnnie Gaff, you and your neighbours be answerable with the prisoner, by seven o'clock in the morning. But, gentlemen, this discovery, anent the wanton Lady Knockwhinnie, that we have with so much inquisition made this night, is a great thing; for no doubt the French Count will relent, and recall the warrant that's out at his instance. As for you, Auchenbrae, it is well known that you are both by habit and repute little better than a malefactor, and you had better leek to what Knockwhinnie will say when he hears that it was you who did him the wrong."

Auchenbrae, who had, during the whole process, treated the magistrate and council with scorn and derision, burst into the most outrageous passion when Johnnie Gaff said to the Provost,

"Dianna ye think, my Lord, he would be the better o' a bit iron round his coots and shacklebanes, and then he'll no be in *periculum;* the deepest den o' *squalor carceris* is o'er gude for the theif o' Knockwhinnie's bonnie blameless leddy. Hech, hech! she maun be fond o' a bird that would tak' for her pet a corbie!"

"Put him up in the traitors' hole," said the Provost; "and as he has once already slipped through your fingers, you may as well shorten his step and stint his stroke in any advisable manner."

The officers accordingly removed the prisoner, and the Provost rising, said to the clerk,

"Enter the adjournment; and now that I think o't," continued he, addressing the magistrates, "I hope my friends, amang the trades, are no' slack in getting our vestments ready for the ploy, wherein we are to do our ceremonies to the Queen's Majesty. Bailie," said he, turning to the one on the right hand, "I trust your lad found velvet enough in the town for our mantles and doublets, and that your needlemen will be industrious, that we¹ may not be disappointed: but this is dry work, and I see as ye're all exhoust, we'll be none the worse, before we go to our several places of abode, of a preeing of sack or hippocras, and so I thought some time ago, and sent Allister, the town-crier, to tell our old friend furthy Lucky Bickers to have a rizard haddie and a stoup of the right liquor ready for us about this time."

All the bailies and council highly applauded this forethought of the provost, and adjourned with him to the house of the worthy hostess, where, after occasions of nocturnal deliberation, they were wont to find solace.

CHAPTER XX.

"I'll fetch a turn about the garden, pitying
The pangs of barr'd affections."
CYMBELINE.

DEEPLY as Southennan felt for the misfortunes and perplexities of Knockwhinnie, they did not so entirely engross his mind, as to prevent him from thinking of the delightful vision he had seen gliding across the gallery of the palace. When he returned to his lodgings, and had retired to his chamber for the night, it came upon his remembrance with renewed brightness; but not with such intensity as to dazzle away the solieitous sleep, whose soft influence was rendered irresistible by his day's hard journey, and the busy variety of incidents in which he had subsequently been engaged. But, nevertheless, it had the effect of making her spell of shorter duration than usual, and he rose at an early hour, full of the recollection, and proceeded to the palace in quest of Dufroy, according to the promise given to Knockwhinnie.

The morning, even for the season, was beautiful. It was one of these soft hazy mornings which are only met with in the vallies of mountainous regions. The top of Arthur's Seat was covered with a cowl of mist, and a hoary wreath of similar vapour hung round the rocks of the castle, and gave to the towers and battlements the magical appearance of floating on a cloud. The sun, through the smoke of the eastern part of the city, shone like a golden orb; and although within the narrow streets and wynds through which Southennan picked his way, there were other airs and sounds than those which freshen and enliven the early day in rural scenes and sylvan solitudes, yet all around was cheerful and exhilarating. The house-maids, as they unclosed their windows, smiled to see the promise in the skies; the children were jocund and bounding; and the cadgers and country lads, bringing their wares to market, whistled gayly as they passed along. An old widow, who kept a little fruit and gingerbread stall near a private gate in the wall which in those days enclosed the palace, appeared dressed in her holyday clothes, patched but neat. As Southennan approached the gate, she was spreading her table for the exhibition of her merchandize, with a dornick table-cloth, bright and fresh from the fold, and congratulated the young Laird on the beauty of the morning, as he went through the gate, hoping that blither times and more courtly festivals were come again, and she told him, as news of good augury for her own vocation, that the city trades and bodies intended to entertain the Queen, for a welcome home, with pageantries and other shows, such as had not been seen in all Scotland since before the royal raid to Flodden Field.

On inquring for the Count Dufroy, Southennan was disconcerted at being informed he was already abroad; that he had gone up to the council-chamber of the city, in consequence of a summons which had been received from the Magistrates during the night, and that he was not expected to return for some considerable time, having left notice to that effect.

Somewhat chagrined at this disappointment, he was about to return to his hostel, where he expected his boy would be with information regarding the place of Knockwhinnie's concealment, when in retiring from the portal he met Chatelard. The Frenchman, exulting in the infatuated hopes which he indulged, received him with more than his wonted characteristic buoyancy, nor was Southennan less happy at their meeting, as it afforded him an opportunity of inquiring respecting the fair unknown, in whom he had become so suddenly and tenderly interested.

After the customary salutations of the morning, Chatelard invited him to walk in the palace gardens, an invitation which was courteously, or rather it should be said, joyfully accepted.

They had not taken more than a turn or two when Southennan mentioned the distress in which he had accidentally seen the young lady come from the Queen's chamber, with some encomium on her beauty, affecting, at the same time, more indifference in his inquiries than was consonant to the impression she had made, though natural to the sentiment which her sorrow and loveliness had inspired.

Chatelard, with the gay legerity of his countrymen, readily replied to all the questions of the enamoured Southennan, and conceitedly insinuated that he was probably cruel enough to be in some measure the cause of the tears he had witnessed. These insinuations were not calculated to sooth the mind of Southennan; but his natural quickness of discernment soon enabled him to discover, that if the gentle stranger was indeed attached to Chatelard, it was a passion without return. This discovery had the effect of awakening some suspicion of the purity of the Frenchman's declarations, especially when, in a short time afterward, he began to profess, with more vehemence than the occasion seemed to require, the love which he had determined to assume in order to mask his passion for the queen. Moreover, the caution of the young Southennan was surprised at the loquacity of Chatelard, and he could not but regard as something extraordinary, that he should, upon so slight an acquaintance, talk so openly to him of feelings which delicacy and genuine affection teach the sincere lover to conceal. He learned, however, from him, but without disclosing in any degree the emotion with which the intelligence affected him, that the fair unknown was no other than Adelaide, the adopted daughter of Dufroy. Could it be possible, thought he, that she is the child of Knockwhinnie; but upon this point Chatelard could give him no information. When he was engaged himself to come to Scotland with the court, Adelaide was already a favourite attendant on the Queen, and he had not, until during the voyage, any opportunity of becoming acquainted with her.

Although this conversation did not last very long, it yet served, to the instinctive quick-sightedness of Southennan, to disclose much of the latent vanity and secret ambition of Chatelard; for, in speaking of the feminine superiority and graces of the Queen in terms natural to their years, Southennan observed, with a kind of suspicious curiosity, that his companion affected greater coldness on the subject than any other who had ever beheld his royal mistress. On her intellectual qualities he was abundantly eloquent; he spoke of her personal courage and decision of character as if he had been praising the bravery and enterprise of a young knight, and he applauded the aptness of her scholarship as if he had been commending the genius of a student; but he never alluded to those charms and endowments which were far more attractive to youthful admiration. In this his hypocrisy overreached itself; for though the thought of his aspiring to the love of the Queen could not infect the reverential loyalty of Southennan even with the bare imagination of a possible presumption, he could, nevertheless, discern that Chatelard's guarded and circumspect language, in speaking of those qualities by which she was so personally distinguished, sprung from some resolution that had its motive deeper than the duties of his servitude, and his distrust, in consequence, of the truth and integrity of the Frenchman, was thus, in their first familiarity, heightened to a vigilant suspicion of his honour and principles.

CHAPTER XXI.

"The Duke's in council, and your noble self
I'm sure is sent for."
OTHELLO.

THE Count Dufroy was in the council-chamber before any of the magistrates made their appearance. Although he was unable to divine the reason for which he had been invited to come before them, he had yet a vague notion that the business had something to do with his adventure when formerly in Scotland and this preconception assisted in some degree to prepare him for the investigation.

At last two of the bailies appeared. They looked around them with that consciousness of superiority which befits and is so requisite to support civic dignity: one of them recognised, with a tacit and inscrutable wink, a customer in the crowd which pressed upon the council-table; and the other with a nod and some familiar phraseology, augmented the consideration of a friend whom he saw at a distance also in the crowd. Others of the Council then began to assemble, and after the compliments of the morning, they spoke together with many sentiments of admiration, all agreeing that " My Lord," meaning the Provost, had never been so jocose as on the preceding night. Then his lordship came in, and they took their seats with every proper demonstration of dutiful homage and respect; to all which he made a suitable return, becoming a chief magistrate on such a solemn occasion.

The Council being formed, the Provost rose, and said that he had the honour to report, " that by reason of the great stress of business thrown upon the Council held last night, because of the multitudinous state of the city, occasioned by the arrival of the Queen's Majesty within the realm, the sederunt thereof had been prolonged to a late hour; by which the members were sorely forefoughten, insomuch, that when the Council adjourned, at the late hour of eleven by Giles's clock, it was thought necessary, and to show their loyalty to the Queen's Majesty, that they should partake of some refreshment, as a solace after the arduous duties they had so strenuously performed, in the house of that most reputable vintner, Marion Bickers. He therefore submitted for the consideration of the Council, before going into the business of the day, whether the expense, being as he conceived on account of public duty, should be borne by the magistrates and council on their own pock-neuk, or, as it ought to be, made a charge on the community."

The question arising thereupon was moved by the Lord Dean of Guild, and seconded by past Bailie Brown, " That inasmuch as their sore labours and their great loyalty brought on the needcessity, the cost of the refreshment ought to be charged to the public accounts."

For sometime a patriotic diversity of opinion appeared on the subject; but in the end it was carried *nemine contradicente,* and the clerk was ordered to record a minute of it in the usual manner, and to read what he had recorded. This was accordingly done, and he read as follows:—

"That forsameikle as the Queen's Majesty cam yesterday, from o'er sea, into this her auncient kingrik and realme of Scotland, to the great joyaunce of her leil subjects, and the contentation of all her trew lieges, it behoved the Provoste, Bailies, and Counsale of the Burrow of Edinburgh, to demonstrate and mak manifest their hearty gude wull thereuntil; for the whilk reason, there being divers sorners and others misleart persones in and about the town, causing by their appearance, panicks and apprehensiones in the mindes of the weel-disposed lieges, it was fund expedient and necessar, to keepe a session and sederunt of the counsale intil æn late hour; by whilk great exertion, and through the labour of examinating malefactors and other ill-doers, the Provost, Bailies, and Counsale aforesaid, were meikle exhoust; insomuch, that it was thocht due in reverence and thankfulness, for what had come to pass by the Queen's Majesty's safe return, and the debilitation whilk the foresaid Provoste, Bailies, and Counsale had suffered in the said quest, to seek in the house of æn Marion Bickers, a reputable widow woman, a vintner forenent the Luckenbooths, some moderate refreshing; and the said Provoste, Bailies, and Counsale having adjourned until the samen, thea were there conjunctly and severally pleasauntly solaced with kippered saumon, rizard haddies, partens, and other shell-fishes, together with a certain part and portion, of ane chappin stoup of the French liquor, and fifteen stoups of sack wine, being ane stoup for ilk man, and ane double stoup for the Provoste; and the samen being this day taken into consideration by the said Provoste, Bailies, and Counsale, they unanimously appruved of the samen, and authoreezed and empoured as they hereby authoreeze and empour the Treasurer, to pay and defray the cost and charge thereof, and to put the samen to the count of the cost of receiving the Queen's Majesty."

"On the minute being read, the Lord Dean of Guild rose, and said—

"Altho' every kything of loyalty has my most hearty approbation, yet I have a duty to perform, and I am sure that all my colleagues will be as liel as myself in this matter. It was an occasion last night, caused upon us by a great event, but it would be most wrongous were we to establish a precedent, that whenever a Queen's Majesty, or a King's either, returns upon us, that we should put the community to a dreadful outlay for our particular behoof, I therefore, beg that it may be entered in the minutes of Council, that the community is never hereafter to be burdened with the cost and outlays of such banquetings."

All present ruffed upon the table their high admiration of this magnanimous patriotism, and the clerk was directed to make a record of the same.

When this important part of the business of the morning was determined, and when the town-clerk had read over the minute of the proceedings in the case of Auchenbrae, on which the Court had adjourned, that delinquent was again ordered to be placed at the bar; and the Count Dufroy then called by name, immediately presented himself, and was most courteously invited by the Provost to take a seat within the bar.

Some little time elapsed before the halberdiers appeared, and in the mean while a number of pleasant and facetious bagatelles passed between the Count and the Lord Provost, who politely recollected that he had seen him during the siege of Leith; and past Bailie Brown inquired of the Count, in a most debonair manner, concerning a certain very remarkable French officer of distinction, with a Roman nose, and large black whiskers, whom he recollected in the French army, but whose name he did not then exactly remember.

"He was," said the Bailie, "a most entertaining lad, and could play on the lute with the dexterity of a trumpeter, or a troubadour, the sort of musicants ye have in France: for my part, however, though I will allow their music to be most soft and melodious, I yet cannot but say, that I think every man of a correct taste will acknowledge that the bagpipes on the far side of a Highland loch, are to the full more commendable."

The Count replied, that there was no accounting for tastes, and to some ears there might be a fascination in the bagpipes, especially at a distance.

At this moment Johnnie Gaff came forward followed by his compeers, with considerable consternation in their faces.

CHAPTER XXII.

"*Mer.* You gave us the counterfeit fairly last night.
Rom. What counterfeit did I give you?
Mer. The slip, sir, the slip."
ROMEO AND JULIET.

On seeing the halberdiers, the Provost exclaimed, with some impatience,

"Bring forward the prisoner? What for will ye no do your duty?"

Upon this Johnnie Gaff stepped forward, and said—"*Non est inventy.*"

"None of your Latin havers, Johnnie," said past Bailie Brown: "but tell us in the language of Christianity, where's the prisoner?"

"Na!" said Johnnie, "that would puzzle a soothsayer; but he's either aff and awa, wi' a whisk like the wind through a key-hole, or he has undergone some unco metamorphoze."

"What is it you mean?" said the Provost.

"Just nae mair than, that where he should hae been in the iron room, instead o' him, we found his servant man, Watty Wallace."

"How can that be possible?"

"As to the possibility, I hae little to say, but it's true; it's neither in *essy*, or in *possy*; it's just a certainty."

"This is most extraordinary!" exclaimed the Provost, Bailies, and Council.

"And how can you account for this neglect in your warding, Johnnie? I never heard the like of this," said the Provost.

"It wasna our faut, my Lord! it a' cam o' the crowd that fallow't us up the steeple stair. In that crowd there happened to be the foresaid Watty Wallace in *pro: per:*, wi' a plaid about him the very marrow, I would say the ilk in a certain sense, o' the ane his master had on. Weel ye see, my Lord, when we were in the mirk o' the stair, the bowet wherewi' Robin Lockie was lighting us up, was driven out o' his hand by the said Watty Wallace, greeting like a bairn, and forcing himself in on a pretence to tak a loving leave o' his maister; by the whilk thing, somebody put their feet on the said bowet, and smashing the horn, quenched the candle. So being a' in the dark, we somehow, *non clary constat*, rammed Watty Wallace intil tha hole, a substitute for his master, wha maun wi' a sort o' glamoury hae slippit thro' our fingers like an evil spirit, for we kent naething o't till we ga'ed to bring him hither this morning."

"Weel," said past Bailie Brown, "I ne'er heard o' sic a supple trick, and is't a possibility that the prisoner has really absconded?"

"He's *fugæ*," said Johnnie.

"Clerk," said the Provost, "ye must send a hue and cry out directly."

"*Esto!*" said Johnnie Gaff.

The Provost then addressed the Count.

"You have heard, sir, of the accidence that has befallen the man that you were called hither to confront, and as he has in a manner so singularly fled from justice, it is not very clear how we should deal with you; but since you have obeyed in so discreet a manner, our summons, we will just ask you a few simple questions, to the end, that it may not be said you were troubled to come from the palace to the Council Chamber of Edinburgh for nothing."

The Count assured the Provost, that he was ready to answer any question which might be put to him.

"Nothing can be more civil and polite than that," said the Provost; "now clerk, take your pen."

"Well, Count, was it you that broke into the Lady of Knockwhinnie's bower chamber, and stole her away?"

The Count, without answering the question, expressed himself happy in being at last placed in a situation to enable him to explain his part in a transaction which was still involved in mystery. But before we relate the statement of the Count, it is here necessary to mention some circumstances in the previous history of Knockwhinnie.

In early life, almost in his prematurity, in consequence of an agreement between their respective fathers, Knockwhinnie was married to the Lady Ellenor, a daughter of the Lord Kilburnie. Contrary to the course of such marriages, their union proved affectionate and happy. From the day of their betrothment, to that of their nuptials, a period of twelve years, they had lived together in the castle of Kilburnie. Knockwhinnie, however, was too bold and adventurous to remain always content with the blandishments of his bride. After the birth of a daughter, he was induced to visit Paris, then much frequented by the young nobility and higher gentry of Scotland; and while there was persuaded to become a member of the Scottish Guards, which at that period were the distinguished attendants of the French king. He then returned home for the purpose of carrying his lady and child to France; but to his extreme disappointment she was averse to go abroad, a circumstance which for the first time caused discontent between them, and he was in consequence obliged to return without her; in the hope, however, that she would yield to the influence of his absence, and voluntarily follow him.

When the Queen Dowager was Regent of Scotland, an army was lent her from France, to enable her to subdue the Protestant malcontents, and the Count Dufroy held in this army a high appointment under the Count D'Oisel. On his arrival at Linlithgow, where the dowager held her court, he found the Lord Kilburnie there with his family, and the Lady Ellenor and her child. Dufroy was previously acquainted with Kilburnie, who had been several times at Paris, and they were both equally happy to renew their former intimacy. It thus happened that the Count became a frequent visiter at the house of Kilburnie, and the freedom which he enjoyed there, with the gay affability of his own manners, was ascribed by some of the friends of the family to an attachment to the Lady of Knockwhinnie.

In the mean time Auchenbrae, a profligate scion of the Montgomeries of Eaglesham, had become deeply enamoured of the Lady Ellenor, and, being regardless of the means he employed to attain his ends, resolved to carry her off. This, as the reader is already informed, he had nearly effected, but was interrupted by an accidental encounter with the Count.

The previous rumours, which were altogether unfounded, to the prejudice of her honour, seemed to be verified to the servants, who in the pursuit, found her as already described, senseless in the arms of Dufroy. These rumours and the history of her elopement reached, without any allaying circumstance, Knockwhinnie, at Paris; and he, as the reader is informed, came instantly to Edinburgh, and attempted to satify his revenge by stabbing the Count at the Cross; an event which led to his own outlawry, and induced the Lord Kilburnie to persuade Lady Ellenor, with her child, to retire to a convent in Normandy, as the worthy host of the Unicorn, the Maister

Balwham, had related. The Count, on his return from the Scottish war, moved by his compassion for the unfortunate lady and her innocent misfortunes, and also by his attachment to the Lord Kilburnie, adopted her daughter Adelaide, gave her his name, and finally procured for her that place among the attendants of the young Queen, which ultimately brought her home to Scotland.

His explanation to the magistrates did not, of course, touch upon so many particulars; but it was so far in unison with what Johnnie Gaff had set forward in his declaration, that the only hiatus remaining unexplained, was the interval between the flight of the Lady Ellenor, and the finding of her with the Count; upon which point, he observed, that although not acquainted with Auchenbrae, he had no doubt whatever that it was him who had committed the abduction. "In the dark we met," said he; "and it was only by hearing the screams, and knowing the lady's voice, that I was led to interfere in her rescue."

CHAPTER XXIII.

"What news?
Hast thou met with him?"
ROMEO AND JULIET.

In the mean time, Southennan returned to his lodgings for Hughoc to conduct him to the house where Knockwhinnie had gone to conceal himself, but the boy was not there. He found, however, Baldy waiting for him, with considerable anxiety.

Baldy had been that morning early a-foot, in quest of a more becoming domicile for his master, and was now desirous of permission to remove their luggage.

"I hae," said he, "met wi' very creditable dry lodgings in Crichton's Land, ayont the Luckenbooths, only up nine stairs, in the house o' ane Mrs. Marjory Seaton, a leddy o' the single order, no being married, and haeing nae childer; she's a maist sponsible character, well stricken in years, and as prejinct in a' about her dwelling, as it's possible for our ain Abigail Cuninghame for her life to be."

Southennan expressed himself satisfied with the arrangement, although nine stairs up sounded somewhat above his wishes.

"Deed!" quoth Baldy, "I will allow it's taking you a thoct nearer heaven's yett before your time; but if ye heard what a panic's in the burgh on this occasion for lodgings, ye would be content wi' thae that I hea gotten, even if they had been nine stairs towards the entrance of anither place."

"Well," said Southennan, "let the things be taken there; but where is the boy? I want him."

"I trow," replied Baldy, "he's to be a fash to us. He's glaikit and ta'en up hither and yon, wi' Gude kens what: he was up and out this morning afore the skreigh o' day, and I misdoot if he hasna' gi'en himself o'er wi' mair gudewill towards that unco Knockwhinnie, than comports wi' faithful service to you, Laird: ye'll hae to gie him counsel, if it should be on the breadth o' his back, wi' a rung, no to be sae neglectfu' o' his rightful service."

While they were thus speaking, Hughoc made his appearance, and in approaching, gave his master a sign that he had something to tell not proper for Baldy to hear. Southennan, in consequence, repeated his order to remove the luggage without delay; and stepped towards the boy, who said, warily, in a whispering voice,

"I'm thinking we hae gotten into an awfu' trap. I did, yestreen, just what ye bade me. I ga'ed wi' Knockwhinnie to the house he has made his howf. It was up Gude kens how mony stairs, and its keepit by a long lean leddy, ane Mistress Marjory Seaton: she's a narrow woman, yon!"

Southennan was a little disconcerted that Baldy should have made choice of the same house; and was on the point of directing the boy to bid him suspend the removal of the luggage until he should have accommodated himself elsewhere, when Hughoc subjoined, still more impressively,

"And do ye ken, Laird, just when I had gotten Knockwhinnie weel within the door, and was coming down the stair, wi' a match in my hand for a light, wha should I meet coming up, wi' a flaught like a whirlwind, but Friar Michael, that was catched, ye ken, by the town offishers, talking high treason wi' our auld doited Father Jerome. What could be the meaning o' that, Laird?"

Southennan being altogether unacquainted with what had taken place before the magistrates, saw nothing very extraordinary in the circumstance which Hughoc had observed; and said, "Well, what then?"

"What then, sir!" exclaimed Hughoc, "wasna he on leg bail! But the wonderfu' thing o' a', sir, he ran up the stair, and I couldna' but blaw out my match, and creep after him; and what do ye think happened?"

" And what did happen?" asked Southennan, impatiently.

" He chappit at the door wi' his knuckle, and it was opened by Mistress Marjory herself, wi' an iron croosie in her hand. ' Eh cousin!' said she; ' Scog me!' quo' he, so in he went, the door was shut; and wasna' that a wonderfu' thing?"

" Is he too a lodger there," said Southennan, to himself, " that settles the point;" and he called aloud to forbid the removal.

" But that's no a'," said Hughoc, " I cam down the stair and out on the causey; and sic a stramash as there was in a crowd concerning ane Auchenbrae that had loupet out o' the hands o' the Lord Provost, when he was standing before him to be hanged for something that wasna canny. But, sir, for a' that, I cam hame and I gae to my bed, but I couldna sleep; so I rose at the gray day-light to see what Mistress Marjory was making o' her bonny birds. Now, sir, I'm gaun to let you into the marrow o' the fact."

" Well, go on," said Southennan, beginning to be more interested in the story; " You went there this morning—"

" I was so minded," replied Hughoc, " but just as I got to the foot o' the stair out cam a terrible stalwart gruesome randy carlin, wi a rung for a staff that would hae made a bawk to our barn; and wha do ye think it was? If I can trust my eyne, it was Friar Michael again; and he had a creel on his ba fu' o' gear like a fish-woman. Wasna this an extraordinar' thing?"

" And what did you?" asked his master.

" I had heard o' plots and conspeeracies about Courts, ye ken, Laird; and I said to mysel, surely this maun be ane o' them, but please Gude! I'll see the bottom o't, for maybe I'm ordained to be a mean o' saving the Queen's life, and may get something worth while for my pains. So ye see, maister, I just took my heels ahint me and fallow't madam that was the Friar Michael; and whar do ye think she gaed to?"

" Be more connected," said Southennan, " tell me, at once, what all this is about; for I have no time to listen."

" It's no possible," replied the boy, " to mak' the tale shorter; but I can skip the particulars till anither time, and tell you that I fallow't Friar Michael in his glamoury down to the ferry at the water o' Leith, and there he crossed, and for aught I ken, is aff and awa' to the Highland hills. Doesna' that cow a', Laird?"

"But what of Knockwhinnie? What have you seen or heard of him this morning."

"If ye would be a wee patientfu', Laird, I would tell you, for I canna mak the past and the present ae thing; but the come-to-pass was, when I saw Friar Michael o'er the water, back cam I to do my devoirs to Knockwhinnie, an' ye see I was soon again at the foot o' the mistress Marjory's stair, and I ran up; odd! yon's desperate stairs, they put me out o' breath before I got to the door; but to the door I did get, and tirled at the pin; and wha was sae ready at the sneck as the leddy hersel', to open and let me in. Then I said to her, that I cam frae you, and was sent to speer for Knockwhinnie: that was nae lee, Laird, for ye kan ye intended it should be sae. Odd! but she's an elsin, yon leddy; her eyne kindled, and she looked at me as if they had been wimbles, that would hae gaen thro' me. So I put on a weel-bred saft manner, and told her how my maister—that was you, sir—was a condisciple o' Knockwhinnie's, and how we had travelled intil Embro thegither, and how ye were concerned for fear he would this morning be the waur o' his journey, and I was come to speer for him. This beguiled the leddy, and she bade me come in, and be sure and dight my feet; she does keep a clean house, and that I'll tell my aunty Abigail, when, please fortune! we're a' back and safe at the Place again."

"Did you find Knockwhinnie there?" interrupted his master.

"Oh, no," said Hughoc, "he was out, and the leddy couldna' tell where. But she said he was in a very-weel-I-thank-you way; and that's a' I ha'e gotten, Laird, to tell you."

Little as the boy's story seemed to be to any purpose, it yet contained some tidings which interested his master. The conduct of Friar Michael seemed to be involved in some guilty mystery, and he was uneasy in reflecting that he had been first arrested in the company of his own chaplain. But the strongest impression which he received from the story was the curious accident, as it seemed to him, by which Baldy had been led to choose his lodging in a house frequented by characters in the hunted state of Knockwhinnie and Friar Michael. It appeared, however, that the latter was related to the hostess, and it might indeed be but by chance that Baldy had gone there; still he was perplexed, and without absolutely deciding not to go to his new lodgings, he ordered Baldy to postpone the removal till another time.

CHAPTER XXIV.

"Heaven has a gentle mercy
For penitent offenders."
THE LADY'S TRIAL.

SOUTHENNAN went into the house, and had scarcely seated himself in his own apartment, when the Count Dufroy, from the Council chamber, was announced. The visit was unexpected; but it had happened that after leaving the Tolbooth, the Count met Chatelard in the street, who informed him of Southennan's early visit to the Palace and the particular anxiety which he had evinced to see him.

Unaware of the interest which so many curious accidents and circumstances had excited in Southennan for Knockwhinnie, the Count, after a few civilities had passed between them, began to speak of the occasion which led him so early to attend a summons from the magistrates.

"I am in hope," said he, "that the time is come when Kockwhinnie will be disabused of the delusion under which he labours with respect to me."

He then recounted what had taken place before the magistrates regarding Auchenbrae, adding,

"I have no doubt by the description which I received from the Lady Ellenor on the night of her abduction, that he is the guilty party. There was great weakness in me at the time, in not making more sure of him, but my attention was absorbed in her condition, and he was permited to escape. I wish it were possible to convince Knockwhinnie of the truth of this. On many accounts I desire it; but chiefly on his daughter's, whose situation with the Queen, though honourable and distinguished, is not happy."

Southennan assured him that Knockwhinnie was inclined now to listen to every reasonable explanation, and had commisioned him to wait on the Count for that purpose.

"I can only," replied Dufroy, "repeat to you what I have said to others, that it was not by me the Lady Ellenor was stolen from her own house; that I found her in a state of insensibility in the possession of another; that I rescued her from the outrage ; and that it was in the crisis of rescue her own servants came up. Her father, the Lord Kilburnie, was so far satisfied with the purity of my conduct, that when he himself conducted her to Normandy, he placed her in the convent of the Ursulines at Caen, of which the abbess is my aunt."

Southennan then inquired how it had happened that no endeavour was ever made on the part of Lord Kilburnie to inform Knockwhinnie of these circumstances.

" Your observation is just," replied the Count, " but had you known the man you would not have been surprised at his conduct. He is no more, and I may speak of him truly as he was : it can now do him no harm, nor is there any lack of discretion in the freedom which I may take with him. He was a Scottish baron of the sternest breed, somewhat, it is true, tamed by occasional visits to Paris, but it was a mere habitude, no change had been produced upon his proud and fierce nature. The iron was not transmuted : it was only gilded. Something which was never explained to me, had filled him with resentment against Knockwhinnie, for having as he alleged, deserted the Lady Ellenor and her child, and this it was which prevented him from seeking to conciliate Knockwhinnie after the abduction. Satisfied with the innocence of his daughter, he disdained to explain as much to her husband, whose desertion he often wrathfully said, was the cause of the outrage to which she had been exposed. His death, soon after her retirement to France, left the affair in this unfortunate and undermined state."

" You must acknowledge," said Southennan, " that the affection you have shown to the Lady Ellenor's daughter, was calculated to confirm the jealousy of her husband."

" The child was helpless. I thought in no particular manner, either of her mother's wrongs, or of her father's attack on my own life. I was pleased with its beauty when I saw it with other noble children, who were placed for their education with my aunt the abbess. It was for it's own sake, having no family of my own, that I adopted it ; for though the Lord Kilburnie was reckoned among my friends, yet I regarded him with no such particular affection as to have adopted his granddaughter, had there not been other motives in the beautiful creature itself to attach me to her."

Southennan acknowledged that the explanation of Dufroy was to him satisfactory ; but there was still something unaccountable in the reserve with which the Count appeared to withhold his adopted daughter from her father ; for he remarked that Dufroy, though frank in the vindication of himself, evinced no wish to introduce Adelaide to her father. On the contrary, though he said nothing, it was evident by his manner, that he bore a secret dislike to Knockwhinnie. This was perhaps natural, considering what had taken place between them. Still to the young and generous mind of Southennan it seemed harsh: he thought that Dufroy should make more allowance for the wounded sensibilities of the Outlaw, and he was disappointed that he had not of his own accord offered to procure a pardon for Knockwhinnie, for whom, as the father of Adelaide, he felt a growing and more tender interest.

"Surely, Count," said he, "it cannot be, that doting with such paternal affection on the child of Knockwhinnie, you would not wish to promote her happiness, by enabling her father to join his affection to yours at this particular time, when you say that her situation with the Queen is so far less desirable than you had expected it would have been."

"He has done me an injury," replied the Count, gravely. "I speak not of what he did by his dagger; but the wound inflicted on my honour: he has yet to atone for that. Nor was it all regard for Adelaide that brought me at this time to Scotland."

Southennan was struck with the feeling which evidently agitated the Count; he thought it unwarranted, and expressed, with some degree of firmness in his manner, his surprise that the Count should think so sternly of an incident which partook so much of mistake and chance.

"By what you have stated," said he, "you admit that there was strong reason for Knockwhinnie to believe that it was you who had withdrawn his lady from her house. Every thing in the advent and first rumour of the affair was calculated to make Knockwhinnie believe you had done him that irreparable wrong; and he sought to gratify his revenge on you, believing you to be so guilty. Had he known then what you have now explained, he could not have felt against you what he then felt; and you should, therefore, think of what he then did as unintentional. Had he known the truth of the case, he could not have been your enemy; and, for the error under which he was impelled, should you not therefore forgive the act?"

The Count listened without emotion to what Southennan urged; he even appeared to acquiesce in the justness of some of his observations; but when the young Laird, with redoubled earnestness, entreated his assistance to obtain a revocation of the outlawry, and a pardon for Knockwhinnie's uncompleted offence, he looked at him with a steady eye, and then said, " What do you ask—what do you expect from me ?"

" I have said," replied Southennan, calmly, but with a tone more solemn than he had yet employed; I have said, considering the delusion under which Knockwhinnie acted, what he is justly entitled to receive."

" What is that ?"

" Your forgiveness, and the Queen's pardon."

A pause ensued. Southennan stood in visible expectation of an answer; but the Count cast his eyes upon the floor, and seemed thoughtful. At last, the young Laird said—

" Will you assist me to procure his pardon ?"

" No !" was the answer ; and the Count, at the same time bowing with particular respectfulness, immediately retired.

CHAPTER XXV.

" A fearful storm is hovering ; it will fall,
No shelter can avoid it."

FORD.

SOUTHENNAN was troubled. The reluctance which Dufroy showed to peform what honour and humanity equally required, appeared to discover the existence of a spring amid the motives of the heart, of which he had formed no previous conception. At first he was disposed to treat the refusal of the Count as weak and unworthy; he thought his antipathy to Knockwhinnie like the anger of the child at the stone by which it has been injured. But as he reflected more deeply, he began to suspect that through the predicament in which he had been placed by his connexion with the lady Ellenor, and by the story of the attempted assassination, he had incurred some other misfortune, and that it was perhaps the recollection of it which made him so calmly reluctant to abate the sufferings of the Outlaw; nor was he erroneous in this conclusion.

The Count Dufroy, at the period when the abduction of the Lady Ellenor took place, had become enamoured of Lady Margaret Douglas, a fair and pious votary of the reformed religion. Severe, according to the rules of those champions of the Reformation, whose doctrines she had embraced, she regarded the slightest aberration in morality as a greater offence than even adherence to the errors of Rome. She could look with favour on the accomplished Couut, while she lamented his religious obstinacy ; but the slightest stain upon his purity was in her eyes inexpiable : she heard of the assassination, of the cause to which it was imputed, and all partiality for Dufroy was at once erased from her heart. She saw him no more, and he was informed that it was in vain to expect she would ever permit him to renew his suit ; a decision made unalterable by soon after accepting the hand of the Rev. Simeon Glossar, an eminent divine of the new sect, and of great repute and efficacy as a preacher.

The knowledge which Dufroy obtained of the cause of her sudden and decided estrangement, made him feel as if the misfortune had not only come immediately from Knockwhinnie, but had been the result of some deliberate machination of his invention. We are not to examine the reasonableness of this feeling : it existed : it inspired motives which, though they did not draw the Count on into any active retaliation, yet caused him to regard Knockwhinnie as the adversary of his fortune.

In characters composed of more austere elements than those of Count Dufroy, it is probable that the feeling we have described would have instigated some darker purpose than any thought or wish which the generous and noble nature of that accomplished person could entertain. But still it affected him to the utmost degree of which his character was susceptible ; he was too honourable to indulge his animosity in sinister designs, and too just to think of revenging a wrong which, however deeply he felt, he could not conceal from himself was not voluntarily committed. But he could not so master the infirmity of man as to regard the sources of his disappointment in their true light.

" I have suffered," said he to himself, as he left Southennan : " and why should I involve myself more with the cause? This Knockwhinnie and his concerns are the sediment in my cup. I can but cast them from me ; and I wish myself well rid of the puling girl, in whom I have taken too long too fond an interest."

Scarcely had the expression escaped him when the wonted tenderness of his disposition returned ; he felt almost remorse at the idea of withdrawing his paternal protection from Adelaide, and he hastened towards the palace, anxious to ascertain the source of the distress with which she had been affected the preceeding evening; for he had learned that she had left the Queen's presence in tears, and was observed more dejected than she had ever been seen on any former occasion.

He found her in her own own apartment, a small dark triangular room, with only one window, the casement of which was open: a pitcher with flowers stood upon the sill. The chimney was in one corner, and was filled with green boughs. The walls were hung with ancient tapestry, representing the story of Æneas's departure from Didoit: was old and faded, but the tale was well told. The galley which bore the hero from the shores of Carthage was seen at a distance, and the attendants of Dido were represented as wistfully pursuing it with their eyes from a terrace of her palace: she herself was seen reclining dejectedly on a couch, near a huge pile of fagots, the funeral pyre prepared for herself. She was the principal figure in the picture, and appeared pale, young, and beautiful, immediately behind the seat on which Adelaide was sitting.

As the Count entered the room, the disconsolate attitude of his adopted daughter seemed to him strikingly similar to that of the forsaken Queen; and the air of her despondency to resemble the melancholy which heightened the beauty of Dido.

Adelaide was leaning her cheek upon her hand, resting her elbow on a small table of ebony, on which stood a little mirror in a silver frame. A string of pearls, which she had worn the preceding evening, hung over it in a careless festoon; on the table lay several little articles of Parisian bijouterie, and three or 'four artificial flowers, which, in the liveliness of their appearance almost surpassed nature; among them lay also a set of ivory tablets, fastened to each other at the corner by a silver pivot, studded with a small ruby.

A few words were inscribed on one of the tablets, it would seem newly done, as a pencil lay beside it. At the foot of the table, with loose sheets of music, stood a Florentine lute, and in a chair, on the opposite side of the table to that on which the pensive lady was leaning, lay a rich robe, selected for her appearance in the Queen's circle in the evening, with gloves and embroidered shoes, befitting the elegance of her hands and the beauty of her feet.

The Count halted at the door as he entered, and regarded her for a short time with compassion and sorrow. He saw that her bosom was pierced with an anguish which she indulged, and that she was yielding with the helplessness of despondency, to the impression of some misfortune, with which her disconsolate attitude indicated that she felt it was in vain to contend. For a moment he fancied that possibly her grief had its origin in some of those manifold little slights which are so deeply felt, however unintentionally given, by those who are doomed to move in the ephemeral splendour of royal favour; but her meek and gentle attitude, so resembling that of the forlorn Dido, excited his attention, and he could not but acknowledge that the same mournfulness of look and air might arise from a similar cause. He approached softly towards her, and touched her before she was aware that he was in the room. It dissipated her trance of thoughtfulness, and in the same moment she started from her seat, and falling on his arm, with her forehead on his shoulder, burst into tears.

CHAPTER XXVI.

"A melancholy, grounded and resolved,
Received into a habit, argues love,
Or deep impression of strong discontents.
In cases of these rarities, a friend,
Upon whose faith and confidence we may
Vent with security our grief, becomes
Oftimes the best physician."

FORD.

The Count kindly endeavoured to sooth Adelaide, and disengaging her from his arm, replaced her on the chair, and took a seat beside her.

"I am afraid," said he, "that this voyage from France has taken you far from some dearer object than any you have yet met with in your native land."

"Alas! it is not so: but why did I ever leave France; I share with my royal lady the sorrow she felt at bidding it adieu. But it is not for aught I have left behind that my tears flow; nor do I well know wherefore my heart is so heavy."

The Count smiled, and said, with pity mingled with gayety—

"I think, Adelaide, it would not be difficult to guess the cause of your sorrow."

She was a little startled at this, and wiping hastily away the tear which stood in the corner of her eye, said, with a look of alarm and solicitude—

"What do you mean?"

The Count took her hand, and smiling a little more expressively than before, said—

"Don't be frightened: I only fancy that there is no wound in your grief which may not be easily cured. Come, confide in your father. It must not be that you sit sighing here alone, and perhaps, at the same time, by your seclusion breaking another heart."

"Ah!" exclaimed Adelaide; and stooping her head to hide her blushes, she affectionately kissed his hand.

"I thought it was so," said the Count, cheerfully; "Pray, for whom are all these tears so tenderly shed. May I guess?"

"You cannot," replied she in a tone of hopeless pathos. "He for whom they fall shall never know of them. Ask me no more, and I will try to subdue a sentiment that is hopeless."

"Why hopeless?" inquired the Count, with some degree of earnestness, touched by her candour and sensibility. Who is there among all the gallants of the court that might not be proud to win this gentle hand?"

Adelaide answered only with a sigh, which told still more expressively the dejection of her heart.

"Ave Maria," exclaimed the Count, "protect my child! Hast thou then unworthily placed thy affections? I beseech thee, sweet Adelaide, to make no more concealment!"

"No," was her firm reply, "but nevertheless there is no hope for me."

"It must be so then," cried the Count, anxiously; "he is wedded to another."

"Oh no," cried Adelaide, with an eager and terrified tone, "I could not be so guilty."

"Then he is engaged to another," said the Count, compassionately.

Adelaide made no answer, but rising, which the Count also did at the same time, she wiped her eyes, and appeared for a moment thoughtful.

"What would you, Adelaide?"

"You have come, my lord, when I should not have been seen, and I have told you more than befits maidenly diffidence. yet I wish not to recall what I have said. It is true that my heart hath gone away from me, but hath not taken my reason with it. I forget not my birth, nor the dignity of the lessons I received from the Lady Beatrice in Normandy: and therefore,

8*

though my love is hopeless yet it shall be free from shame. I will conquer it if I can, and if I cannot I can die."

"Come, come," said the Count, laughing, "not so fast; you may change. But to leave this common version of true love's fond tale, I have come to tell you news. Your father, Knockwhinnie, is in Edinburgh."

"I know no father but yourself," replied Adelaide; "of Knockwhinnie I have heard but the name; and it was not spoken by those who used it with much kindness. Tell me something of him. Ah me! I hope I am not much undutiful; but now I do remember that my mother told me that he was a brave and gallant knight, though wilful in his humour, by which he bred to her many sorrows. Will he come here to see me? Methinks I should like to see my father. Alas, I can never love him as I do you!"

The Count caressed her affectionately, and bidding her be again seated, related to her so much of the story of her parents as prepared her to understand that her father was in a state of outlawry.

"Then," said Adelaide, "that will soon be reversed."

"How?" inquired the Count, a little gloomily.

"Because it will give me pleasure," said she; "and you have been always so kind you cannot but for my sake solicit his pardon."

The Count avoided the earnestness of the entreating look with which this was said. She observed it, and it overawed her.

"I fear," she cried with anxiety, "that you have not told me all. Has my father done you any wrong, that you are so averse to extricate him from his present perilous state?"

"Let us speak no more of it at present," said the Count; "we shall talk of it another time."

"It must not be so," exclaimed our gentle heroine, with more than the wonted energy of her meek character; "I will myself go straight to the Queen, and beseech the grace of her pardon."

"You said but now," replied Dufroy, "that you felt but little for your father, and that you loved me in his stead."

"True; but you had not then told me of his danger. What should I be, were I not to help my father? If he hath made himself your enemy it is to me a great misfortune; and if you are his, it is still greater; for I can never look on you as I should do on my father's enemy.

The Count was greatly moved; he could not but acknowledge the justness of her sentiments; still he thought that such a blight had fallen on his happiness by Knockwhinnie, that to seek the reversal of his outlawry was a thing that lay not within the scope of his duties.

Adelaide, however, was not to be repulsed by the coldness of his manner, and she again expressed her persuasion that he would aid her to procure the pardon. Before he had time however, to make any reply, the voice of Chatelard, passing beneath the window, was heard humming the air he had sung the knight before to the Queen. It caused Adelaide to pause abruptly in her solicitation, and covered her face with blushes. The Count observed her emotion; in the same moment he rightly conjectured that Chatelard was the object of her attachment, and looked at her sharply as he said,

"What hath overcome you? You were speaking of your father."

Her answer was confused, and the crimson of her countenance deepened.

"Ah," said Dufroy, "I need no one now to tell me who is the cause of your disquietude!"

"Is it not natural," said she, "that a child should be disquieted for a father so unhappy as mine?"

The Count looked archly at the little address with which she had thus parried his remark, and added without seeming to have noticed her answer,—

"I do not say it is an ill-placed attachment; but he hath lived too lightly in the world to value properly the warmth and faithfulness of such a heart as yours."

Adelaide perceived that he had discovered her secret; but rallying her spirits, she evaded his scrutiny with that instinctive address with which even the most innocent maiden knows how, in similar circumstances, to extricate herself. She reverted with increased zeal to the unfortunate conditon of her father; and the Count, to avoid her importunity, hastily promised to consider the matter when he had more leisure, and left the room.

CHAPTER XXVII.

"Religion harsh, intolerant, austere,
Parent of manners like herself severe,
Drew a rough copy of the Christian face,
Without the smile, the sweetness, or the grace."
COWPER.

The day, as we have already described, was sunny and inspiring. The spirit of universal gayety pervaded every heart. The city rung with cheerfulness, music, and preparation. Every countenance was lighted up, and even the solitary royal Mary partook of the gladness around her, and the joy that her own presence awakened.

At the moment when the Count Dufroy came from the apartment of Adelaide, her Majesty was passing through the gallery, attended by her ladies, to receive some of the reformed clergy, who, in disregard of the established etiquette of the court, had obtruded themselves at that early hour upon her attention, and had requested an audience with rather more pertinacity than exactly befitted their business, or the respect due to their young Queen. Mary, on seeing Dufroy, gayly invited him to come with her, and laughingly remarked to him, how soon she had been summoned to recant her errors.

"Mary Livingstone here," said she, pointing to one of her ladies, "saw them come into the court, and she has described them to me as grim carles, whose visages are so knotted with godly displeasure that no blandishment, she is sure, can untie them to a smile; but we shall be gracious, and see what influence we may possess when we would subdue or tame;" and with these words she presented her hand to the Count, who led her into the apartment of state, where the reformed ministers awaited her appearance.

On her entrance, these venerable men regarded her, for a moment, with a predetermined severity of aspect, but she approached them with an air of such filial deference that they were suddenly discomposed, and looked confusedly at one another. In the same moment she cast her eyes towards the Lady Mary Livingstone and the Count Dufroy, with a side-look of conscious triumph.

She happened to wear at her girdle a rosary and cross of gold. This soon attracted the attention of the reverend divines, and Dr. Glossar who was of the party, stepping forward, took hold of it, and said,

" What is the use of this bauble ?"

Mary smiled, and withdrawing it from his hand, said, " It is a remembrancer. It reminds me that meekness and humility are the weapons with which I can best hope to resist the rudeness of this world."

Mr. Glossar was rebuked, and retired.

Mary then addressed herself to another of the party, an old, gray-haired, venerable-looking man, with a pale and thoughtful countenance, which indicated a mild and gentle disposition.

" But that I see you here," said she, " and with these worthy men, I should have thought, father, you were too old to be of the new faith !"

The divines looked a little sullenly at one another, but Mr. Allison, the old man, pleased to have been so distinguished, replied with great courtesy, but with firmness, " that heaven's grace never came too late, when it came at all."

" Alas !" said the Queen, with one of her most fascinating smiles, " how changed I must become, if age be merit, before I can hope to share the grace that has fallen on you."

" Say not so," replied Mr. Allison, " grace cannot but be soon mingled with such graciousness. It would have been too much had your Highness been so early adorned with heaven's holiness as well as with such temporal beauty !"

Mary appeared delighted with his adulation, and presented her hand, which the old man, bending his knee, respectfully kissed.

" Brother Allison," cried Dr. Glossar, " we came not here for purposes so idolatrous !" and turning to the Queen, whose countenance had changed at his austerity, he said, " Madam, we have come hither to tender unto your Highness our willing service to unbind the errors wherein you have been swaddled from the womb.

Mary looked at the Count, as if to ask him what answer to make, or to request his assistance to put an end to the audience ; but she saw that he was burning with indignation, and that her ladies were pale and alarmed. She felt, however, that the moment was critical. She was aware that the austere personages before her were men, with whom the spirit of the times was proud and influential. Upon the report of their reception much, she knew, depended, and accordingly, with that dignity and presence of mind which she ever evinced on the most trying occasions, she thanked Dr. Glossar for the charity of their intentions towards her. She assured him of her desire to deserve the good opinion of all just and wise men ; and that she trusted, with God's blessing, so to deport herself as to merit a continuance of the love and loyalty of which their zeal was so remarkable a testimony ; and presenting her hand to the Doctor, he condescended to bow over it with more deference than might have been expected from the severity of his address. She then, with her wonted affability withdrew ; but, instead of presenting her hand to the Count, to lead her away, she leaned upon his arm, and he felt that she was fluttered and disturbed. She, however, concealed her emotion until they were returned into the gallery, when, with a slight hysterical exclamation, she burst into a momentary fit of tears, and said,—

" I hope we are not to have too much of this. I was told what I had to expect, but it is more racy than the description. Cannot these good men be admonished that queens expect courtesy, and that ladies look for fair speeches ?"

The Count expressed himself with so much vehemence against the rudeness of the divines, that Mary was obliged to repress his fervour.

"Truly," said she, turning to the Lady Mary Livingstone, " thy account was none too rough ; they are grim carles, but that old man had in him something of the leaven of more courtly breeding : he was born before rudeness was esteemed a grace of virtue. What think you, Count, of that gaunt dominie ? He is a fellow of excellent impudence ! but it were not wise to tell the world what we think of him."

The Count at the moment recollected that he was the same person who had supplanted himself in the affections of the Lady Margaret Douglas, and, emboldened by what the Queen in her vexation had expressed, spoke of him with derision and unmeasured contumely.

Mary, however, suddenly interrupted him.

"Hush, my lord!" said she ; "I thought you a more discreet courtier, than to think aloud in a palace."

And it was fortunate for Dufroy that the Queen was so

much on her guard; for just at that moment, the Prior of St. Andrew's, afterward the celebrated Earl and Regent Murray, entered the gallery. He had heard of the audience which the Queen had so readily vouchsafed to the Protestant divines, and, being himself of the reformed religion, was hastening to grace the interview with his presence.

" You are too late," said the Queen; " and you have missed a lesson of sweet counsel."

" So that your Majesty," replied the Prior, " lay it to heart, I shall not lack of the fruits of it."

" Verily," replied the Queen, and she looked at Count Dufroy, " we shall not soon forget it. Tell me, I pray you, my Lord Prior, if your reformed divines are all such plain-spoken men ?"

The Prior looked at her for a moment, and then said, " I know of none among them who fear to speak the truth."

" I would that it consisted with their integrity," said Mary, " to amend their manners, as well as to reform the Church."

This little sally of her unsuspicious temper was not forgotten by the Prior; but he regarded her with brotherly affection; and, though he wrote it down in his heart, he yet, out of the love and pride with which he regarded her, as his sister, kept it at that time from the world; but he augured ill from it to that religion in which he was at once so piously and boldly engaged.

CHAPTER XXVIII.

> " He reads much;
> He is a great observer; and he looks
> Quite through the deeds of men."
>
> JULIUS CÆSAR.

WHEN the Count Dufroy left Southennan in his apartment at Luckie Hutchie's, our hero remained for some time by himself, thoughtful almost to regret. He had long esteemed the character of the Count, respected him, indeed, as a nobleman of lofty bearing, and he was disappointed at discovering the latent antipathy with which he seemed affected towards Knockwhinnie. But this feeling was in some measure compensated by the circumstances which Dufroy related concerning the abduction. It seemed that he had it now in his power to assure the Outlaw of the innocence of his lady, and that the profligate Auchenbrae was the guilty party.

As he was ruminating over these topics and of the incidents his boy had told him, respecting Knockwhinnie and Friar Michael taking refuge in the house in which Baldy had provided him with lodgings, a letter was brought to him from Knockwhinnie, the contents of which surprised him not a little.

The Outlaw stated, that the information he had received from Balwham, the inn-keeper, had greatly affected his mind, and that in consequence, and until his outlawry could be reversed, he had determined to avail himself of the return of one of the French vessels which had come with the Queen, to go over to France, and to ascertain at the Ursuline convent at Caen, into which his wife had retired, the facts of her story. The vessel was to sail that morning; and he concluded by entreating Southennan, in the interval, to procure for him the pardon.

This letter exceedingly disconcerted the young Laird: he saw in it the characteristic precipitancy of Knockwhinnie, and could not but lament that he should, on the very eve of explanation, have withdrawn himself from the scene where he was most wanted. His absence, during the process of soliciting the pardon, was in itself prudent enough; but he could have retired into the country, and awaited the result there.

It seemed also strange that Knockwhinnie should have appeared so little interested in his daughter, as to think of leaving Edinburgh without making even an attempt to see her; but in this our hero reasoned more from his own feelings, than from the common nature of man. Knockwhinnie had scarcely ever seen his child; her image occupied faintly but a small space in his mind, while that of his lady absorbed, in a great degree, all his thoughts and feelings. Moreover, the bosom of Southennan was filled with the beauty of Adelaide; she was to him the most important object of his ruminations; his interest in her had been increased by his conversation with Count Dufroy, and he could not conceive how she could be regarded with so much indifference by her father. Altogether, he felt himself in a state of disquietude.

At last, he finally resolved to direct the removal of his luggage to the lodgings which Baldy had taken, and to proceed to the palace, in order to obtain an introduction to Adelaide; for although he was dissatisfied with the reluctance which the Count evinced to take any part in mitigating the condition of Knockwhinnie, yet his habitual respect for that nobleman, and the part he took in the affairs of Adelaide, made him still solicitous to cultivate and retain his friendship.

As Baldy had expressed it, the courtiers only engaged dry lodgings, that is, house-room—living out of doors in the hostels and other places, where dinners and entertainments were prepared. In sooth, bating the names, and the style of accommodation, there was no great difference between the mode of life among the gallants of those days and the exquisites of these. Thus it happened, that in proceeding towards the palace, Southennan went to the Unicorn, then a place of fashionable resort, as we have already intimated, to bespeak a place at the dinner-table; for the day was now advanced towards noon, and the dining hour was at one o'clock.

While our hero was settling terms with the host, a young gentleman came in, and inquired for some of the other foreign courtiers who had come from France.

The appearance of this stranger took the attention of Southennan. He was a short, thick, bandy-legged figure, of a dark olive Italian complexion, an aquiline nose, large black whiskers, eyebrows like the night, and eyes vivid, piercing, and intelligent. In his dress he was rather more showy than was then common, except on gala occasions: his ruff and the ornamental parts, were unusually costly, and he wore a gold chain, with a medallion of the Queen attached to it, richer than any which Southennan had yet observed on the other attendants of her Majesty: with the exception, however, of the chain and badge, he wore the uniform of the Piedmontese ambassador, who had accompanied Mary from France, having only that morning been accepted into the Queen's service.

The stranger's language was remarkable for its tasteful propriety: it was clear, apt, and elegant, insomuch that it was immediately manifest he was possessed of no ordinary talent, nor of common acquirements; but rich in both to an eminent degree. It was David Rizzio.

When he had received an answer to his inquiries from the host Balwham, he turned to our hero with a degree of familiarity at which the reserve of his Scottish habits, notwithstanding the softening they had received from his English education, rather retreated. He began by remarking, that the town reminded him of Brussels, and inquired if Southennan had ever been there. The reply was of course in the negative, but a little more stingy than perhaps civility towards a stranger required: it was simply "No!"

"Ah?" said Rizzio, "then you have not been yet abroad?"

Southennan smiled, and replied, "The conjecture is not exactly correct, for I have been in France, and have also spent several years in England."

"I might have thought so," said Rizzio, "for you do not wear much of the Scottish look about you."

Southennan was not quite pleased with the compliment to his country: as it, however, implied the discernment of some superiority in himself, he took no notice of the disparagement, but inquired how Rizzio was pleased with Scotland.

"Bah!" exclaimed the Italian; "it is rich in rocks; the people grimace as if they were eating uncured olives, and the priests are as unmannerly as the winds; five of them, within the hour, have drawn more water from the Queen's fair eyes, than Eurus could have done in a March morning."

Although Southennan was of the unreformed church, he was yet too much of a Scotsman to relish the Italian's sneer at his countrymen, the Protestant clergy; the manner of Rizzio, however, which was playful and easy, took much from the sting of his sarcasms.

They left the Unicorn together, and walked down the street towards the Palace, continuing their conversation, which, as they became better acquainted, grew more interesting to

Southennan. By the time they had reached the gate, it may be said that the Italian had wormed himself a good deal into his intimacy; but still the wariness of Southennan's national character prevented him from explaining more of the object of his visit to Holyrood House, than that he was in search of the Count Dufroy or Chatelard.

CHAPTER XXIX.

"This is the very ecstasy of love,
Whose violent property foredoes itself,
And leads the will to desperate undertakings,
As oft as any passion under heaven
That does afflict our natures."
SHAKSPEARE.

In ascending the great stairs of the Palace, much to the delight of Southennan they met Adelaide and the Lady Mary Livingstone descending with a little dog held by a riband, to walk in the gardens. Rizzio being acquainted with the ladies stopped to speak with them, treating, in the badinage which passed between them, the visit of the divines with even less respect than he had spoken of it to our hero. The Lady Mary Livingstone was still more indignant at their rudeness. With Rizzio it was ridicule and contempt: but with her, anger mingled with dread. Adelaide, who had not seen the reverend gentlemen, took no part in the conversation, and her silence, which was purely owing to that circumstance, appeared to Southennan delicate and becoming. Before they separated, Rizzio introduced Southennan to them in a light and easy manner, as if it were only to get rid of the embarrassment of allowing him to stand in silence beside them.

In a state of ordinary feeling, the distant civility with which the introduction was accepted by the ladies, would have excited no attention on the part of Southennan; but in the warmth of the sentiment which he had cherished from the first sight of Adelaide, it seemed as if her coldness was marked and repulsive. This notion, the mere offspring of his own interested imagination, served him for a new topic to think of, concerning her. He would have been glad had Rizzio proposed to return with them to the garden; but he had himself spoken so anxiously of his own wish to see the Count Dufroy or Chatelard, that the Italian could not, in civility, propose to accompany the ladies;

and thus it happened, that after parting from them, on the stairs, he ascended with his companion, dissatisfied with himself, to the gallery, where they found the two gentlemen, with other courtiers, French and Scottish, assembled.

On seeing Southennan both the Count and Chatelard came towards him. They had been speaking together; and the sharp eye of Rizzio discerned that their conversation had been something more lively than the topics of the day were likely to have suggested. It was even so. The Count had been endeavouring to sound his young countryman respecting Adelaide, and had heard with some degree of surprise the fervour of attachment with which he affected to regard her. At the same time it did not displease him; for Chatelard was wellborn, highly accomplished, and possessed of talents which well qualified him to succeed in diplomatic trusts. Accordingly the Count did not repress his strong declarations, but he did not give him any encouragement: so that although their conversation had been earnest and animated, it yet was in no degree conclusive.

After the customary interchange of the compliments of the morning, Southennan informed the Count that he had been introduced by Rizzio to Adelaide, and in saying this, he threw his eyes inadvertently towards Chatelard, as if he expected the intelligence would produce some effect upon him. The Count did the same thing, and both felt something like disappointment, at observing one so enamoured as Chatelard professed to be, hear it with evident indifference. Rizzio, however, the keenest-sighted of the three, without being aware of the state of the ground on which he stood, began to rally Chatelard on his want of gallantry towards Adelaide.

Chatelard, conscious of the truth, and apprehensive that his passion for the Queen might also have been discovered, looked a little confused; which Rizzio observing, said, with a particular shrewdness in his eye,—

" But you were too much engaged in your own game of cross purposes, to be aware of how much the onlookers were interested in your play."

Neither Southennan nor the Count understood the insinuation: it was not so, however, with Chatelard, who became still more confused. He could not, indeed, conceal from himself that his devotion to the Queen had been detected by the acute and sagacious Italian.

But it was not expedient, in the views and purposes of Rizzio, to appear so well acquainted with matters of that kind as he really was. He had not yet established the fulcrum for his own elevation; he was but casting about for materials to construct it with. The study of character, especially the weaknesses of those about him, constituted, at this period, his principal employment; and the confusion of Chatelard assured him that it would not be difficult to find a spring to render him subservient to his designs. Without, therefore, affecting even to suspect the secret of Chatelard, he took him familiarly by the arm, and left the Count and Southennan together.

"Let us go," said the Count, "and join Adelaide in the garden. I wish you to become better acquainted with her; she is a creature of every amiable quality, and I'm afraid regards, with more kindness, that Chatelard, than he deserves; for though he speaks of her with more warmth than I think true affection would prompt, I should almost be sorry she preferred him: and yet, neither in his birth, person, nor circumstances, is there aught which could be reasonably objected to. His love for her, I doubt, springs from some calculation of the agency he might convert her to."

"It is curious," replied Southennan, "that I should have formed the same opinion. On our first acquaintance he was all flames and darts. It may, however, be the nature of your countrymen, Count, to speak lightly of those they love; but it is not in the custom of humanity to speak unnecessarily, which Chatelard, certainly, too much affects. He seemed to wince a little at what the Italian said; but I did not very well comprehend the meaning of it."

By this time they had reached the bottom of the stairs, and were turning towards the garden, when Hughoc made his appearance with a note for his master.

"I was boun'," said the boy as he delivered it, "to fin' you sleeping or waking; for it cam frae the Queen's chamberlain, wi' an order that by nae manner o' means was it to be stayed or hindered in the delivery."

The note was a command, conveyed through the chamberlain, for the young laird to attend the public Reception that night in the palace. His name had on his arrival been reported to the Queen, at a time when some of the old nobles were with her; and the Earl of Morton being among them, recollected the affair of the Solway Moss, in which Southennan's father had been made a prisoner, and spoke of him in terms of much commendation, hoping the scion would prove worthy of the stock: orders were in consequence given to command his attendance at the Reception.

CHAPTER XXX.

> " It is not wise
> To task ourselves above our duties."
> ANONYMOUS.

On entering the garden, the Count and Southennan saw the ladies at some distance; but as several brilliant groups and other parties were interspersed among the walks and flower plats of the parterre, the Count, not partaking of the eagerness of his young friend to reach Adelaide, conducted him towards her by a circuitous route.

In those days the gardens of Holyrood House consisted of a wide space of several acres, enclosed by a high, rough stone wall. They were laid out in a stiff, artificial manner, with holly hedges and yew trees cut into different forms, such as peacocks and unicorns, lions and eagles. The flowers interspersed among the shrubs were then esteemed rare and beautiful, but they consisted of what are now the commonest kinds. The flower beds rose over each other in low successive terraces, and the centre of the garden was so built up in this manner, and crested with a yew-tree shapen into the form of an imperial crown, that it might, without much exaggeration, have been compared to an ornamental pie. Two fountains, at the distance of a hundred and fifty yards, played at each end of the mound, and seats were neatly disposed in different parts on the lawns and beside the fountains. The whole was trimly kept, and for the rudeness of the climate and the age, was not in its effect without beauty.

On reaching the ladies, the Count addressed himself particularly to the Lady Mary Livingstone, leaving Southennan to make the best of his own way with Adelaide. But she maintained towards him the same coldness and indifference which he had experienced at his first introduction. Their conversation, in consequence, was abrupt and constrained, until, as it were, almost by an accident Southennan spoke of her father.

"And do you know him?" enquired Adelaide, in a tone of tenderness.

Southennan replied by recounting in what manner he had

met him on the moors of Renfrewshire, and the subsequent incidents of their ·journey to Edinburgh. The interest which she took in the narrative, although not of that strong kind which more familiar affection would have inspired, yet showed a filial regard for the dangers and misfortunes of her parent, natural and touching to a pathetic degree.

Upon this thesis Southennan began to lay the foundation of his love. He perceived that she was aware of some prejudice or antipathy on the part of the Count Dufroy, to move in the remission of Knockwhinnie's outlawry, and it seemed to him that he would best promote his own object, by evincing the sincerity of his desire to procure the pardon of her father. In this, though acting from the dictates of his passion and considerations of humanity, he chose precisely the course that a man of more libertine knowledge would have taken to engage her attention. He lamented in terms that awakened her sympathy the original doubt which hung upon the misfortunes of her mother, of which she had heard for the first time that day, but not with so many particular incidents as Southennan's version of the narrative contained. And he dwelt in a more especial manner on the perils and privations to which her father was exposed. Without any intentional exaggeration of the kindness he had himself shown to the Outlaw, he also spoke of it in terms that produced an impression in his own favour, while it was calculated to excite a stronger filial interest in Adelaide. Thus, an effect arose from their conversation which the Count could not have anticipated.

Adelaide became tenderly alive to the hazards of her father; and though no image was associated in her mind with the feelings which the name of parent and the story of Southennan awakened, she yet found herself, as it were, drawn by numberless fibres towards some one whom she pictured to herself for her father.

The Count Dufroy, as he walked on before them, with the Lady Mary Livingstone, engaged in light and general topics befitting the time, looked frequently back to Southennan and Adelaide, gratified to see them apparently so much interested in each other. His affection for her had been truly of the purest parental kind. In her childhood she had acquired a place in his affections at a time when his heart wanted something to be kind to. Her simple character and extreme loveliness as she grew up, increased the influence of that fond and early charm, until his regard, without one tinge of passion, settled into that mild affection which hath its gratifications in cherishing and protecting. No parent could love with more sincerity: but in addition to the pleasing and proud feeling of the father of so admirable a daughter, a sentiment of pity strengthened and exalted his delight in her. The misfortunes of her natural parents had thrown her adrift on the wide world; and with more than common claims to parental love and care, she was exposed to feel much from the want of both. His generosity, as well as his affection, was, in consequence, extended over her; and he not only loved her for her worth, but because he had himself been kind to her.

He had also seen in Southennan, though his knowledge was not of an intimate kind, the many excellent qualities which he has been described as possessing. That he preferred his noble ingenuousness to the talents and address of Chatelard, could not be doubted. Magnanimous minds have a natural affinity to each other; and the Count believed, that among the qualities of Southennan, were many of those merits which had been commended as graces in his own youth. He was likewise aware, that the obligations which he had heard in the morning, Knockwhinnie owed to him, rendered it probable that Adelaide could form no connexion in life more agreeable her to father. But while he admitted this sentiment, he wished that Knockwhinnie had no claim, nor right, nor interest, to affect the destiny of Adelaide; and yet he was almost angry with himself for thinking so: but his heart was rebellious, even while acknowledging that the repugnance which he cherished involuntarily against him, was unjust. It was seemingly a curious and a strange antipathy by which he was actuated; but is it uncommon?

CHAPTER XXXI.

" Where's Potpan, that he helps not to take away? he shift a trencher! he scrape a trencher!"—
ROMEO AND JULIET.

SOUTHENNAN lingered in the garden with Adelaide, until it was near the dinner hour at the Unicorn, when he took his leave, promising to pay his respects to her at the Reception in the evening.

The interview, inasmuch as it had enabled him to cultivate some degree of acquaintance, had been pleasing and satisfactory. He had discovered, in the state of her father, an amulet by which he could affect her feelings; or rather, he had excited, on her father's account, some degree of interest towards himself. But he could not disguise the fact, that she was cold and absent towards him on all other topics; and the knowledge of her affections being attracted by Chatelard, made him full of doubt, and affected him with a painful anxiety.

On reaching the Unicorn, he met the host, Balwham, at the door, with a busy look, bustling and impatient for his arrival, the dinner being ready, and the other guests assembled.

The Maister was a little, fat, short personage, with a round bright bald head, small twinkling eyes, and as chubby in the cheeks as a cherub on a tomb-stone. He had a servit or towel under his arm, and a white linen apron, clean from the fold, tied before him. The day being warm, he had doffed his coat, and wore his shirt sleeves. A leathern strap served him for a girdle, in which was stuck in a sheath a carving knife and fork; and a steel for sharpening, somewhat daintily-fashioned, hung from it. In other respects, he was dressed after the manner of the better sort of citizens; and, with red bows in his shoes, he wore also red hosen, which came over his knees, and were tied below them with black garters.

"Come 'awa', Southennan! 'Od! but I hae been in a ploutie o' het water, for fear ye were na coming! And a' the gentlemen are just wud to see you, and to get their dinner; for I told them that there wasna' a brawer and a braver than yoursel' this day in the Court o' Scotland. Just come in, and I'll hae up the dishes in a jiffey!"

Southennan was accordingly ushered into the room, where the guests were waiting.

It was a large square apartment, very low in the ceiling, which consisted of but the beams that supported the floor of the incumbent apartments. They were of old dark oak, clumsily carved with flowers and true lovers' knots. Time had somewhat opened the seams of the floor above; and to prevent the dust from coming down, they were covered between the beams with strips of paper, dingy and fly-spotted. In one corner stood a huge wardrobe, open; but, instead of being filled with napery and clothes, as befitted its functions, it was garnished with gardevines, drinking-glasses, and blue pitchers of coarse delfware. On the lower shelf stood a range of wickered flasks of wine, some unopened, and others half empty. Near this wardrobe a long narrow table, higher considerably than usual, was covered with a Dutch table-cloth, on which were set out various articles and utensils, that would be wanted during dinner. Among other things it exhibited two large masses of butter, on lordly wooden dishes, and a huge cheese, that was almost still entire ; together with a plentiful assortment of horn spoons and pewter trenchers.

The dining-table, a spacious circle, stood in the middle of the room ; it was also covered with bright Dutch damask. In the centre, a curiously-carved congregation of several salt-cellars and spice-boxes stood, forming an antique ornament, not without beauty. Around this was placed a radiance of pewter spoons, with the handles pointing outward. The circumference without them was formed by a circle of Venetian drinking-glasses, as many as the guests, who, by the preparation of the table, appeared to be expected to the number of a dozen. Four large bright pewter flagons, foaming with ale, formed the angles of a square on the outside of the drinking-glasses. The space between them and the edge of the table was appropriated for the reception of the dishes and the covers of the guests.

The architecture of the table displayed considerable taste, something even of style, every thing was neat, the order was formed with some perception of elegance, and gave good assurance of an abundant entertainment. Nor were the hopes it inspired disappointed.

Maister Balwham himself brought in the first dish—a large cut of boiled salmon, split open and lying on its back, with the bone which had been taken out, seasoned and grilled, lying across it, like a baton sinister on a shield of bastardy. Opposite to this majestical dish was placed an equal ashet of crappit heads—an ancient and much approved dainty of the Scottish nation. At right angles were placed, on the one side a capacious tureen of savoury broth, from the centre of which the black muzzle of a singed sheep's head looked as if breathing ; on the other, opposite, a haggis. These were the cardinal points of the feast. Between them, with an equal attention to symmetry, stood in each space a boiled and roasted fowl on the same plate ; flanked, on the one side, by a hecatomb of mutton chops, and on the other a black and white pudding *en saltier*. In the innner space, between this zodiac of substantials, were placed various constellations of tartlets, confections, and other stellar-shaped preserves and comfits. But the pride of the feast was a large haunch of venison, placed upon the sideboard, at which, whetting his carving-knife, the host took his station to do duty. Looking around with a self-complacent smile of pride and triumph, he called on our hero aloud by name, and requested him to take his seat, the rest of the guests standing until he had done so :—then was the onslaught and the battle.

Besides the host, the guests were attended by some of their own servants. Hughoc waited on his master. But, independent of the gentlemen's servants, there were two others belonging to the house. One of them was a tall, thin, sallow-faced, lank-haired, elderly person, steaming with perspiration; the other, his wife, a dame of considerable antiquity; she wore a large flannel hood, with long lappets, that swept the covers with their corners as she moved or presented them to the guests. She too, having assisted in the cookery, was not in coolest condition; but, nevertheless, there was no hinderance in the service, and the guests did justice both to the quantity and quality of the provender. When the edge had been taken off their appetite, some of them called for wine, and the flasks which we have before described were distributed among their respective owners. A fresh unopened one was placed before our hero, and the Venetian goblet, from which he drank of the ale in the flagons, served for a vehicle to his wine.

During dinner, a commendable taciturnity was generally observed. The guests, for the most part, were well-born French gentlemen: civil, not only to each other, but polite and even officious in their attention to the Scottish guests among them, some of whom did not appear to be well acquainted with the uses of the utensils on the table. They all knew, however, somewhat of the occult purposes of knives and forks, for they cut up the meat into morsels, and then laying down the knife and fork, employed their fingers, according to the most primitive practice, in conveying it to their lips. But, nevertheless, all passed cheerfully, and when the table began to be denuded of its ornaments, there was an evident disposition to hilarity among the French, and something very like domestication and docility among the Scots.

CHAPTER XXXII.

"No offence to the general, or any man of quality!"
                                        OTHELLO.

ALTHOUGH the dinner at the Unicorn was not the first of which Southennan had partaken in public, yet it was, in many respects, a novelty to him. In the character of the guests he early perceived there was considerable diversity. The smoothness of the French was engaging and conciliatory; and the stiff self-opinionated conduct of his countrymen was not disagreeable; it was even picturesque. Though in the parties themselves there was great solemnity about many things, still it was a solemnity so much above the occasion, that it could not be observed without affording tacit amusement.

Southennan was first made aware of what might justly be called the awkward attempts at civility on the part of the Scots, by observing that they were rather tolerated by the Frenchmen, than considered upon a par with them. This was particularly the case with a sturdy homespun laird, known to the party by the name of Cornylees of that Ilk.

That gentleman had not benefited, as his own man said of him, "a great deal by the kittle craft o' the dominie; nor indeed, was it to be expected that a personage o' his acres, would tak' meikle trouble wi' sic crockit curiosities as the A. B. C." Cornylees, however, had a great deal of mother-wit. He carried a shrewd eye in his head, and had a mind in his breast that was not without reflection. At home he was a stirring, active, looking-to-all-thing carle. His beasts were about the best, and the best tended in the West country. His servants were buirdly bustling fellows, on jocose terms with himself. No laird of double his means, in all the country side, rode a better horse, or could give to the stranger within his gates a more hearty round and rough kitchen to his welcome. Cornylees was, indeed, a sort of paragon among the western lairds; he kept, what was well described by his neighbours—

"a het and fu' ha; few went thither that cam awa' hungry, and that they stood weel on his books, aften experienced the potency o' his cup and stoup."

It was thought that the cost of Cornylees' furthy hospitality led him just as far as his incomings and mail and kain would allow; but there was in the midst of the hurry and hasty handlings ever about his doors, an order and custom which, though rude in its kind, was efficacious in its consequences. He little heeded the decorum which might have been expected at his place and steading; but there was a limit and restriction put upon the amount of what was in use, which in the midst of the seeming confusion, prevented any great wastery. In short, the Laird of Cornylees was a ranting, but a shrewd landlord and master; and there was more in the coffer-kist, when he resolved to pay his respects to the Queen's Majesty, than in the sorted hoards of men of better incomes and more gentility.

He had a considerable dash of humour in his nature, and great good-will to a practical joke; nor was he ill-pleased when he could bring his friends into a difficulty without much danger. The habits of his life had not, however, greatly qualified him for a courtier of any time, far less for that of a delicate and accomplished queen: but he was not sensible of being in this respect deficient. Like most worthy Scottish country gentlemen, he had a comfortable opinion of his own sagacity, and this tended in no degree whatever to make him diffident of his own powers to please. Yet, to do him justice, he was not more than his compeers likely to overstep the boundaries of respectful behaviour towards his neighbours, though sufficiently jealous of any thing like competition with himself from an inferior.

Of Southennan he had before heard, and knew something of the high breeding of his mother, and also of his English education. The pedigree also of Southennan was respectable in the eyes of Cornylees, as well as in that of all the county. He was therefore exceedingly rejoiced at the opportunity of making his acquaintance, which their dining together at the Unicorn afforded. But it happened during dinner, and while the French gentlemen were at table, that he could not approach near enough to Southennan to enter into conversation with him. The obstacle, however, only served to goad his desire to become acquainted with the young Laird; and accordingly, as soon as the cloth was drawn, and the flasks of wine placed orderly on the table, he rose from the place where he was sitting, and going to where Southennan was

Vol. I.—10

seated, engaged in conversation with one of the French gentlemen, he pushed his chair in between them, and thinking to make himself better understood by loud speaking, he bawled into the ear of the Frenchman, as if he had been deaf, saying he had a word of confidence to say to Southennan.

The Chevalier, for he was of that rank, was a good deal astonished at the intrusion, but not understanding his language, yielded seemingly to his request by pushing back his chair, while, at the same time, he regarded him with a degree of *fierté* that, though unobserved by Southennan, was not unnoticed by the rest of the company.

Cornylees, altogether unconscious of having discomposed any one, or done any thing in the least degree likely to disturb the harmony of the party, introduced himself cordially to Southennan, shook him heartily by the hand, and filling his Venetian goblet from his own flask, which he had brought round from the other side of the table in his hand, chuckled and hobber-nobbed in the most facetious and familiar manner to their better mutual acquaintance, talking to him a great deal about many things which Southennan did not very well understand, farther than that he was going in the evening to the Reception at the palace, and proposed that they should go together.

The proposition was not entirely agreeable to Southennan; there was rather, even in that day, too much of the grange and dairy about Cornylees to make him acceptable as a companion to one who was affecting the gallantry and debonair manner of the court. But Cornylees was not to be repulsed by any denial so slight as a cold evasion.

"In verity," said he, "Southennan, ye'll be surprised, in course now, to see what a pomp I mean to mak mysel'. I hae coft a new suit o' Geneosy velvet in the shop o' Bailie Brown, and he tells me, there will be no this night in Holyrood House afore the Queen's Majesty, in course now, a man o' my points and bravery."

"While he was thus speaking, the French gentleman whom he had so rudely displaced was waxing more and more indignant, until at length he could no longer repress his choler, but rising touched Cornylees on the shoulder with the two forefingers of his right-hand, and told him in French, that as he could not speak his language, he would send a friend to know what he intended by the manner in which he had treated him.

Cornylees, who did not understand one word of what he said,

gave him a nod, saying, " Very weel, in course now," with as much coolness as it was possible for one to do who was answering a civil notice.

Southennan understoood what the Chevalier meant, and looked considerably surprised at the equanimity of his new acquaintance, but he was still more amazed when the other said—

" What was it that chap was saying through his nose to me ?"

Southennan perceived by this that the Laird was altogether unconscious of having given any offence, and somewhat lightly and jocularly endeavoured to give him an idea that the Frenchman was offended with him ; but the intimation was incomprehensible to Cornylees, who continued to rub his hands, drink his wine, and become more and more jovial, until it was time for them to think of returning to their respective lodgings to dress for the Reception.

CHAPTER XXXIII.

" Her father was the grave Hans Van Herne, the son
Of Hogen Mogen, dat de droates did sneighen
Of veirteen hundred Spaniards in one neict.
THE LADY'S TRIAL.

SOUTHENNAN, attended by his boy, went to his dry lodgings in the house of Mistress Marjory, to which Baldy had previously transported his valise and saddlebags. Hughoc, until they reached the bottom of the stairs, kept at a decorous and page-like distance from his master, but no sooner had he entered to ascend, than he ran up close to him, and cried,

" Oh, Laird ! what a dreadfu' death is to be done on that gash bodie Cornylees. There's a Frenchman yon'er whom ane o' the servant-men tell't me he heard him say to anither o' the outlandish gentlemen, that this very night, if it were at the black hour o' midnight, he would send day-light through his body !"

Southennan was startled at this intelligence. It accorded with what he had apprehended, and he became anxious to extricate, if possible, the Laird from the scrape into which he had unconsciously fallen, and would have immediately returned in quest of him, but the time pressed. However, he ordered Hughoc to go to Cornylees, and request him to remain, without seeing any one whatever, until he could come to him.

An errand of this sort was congenial to the genius of Hughoc, and he made but light steps in quitting his master to deliver the message.

Southennan, a good deal troubled, ascended the stairs, repining at the vexatious accidents in which he had become involved since he left his paternal mansion.

He was not quite satisfied with himself: he thought that some of his perplexities were owing to the facility of his own temper, and before he reached the top of the stairs, being distented with himself, he was little inclined to be well disposed towards any other person. In this humour he knocked at the door, and was admitted by his servant Baldy, dressed, to his surprise, much more sprucely than usual. He, however, took no notice of it, conceiving that probably Baldy had done so to do honour to himself in proceeding to the Reception. Accordingly, with only some slight order concerning his own apparel, he walked into his room, where he found Father Jerome also dressed with more than usual care. He had not calculated on the attendance of the venerable chaplain, and his appearance had the effect of really disconcerting him.

"How is it, good Father," said he, "that you are thus apparelled in your holyday garb?"

Father Jerome replied modestly, "I am going with the Bishop of Glasgow to do homage to the Queen's Majesty."

"Indeed!" exclaimed Southennan. "I had understood it was not deemed desirable that she should receive the churchmen with any particular distinction. I should have been as well pleased, Father Jerome, had you not been so forward in the proffer of your devoirs."

There was in this something of a querulous tone unwonted in the usual suavity of the young Laird's manners towards the old man, and Father Jerome was hurt by its severity. Southennan had heard of the rudeness with which the reformed ministers had treated her Majesty in the morning, and being well aware of the delicacy of her situation between them and the clergy of the old faith, was averse that his chaplain should take any particular part in their controversies. He thought, like all others not spirited by party zeal, that it would be as well, in the circumstances of the kingdom, that the Queen should be exposed to as little molestation as possible by the religious champions of either side. This feeling, with that which he had brought with him from the Unicorn, and which Hughoc's tidings had excited, made him say to Father Jerome, rather harshly, that he had better abide where he was, and let the bishop go as he thought fit.

Baldy who was present during this brief colloquoy, here interposed with the freedom which the habits of long service almost justified, and said—

" We are weel assured that our apparition will be maist acceptable to the Queen's Majesty, after the grievous insolence she was obliged this morning to endure at the hands o' Doctor Glossar and the ither heretics.'

" We!" exclaimed Southennan ; " then you are dressed to go with Father Jerome. At least I shall control you. Hold yourself in readiness to attend me. If Father Jerome chooses to make himself in what he has never been before, a party to these religious strifes and heresies, he shall not be countenanced by me or by any one of my household."

This language, and the manner in which it was expressed, equally confounded honest Baldy and the Chaplain. They looked at one another, and inquired as intelligently as their eyes could ask, if it were possible Southennan could, in the brief space of a forenoon, be tainted in the purity of his faith ; but they made no audible observation. Baldy retired to prepare his master's apparel, and Father Jerome sat confused and dejected.

In this crisis Mistress Marjory, who had not before seen her new lodger, came into the room with something much more familiar than the young and somewhat irritated gallant was exactly prepared for; moreover, the description of her long and lean figure, which he had received in the morning from Hughoc, had not prepared him for such a phenomenon as then appeared before him.

Mistress Marjory was a woman of family—she could count kin with more than one Earl, and her kith among the gentry was without number. How then, could she do less than pay her respects to the Queen's Majesty, though necessity and the wrongous times of the Queen Dowager's regency had reduced her to the necessity of letting her rooms to the quality. It thus happened that she was arrayed in all her paraphernalia for the Reception.

Her head-dress was stupendous : on the top stood a mighty

pile of lace bows, that had been worn by her grandmother at the ball at which King James the IV. danced with the Lady Heron, before the fatal field of Flodden. Lappets of curious needle-work, rich and dingy, and of more recondite antiquity, streamed behind. A vast drapery of the like curiously worked lace and cambric hung at her elbows. Her waist was an inverted cone, studded with beads and buttons, and her other garments, of a venerable brocade, were " in longitude sorely scanty." She held in her hand a fan of peacock-feathers, that had dispersed the sighs of many a knight who had knelt at the feet of the gorgeous dames of other years.

After welcoming her new lodger with many congees and dignified alamodes of her lofty head, she, in pleasing and soft accents, told him that she had heard he was going that night to the Reception at the Palace, and she would have the felicity of bearing him company. This was more than he was quite prepared for: he had resolved to set his cap for higher game, and to make his appearance with such a faded effigy of departed pomp, was not within the compass of his good-nature to think possible.

He looked at the lady with astonishment; he then surveyed her figure from head to foot with visible alarm; and suddenly rousing himself from the indecision which had infected him, he said decisively—

"Madam—Father Jerome goes to the Reception. I am already engaged."

Mistress Marjory made no answer; but seating herself in a chair, looked unutterable things. Anon she began to clap with her hands, and to ruff with her protruded heels, till a violent hysterical cry of mortification burst from her, at which Southennan, unable to preserve his habitual serenity, hastily retired to his own room.

CHAPTER XXXIV.

" It had been pity you should have been put together with so mortal a purpose, as then each bore, upon importance of so slight and trivial a nature."

CYMBELINE.

By the time Southennan was dressed for the Palace, his boy had returned from Cornylees; and, according to his report, that stalwart personage was in considerable amazement at the message, and had informed him that he was not well in his room, after Southennan had left him, when a French gentleman, whom he had never seen before, came to him, talking most vehemently to some effect, of which he did not understand one word.

Our hero was at no loss to comprehend the object of the Frenchman's visit. Desiring Baldy and Hughoc to follow him, and to give him their attendance to Holyrood House, he hastened to the lodgings of Cornylees, which happened to be next door to the Unicorn.

On reaching his chamber, he found him dressed in his new suit of Genoese velvet, which, either by some defect in the making, or some contrariety in the Laird's habits, unaccustomed to such fine array, sat uneasy upon him.

" Ods-sake, Southennan," said he, " but I'm blithe, in course now, to see you. Never had honest man such a peck o' troubles as I hae gotten! Here is a costly suit of cla'es, such as never was, in course now, on the back o' one o' the breed o' our family before. I darena' tell the price o't; but it's sae saft and fine, that I'm just terrified to use or sit down in't, as if it were made o' egg-shells: but that's naething, in course now, to what I have met wi'. Ye werena' weel gane, when in cam' a worricow o' a Frenchman, wi' a tousy black head, a yellow face, and a nose the shape o' an owlet's neb. He was very weel-bred at first and spoke, in course now, wi' an air really very much like a gentleman; but I told him, wi' equal politesse, that I didna' understand him, whereupon he began to speak louder and louder, till at last he roared like a lion in my lug, and shook his twa hands at me, showing me his loofs, as if he daur't me, in course now, to say they werena' clean. What could be the meaning of so loquacious mumming?"

Southennan explained to him, that he apprehended the chevalier who sat next to him at dinner, had been in some manner offended by the way in which he had displaced him; indeed, that he had heard as much and was anxious to see him before any other person, to prevent a quarrel.

"It's no' a possibility," said Cornylees, " that I could offend him: wasna' he done wi' his dinner, hadna' I, in course now, something particular to say to you. A' that I did, was just shoving him a bit out o' the gait to let me in next till you: thae maun be thin-skinned that would make a quarrel, in course now, about a civility o' that kind."

Our hero endeavoured to convince him, that the fashions, both at Paris and in London, regarded such things as unbecoming; and that, since he was conscious of displacing the chevalier, he had as well authorize him, as he did not speak French himself, to make an apology for the unintended and, as it were, really accidental offence.

"Me ask his pardon!" exclaimed the astonished Cornylees, "I'll just, in course now, as soon chap aff this, my right hand, wi' an axe, as do any such cowardly thing!"

"Then," replied Southennan, "you must fight him. You cannot escape the duello, or you will be shunned by every body. It will be impossible even for me to speak to you again."

"Keep us a'!" cried Cornylees, in a consternation; "and is this court manners? He may just do as he likes, but I'll fight none."

While they were thus speaking, the French gentleman returned, with Rizzio to act as his interpreter. Southennan was glad to see Rizzio; and being anxious to extricate Cornylees as soon as possible, began at once to explain to Rizzio and the Frenchman, that his friend was totally unconscious of having given the chevalier any offence; and begged the good offices of Rizzio to make the matter up.

"My friend here," said he, "has lived all his days in the west country, a region not distinguished for debonair customs; and the little rudeness which he may unintentionally have committed ought rather to be ascribed to our particular manners, than any feeling of disrespect on his part."

Rizzio at once saw the true merits of the case, and found no great difficulty in making the French gentleman understand them: but in doing so, he happened to turn round to Southennan, and enter a little more largely than the occasion required, on the rude and barbarous manners of the Scotch. As this happened to be said in language of which Cornylees comprehended the meaning, he grew exceedingly wroth at Rizzio, and a quarrel between them appeared to be inevitable. Rizzio, however, retained his coolness and self-possession so completely, that he regarded the noise and baying of the west country laird with feelings of as little deference as if he had been an angry cur.

Southennan was greatly perplexed, and wist not well for some time what to do. At last he addressed the French gentleman, and requested him to explain to the Chevalier how little there was, either of design or disrespect, in what Cornylees had done, and to beg him to overlook the matter entirely, and to assure him that it was wholly owing to his ignorance of the usages of society that had led him into the commission of his unintentional rudeness. The Frenchman was, indeed, by this time quite aware of the propriety of Southennan's explanation, and was not a little diverted at the violent altercation between Rizzio and Cornylees. However, he took his leave, promising to pacify his friend, and to make him acquainted with the character and habits of Cornylees. In so far the affair was happily ended; but Rizzio remained behind, and seated himself in cool contempt of the rage of Cornylees.

The contrast which the serene, gaudy, self-possessed Italian presented to the agitation of the Laird, as well as the apprehension which the latter felt for his velvet dress, as he rampaged through the room, rendered Southennan unable to keep his gravity; insomuch, that he was at last constrained to laugh heartily, to the astonishment of the indignant Cornylees, who began to suspect that the whole affair was a little more extravagant than the occasion required. He was, however, constitutionally a good-natured man. The idea had an instantaneous effect on his behaviour, and, bridling his wrath at once, he went cordially towards Rizzio, holding out his hand, saying—

" I'm thinking, sir, there are, in course now, twa fules of us."

" There is one," replied Rizzio, and coolly stooping forward, examined the proffered hand a little curiously.

The wrath of Cornylees was on the point of blazing up afresh at this contumely. But Rizzio, with the address and dexterity of his character, instantly repressed the flame, by smiling good-humouredly in Cornylees's face, and warmly shaking him by the hand. So the matter ended, and Cornylees proposed that they should all proceed to the Reception together, where, as he said, he would make friends with the French gentleman that was so skinless in his politeness. Rizzio, however, was obliged to decline the proposal, saying, that as he was of the Queen's train, it was necessary he should be there before the hour appointed for the Reception; and after some farther interchanges of courtesies he went away.

"Weel," said the Laird to Southennan, "that's a pawkie loon, or I'm, in course now, mista'en. Did ye see how upsetting it was towards me; the creature, a mere fiddling adventurer, to make so light, in course now, o' me, a stated gentlemen, come o' ane of the ancientest families in the shire o' Renfrew!"

Thus early was the true character of Rizzio penetrated by the shrewd common sense of the rough diamonds of Scotland. The influence of his adroit manners, and his acute perception of the dispositions and qualities of others, enabled him to disarm the rudeness which his contempt of them provoked; but their antipathy to him both as an alien and a man, with their conscious inferiority in the arts of pleasing, he could not extinguish. It lay in their hearts like embers in ashes, and was ready, on the slightest provocation, to burn and blaze again.

CHAPTER XXXV.

" 'Tis told me he hath very oft of late
Given private time to you; and yourself
Have of your audience been most free and bounteous."
HAMLET.

SOUTHENNAN had scarcely left his lodgings to go to Cornylees, when a message came from the Abbot of Kilwinning requesting Father Jerome to come to him immediately. The old man, as in duty bound, instantly obeyed the summons, and Baldy, thinking there would be time enough for him to lend Father Jerome his arm in walking to the Abbot's lodgings before he would be required to accompany his master to the Palace, prepared to do so. Accordingly, leaving Mistress Marjory to recover from her hysterics, they left the house together.

In descending to the street they found an unusual stir and bustle, and a flowing of the multitude towards the Palace. The halberdiers, in their Sunday suits, with Johnnie Gaff at their head, were standing at the door of the Clerk's chamber, waiting to attend the Provost, Bailies, and Council, who were going in state to the Reception. Many of the shops were shut, and the people were in their best attire. It was a cheerful and lively sight. But when Father Jerome appeared, leaning on the arm of Baldy, the good-humour of the crowd became a little harsh. At first, passage was freely afforded to the old man. His papistical garb was, however, displeasing to many of the spectators, and before he reached the Abbot's door, there was both shouts and yells raised against him, and more than one handful of mire had sullied his robe. This Father Jerome himself endured with patience. He merely pitied the misled and erring multitude, and spoke, as it were prophetically, of the time being at hand when they would return to their old pastors and folds.

Baldy had less of the spirit of martyrdom. His temper was naturally brittle; and the profound reverence in which he held the Romish religion made him feel with indignation the revilings with which the venerable chaplain was assailed. He, however, said nothing, but walked as briskly as the old man could go with him to the house wherein the Abbot resided. Here, when the door was opened, and Father Jerome safe within, Baldy halted on the steps, before entering, and addressed the crowd.

"Ye hae had," said he, "for some time the power in your ain hands, but I trow misrule is coming to an end."

At these words a huge clash of mire was thrown from the crowd, and shut Baldy's mouth. It would have been as well, both for himself and others, had the matter ended here; but the bravery with which he had spoken struck some of the most observant of his auditors, and they made their own comments upon that circumstance.

For some time previous the unreformed priesthood had moved with humility and moderation. They saw that the tides of the time were against them, and conducted themselves, under the reproaches of the Protestants, in such a manner as to save themselves from any particular disparagement or obloquy. This, however, applied only to those who frequented the great towns. In the neighbourhood of their own abbeys and monasteries they still exercised their wonted arrogance, even perhaps more decidedly than when they were in less danger;

and Baldy being bred up in the country, and favourable to the papistical cause, was little prepared to brook the rough treatment he had received. The effect of his bold attempt to harangue the mob, raised an opinion in the crowd that the Catholics were encouraged to make a stand. This notion spreading, the zealots began to think it would be expedient to let them know how little this would be permitted. Thus it came to pass, when it was known that many of the ancient churchmen were assembling at the lodgings of the Bishop of Glasgow to go with him to Court, that the multitude went off in the same direction, to give them some taste of their temper.

Father Jerome was conducted into the Abbot's room, a dark, lofty chamber, wainscoted with oak, richly carved with mitres, armorial shields, and other ensigns and emblems of ecclesiastical dignity. A massy table stood in the middle of the room with implements for writing, and a huge chased brazen inkstand in the centre. Around the room were several large chairs, covered with black leather, each of them capaciously formed for the reception of no ordinary corpulency.

The abbot himself was not in the room when Father Jerome was shown in, but one of his chaplains, a little dried sallow-visaged friar, received him, and requested him to be seated, while he went to make his arrival known.

Father Jerome was not allowed to remain long by himself; a shrill bell was rung in an inner apartment, and presently two tall elderly friars came out, and stood at each side of the door. Then came a third, bearing a silver mace, on the top of which, an emblem of the Abbey, sat a figure of the Virgin and Child. Then came the Abbot himself, a capacious, tall, majestical person, with a hoary flowing beard, dressed in his pontifical, wearing the mitre of his order.

Father Jerome, still tingling with the humiliation to which he had been subjected, beheld the gorgeous appearance of the Abbot with mingled awe and dread. He approached him, however, and lifting the hem of his garment, kissed it with profound veneration, while the Abbot laid his hand upon his head and pronounced a brief benediction.

"I have sent for you," the Abbot then said, "to accompany me to the house of the Bishop of Glasgow. I expect certain others of our west country clergy; for the time has come when we should show the reprobates, that they are not always to domineer over us in the way they have of late done."

Father Jerome, with great humility, expressed his apprehension, that in the present temper of the people, it might be as well to postpone any outward demonstration of their confidence in the religion of the Queen's Majesty, until the councils of the kingdom had time to set the realm more in order.

"Ah!" cried the Abbot, "it is such timeserving that has proved our ruin; unless we now show that we have courage and confidence in our ability, to meet our adversaries face to face, there will be but little amendment in our condition. The Queen is a woman young in years, and will, no doubt, be ruled by those that get nearest about her. But, father, it is in your power at this time to be a great instrument in the restoration of the rights of the Church. It has been observed, that Southennan has, in a very surprising manner, speedily become acquainted with some of those who have the private ear of the Queen, and we look to your instrumentality to turn this blessed accident to an efficacious account."

The Abbot then waved with his hand to his attendants to retire, and seating himself, desired Father Jerome to take a chair beside him. He then began to explain to the old man in what way he should exert his influence over Southennan. The consternation of the Abbot was, however, extreme, when Father Jerome replied:

"I doubt, my Lord Abbot, if what you advise is within the compass of any power of mine. In sooth to say, I have within the hour had great cause to fear that Southennan has received an infection of the new heresies, that will mar the hope I had in him. Prudent and judicious he is for so young a man, and I do not say he has lent himself to the sedition of our enemies; but if it be, my Lord Abbot, as you say, that he has formed intimacies with courtiers in the confidence of the Queen's Majesty, I doubt it is not to be the fashion at Court to take up our cause in any determined manner."

The Abbot told him, that certainly it had been the intention of the Queen's Majesty to act an even part between the old and the new clergy; but that she had been that morning greatly insulted by the reformed ministers, and it was thought if the matter were well handled, she would be brought, in consequence, to make a braver demonstration towards the right cause. Some farther discourse took place on the same subject, and ultimately the interview ended by the Abbot consenting, on the earnest exhortation of Father Jerome, to go without the ostentation of his pontificals to the Bishop of Glasgow.

Vol. I.—11

CHAPTER XXXVI.

"Oh, ye mitred heads
Preserve the church!"
COWPER.

At this interesting epoch many of the nobles and great characters of the state were in Edinburgh, and, according to the custom of the age, they had all numerous trains of armed men in attendance. This circumstance, considering the religious controversies among them, might have endangered the tranquillity of the city, but with a forbearance rare in the history of Scottish contentions, they simultaneously, without any compact, agreed, in deference to the festival of the Queen's arrival, to lay the strictest injunctions on their retainers to preserve the public peace.

Thus It happened, that when the crowd ran from the Abbot of Kilwinning's house, yelling and shouting, towards the lodgings of the Bishop of Glasgow, an accident occurred which, at any other time, would have been the cause of riot and bloodshed. The Earl of Glencairn, one of the most distinguished leaders among the champions of the Reformation, was then proceeding towards Holyrood House with a numerous retinue of armed followers, and immediately behind him came the Lord Torphican, a Catholic, also in the same manner numerously attended. The two noblemen, and their respective principles and characters, were well known to the crowd, who, observing them quietly proceeding together, were daunted in their riotous intentions, and still more awed when the Lord Glencairn, seeing the disposition to tumult that was in the multitude assembled before the Bishop's gate, directed his men to halt there, and to repress every symptom of insubordination. By this well-timed decision on the part of that eminent Protestant, the peace of the city was preserved, the Abbot of Kilwinning with Father Jerome were quietly without ostentation allowed to join the Bishop's party, and the whole assemblage of the clergy convened there, were suffered to proceed with their customary paraphernalia to the Palace.

Nevertheless, it was plain to them all, that, as they owed

their protection to Glencairn, the hearts of the people had deserted them for ever. Instead, therefore, of the arrogant anticipations with which they had formed the design of their procession, they advanced with lowly countenances and mortified feelings. It was observed, that many of them had a look of dejection, even of grief, and that, although a few of the prelates and higher clergy still held themselves with a proud port and an undaunted eye, yet the whole presented something of discomfiture and a consciousness of being only tolerated by some forbearance of their adversaries.

The hazard of disturbance to the festivity of the Reception being thus prevented, the Queen had no cause to regret that evening any seeming want of unanimity among the people.

In the mean time, Baldy, having left Father Jerome with the Abbot, safe in the lodgings of the Bishop of Glasgow, returned to Mrs. Marjory's, for Hughoc, in order that they might together attend their master to the Palace.

On knocking at the door he was surprised to be admitted by the old gentlewoman herself, still in full dress. Hughoc, she informed him, had been restless and camstarie, and would not be counselled by her.

"He's gane," said she, "in despite o' my counsel, to seek for Southennan; wha, to tell the truth, Mr. Archibald, is no the gentleman ye said he was. He's a prejinct upsetter, and if he's o' the right faith, he has an ill way o' showing it. I'm sure, had my cousin Auchenbrae no been under a cloud, and he has the double o' a' the estate of Southennan, he would hae treated me in a very different manner. But, Mr. Archibald, what can he want wi' you and the laddie Hughoc thegither? It's just vanity. Let the laddie gang till him, and mak a kirk and a mill o' what they would be at; but I'll lay my commands baith as a gentlewoman and as an auld acquaintance frae the time o' your former maister, that ye gang wi' me for a protection."

Baldy had been so little satisfied with his master's conduct all day, that he was very much inclined to let him know that the man could do without the master, and, accordingly, he said to Mistress Marjory, if she thought she needed his protection, he would stretch a point to attend her. The offer was gladly accepted; and with her towering toupees, short petticoats, and tall red morocco leather high-heeled shoes, she soon sallied forth (followed by Baldy), carrying her feather fan in the one hand, and her sack (as the reticule was called in those days), hanging by a red ribbon from her wrist.

Surely that day had been ordained to be one full of tribulations, to Baldy as well as to his master. Scarcely had Mistress Marjory emerged from her stairs into the street, followed by him, when a shoal of irreverent urchins gathered around her. At first they were respectful and audible in their admiration of her stature and finery, animated by a due respect for the consideration she derived from the attendance of Baldy. They followed her accordingly down the street, with all manner of apparent dutifulness; but as she reached the Nether Bow, a change came over their spirit.

An old woman, one Widow Sybows, who kept a huxtry shop near the Gate, beholding the pomp of Mistress Marjory's appearance, came running out and stopped her.

"Dear me," said Widow Sybows, "but ye're in your best the night, Mistress Marjory! and it' s, considering the straemash in the streets, a gay thing that I hae seen you; for it'll no' lie in my power, on account o' the daffing that's amang our lasses, to send you, this night, the capons and the kipper that I promised."

"Woman," exclaimed Mistress Marjory, "keep your distance: don't you see that I am going to pay my devoirs to the Queen's Majesty."

"Hech, sirs," replied the widow, nettled, "but the Queen's Majesty must be scant o' leddies when she needs such an auld papistical as you."

Mrs. Marjory well knew the import of this insult; but she held her head in a dignified and lofty position, and walked on through the Gate as if inaccessible to molestation. It chanced, however, that the streets of Edinburgh were not then so well paved as they have been since, in consequence of which, as she was stately stepping forward, the heel of one of her lofty red toppling shoes went into a crevice in the causeway, in such a manner that she fell down upon the breadth of her back, and so was rendered totally unfit to proceed towards the Palace. The accident itself was solemn and affecting; and its solemnity was increased by another occurrence which happened most unexpectedly at the same crisis.

The Provost, Bailies, and Counsellors, were coming down the street with the halberdiers before them, and Johnnie Gaff seeing what had happened to so splendid a lady, turned round, and said to the Provost, "My lord, here's a stoppage *in transitu*. A gentlewoman, somewhat scant in her wyliecoat, has had a sederunt on the causeway stanes. Poor leddy, she's had a cauld seat: I hope she's met wi' nae detriment *à posteriori!*"

The Provost was exceedingly indignant that the city pageantry should be interrupted by such an incident, and called aloud, "Halberdiers, proceed!" The procession accordingly moved on, but past Bailie Brown, who had discovered an old friend in the unfortunate Mistress Marjory, stepped forwards, and whispered to the Provost that she was a relation of his own.

"The good of my country," said the Provost, "must not suffer interruption from kith or kin of mine. Halberdiers and Johnnie Gaff, just go on as fast as you can, and let the leddy take her own way of it."

CHAPTER XXXVII.

————"I have seen them shiver and look pale,
Make periods in the midst of sentences,
Throttle their practis'd accents in their fears,
And, in conclusion, dumbly have broke off,
Not paying us a welcome."
SHAKSPEARE.

About the time when the mishap at the Nether Bow befell Mistress Marjory, and impeded the progress of the city dignitaries to the Palace, Southennan and Cornylees left the lodgings of the latter also to proceed thither. We have already said that something had so affected our hero as to make him not altogether in the best humour with the incidents of the day.

Hughoc had come to him as directed, with eyes and ears ready for every hest upon which he might be missioned, but the non-appearance at the proper time of Baldy troubled him. In truth, the conduct of that worthy, both during the journey and subsequent to their arrival in Edinburgh, had been far from satisfactory, and his master not only regretted that he had brought him, but also that he had brought Father Jerome. Indeed, he could never well account to himself how it was that Father Jerome had come at all, and this very circumstance made him repine at being burdened with the old man. With Hughoc he was content. The boy showed himself possessed of a degree of sagacity and shrewdness far beyond the high opinion his master had previously entertained of him; but Southennan could not be insensible, that with all his adroit-ness, he was more interested in the enjoyment which he himself received from the incidents of his duty than from the performance of the duties themselves. This, however, he was good-naturedly disposed to overlook; but there were certain things essential to his own comfort and importance, the neglect of which he was less willing to pardon.

After waiting some time with Cornylees in expectation of Baldy, the patience of our hero became exhausted, and he proposed that they should, without farther delay, proceed to the Reception, telling Hughoc at the same time, to provide links, and to be ready to conduct them home. Accordingly, the two lairds proceeded together, and reached the Nether Bow just at the moment when the magistrates were stopped by the mishap of Mrs. Marjory.

Southennan was little inclined to pass through the crowd. He felt perfectly sensible of his own insignificance in the midst of a town multitude, and was desirous of quietly threading his way through the throng, without exposing himself to particular observation. It was not so with Cornylees: he was a man who stood high in his own opinion; he was dressed in a costly garb for the occasion; the wine he had drank and the bustle in which his quarrel had engaged him had raised his spirits; in a word, he was no mean man at this conjuncture in his own opinion, and, in consequence, was little disposed to seek his way tamely onward: but in proportion to his impetuosity he was repulsed. However, at last he threaded the crowd, and with his companion, attended by Hughoc, reached the portal of the Palace without farther molestation.

They ascended the great stairs together along with other gentlemen who were hastening to pay their respects to the Queen, who had as yet not emerged from her private apartments.

It happened, that on reaching the landing-place Southennan met with the Count Dufroy and Chatelard, who were passing forwards in the throng to reach the gallery in time for the Queen's appearance. Forgetting in the moment his companion Cornylees, he entered into conversation with them, and was gradually drawn on in the crowd, leaving the laird behind to shift for himself.

Few situations are more disagreeable than that in which Cornylees found himself. He was alone in the midst of a crowd, in which all his habits and endeavours in vain encouraged him to think himself a superior. He soon perceived that his habiliments, notwithstanding their costliness to him, were but ordinary compared with the garbs of many around him, and he felt that he was out of his accustomed element, and not exactly in circumstances of equality even with some of those whom he was somehow disposed to consider as his inferiors. But what he felt strongest of all was being deserted, as he regarded it, by Southennan, and deserted too for foreigners, towards whom there could be no reason for such particular partiality. He was thus completely discomposed, and rendered unable to practise that self-confidence in the courtly circle which he had flattered himself, and had indeed boasted, he should perform with great eclat.

But though disconcerted and alone, he was yet too confident in himself to be much disturbed ; and thus it happened, when in looking round, he beheld the Chevalier whom he had offended standing in the crowd, he pressed towards him, and as far as look and manner went, indicated that he regarded him as an old acquaintance. The Frenchmen recognised him at once, and acknowledged the previous acquaintance with cold civility. This Cornylees did not very well understand, and pressed still closer towards the Chevalier, who, on his part, retired and avoided him as much as he possibly could do.

The Laird had never been placed in such an unpleasant predicament before. Imperfect as his experience was, he had tact enough to perceive that he was shunned, and his chagrin was exaggerated by the thought, that foreigners dared to treat him with such contumely in the very halls of his own sovereign. This discomfort, however, was not peculiar to Cornylees; many of the other Scotch gentlemen were similarly situated, and felt equally indignant, without knowing wherefore : an effect of some obscure consciousness of inferiority in themselves.

The crowd moved on, and Cornylees soon after, entering the door of the gallery, found himself more at large, and near again to our hero, whom he immediately rejoined.

Southennan, like most young men on such an occasion, perceived that the Genoa velvet did not sit smoothly on Cornylees. He discovered something uncouth and awkward in his manners, an impress that was any thing but in accordance with the air of a court, and in consequence was little disposed to encourage his familiar address. He did not, however, cast him coldly off, he only did what was equivalent to the same thing ; he put on the mask of a stranger's countenance, was civil, very civil, but his civility wanted that couthiness which better accorded with the disposition of Cornylees than ceremony.

"This is strange breeding," said the Laird to himself; "before we came up the stair, there could no' be a more friendly and jocose companion. What the Deevil's come o'er him now! His face looks as friendly as ever, but there is a foreign softness in his language that would fain mak me trow he scarcely kent me. It may be court manners; but, in course now, its no gude manners: that say I."

A whirl in the crowd brought Cornylees again to a distance from Southennan, and close to Rizzio. This seemed a happy accident. Rizzio recognised him at once, seemingly with a pleasant old friendly freedom. The Laird rejoiced in the cordial recognition; but while they were speaking, another press of the crowd separated them, and Rizzio was brought immediately beside the Earl of Morton, who familiarly, for the first time, saluted him by the name of " Dauvit," a circumstance which the sharp-sighted Italian instantly turned to his own advantage, and with that address and ingenuity of which he was so perfect a master, he endeavoured to conciliate the attention and good-will of Morton. Cornylees, who knew not the rank or consideration of Rizzio's patron, pressed again forward, but to his great amazement, the countenance of the Italian was now changed: he did not altogether affect not to know the Laird, but he looked at him with reserve and surprise, and answered his questions in monosyllables, while he whispered satirical things of him to the Earl, who, without much regard to the effect, laughed loudly, and turned his eyes upon the disconcerted worthy of Renfrewshire, as if he had been a thing of some inferior and uncouth nature.

CHAPTER XXXVIII.

" Give first admittance to the ambassadors."
HAMLET.

MANY of the Scottish gentry were, on the night of that Reception, as much out of their element as Cornylees, and the uneasy feeling which they had in consequence, was ascribed by none of them to their own unaccustomed habits. The foreigners were, in their eyes, alone to blame. They were regarded as encouraged in their supercilious manners by the Queen; and poor Mary, on the very evening of her greatest triumph, was viewed, by those who were loudest in their loyalty, with distrust.

For some time the irksome sensibility of Cornylees was overwhelmed by the interest which the approach of the papistical dignitaries, with the Bishop of Glasgow at their head, excited. He was not exactly of the reformed Church; in truth, he had very little partiality for any sect of clergy at all; but the air of the Reformation had been breathed upon him, and he saw that by the demolition of the pride of the ancient clergy, the consequence of the stated gentry, as they were called, would be augmented; and therefore it might be said that he was in some measure a partisan of the Reformation: he regarded the Romish dignitaries on this occasion as assuming a degree of consideration in the state to which they were not entitled, and this served to irritate his peevishness, already sufficiently offended.

The condition into which he had been cast by the dryness of Southennan, and the more marked and sudden estrangement of Rizzio, ill qualified him to look with indifference on the veneration paid to the clerical procession by the servants and officers of the Palace. They compelled him to stand aside while the Bishop of Glasgow and the dignitaries of his company were ushered on towards the chamber where they were to be admitted into the presence of the Queen, and with others of the same humour he thought this preference great derogation, insomuch that he even complained aloud of it; nor were there wanting around him echoes to his discontent.

Scarcely had the ecclesiastical pageant passed on, when the magistrates of the city were announced. They were all godly men of the Reformation, but it happened that on entering the portal they had been stopped by the guards for a short time, merely to prevent a pressure until the churchmen had ascended the stairs, a circumstance which vexed one and all of them. They thought it was a slight intentionally cast upon the city in their persons, and were in consequence indignant. They all spoke loudly against the audacity of the Papists, and past Bailie Brown did not scruple to observe, that it was a shame they should be permitted to show their faces in a protestant court. The Dean of Guild gently admonished him to speak low, for he should recollect that the Queen herself was known to be of a papistical nature.

At this seditious crisis a flourish of trumpets announced the approach of Her Majesty. The doors of the presence-chamber were thrown open, and Mary, attended by her ladies, the most beautiful daughters of the land, came forward, led by her then favourite brother, the Prior of St. Andrews, who for the occasion, as it was thought, appeared in a secular garb. In the train of Her Majesty several of the old and most esteemed counsellors and nobles of her mother, the late Regent, came forward. Whether this was by accident or command, they consisted nearly in equal numbers of the professors of the reformed and old religion. But it was soon discovered and whispered through the throng, that there was one more of the papists than of the reformed gentry. This, however, was not very clear to those who, like Cornylees, were still at a distance from the door of the presence-chamber; Southennan, however, who was considerably farther advanced, saw that it was so, and saw also with the same uneasiness, arising from another cause, that the gentlemen in her Majesty's suite were, with the exception of the great officers of state and those ancient nobles who could have no meaner place, all her French courtiers; and that Chatelard in a conspicuous manner attached himself with an unbecoming freedom to Adelaide. This particular circumstance induced him to hang back, and to allow the greater part of the crowd to pass on to her Majesty before him. It thus came to pass that he was again brought beside Cornylees, whose dire dissatisfaction at all he heard and witnessed could with difficulty be restrained from being loudly expressed.

In the mean time Mary was receiving, with her best graciousness, the heartless homage of the crowd, until the head of the ecclesiastical procession reached the door of the presence-chamber, when a sudden pause took place in the ceremonial.

The lords and attendants immediately around the Queen, retired behind her, and left Her Majesty prominently in the fore-ground—a profound silence pervaded all the assembled throng—the expectation of some extraordinary incident was visible in every countenance. The Queen alone appeared unchanged and self-possessed. After a short hesitating pause, the Bishop of Glasgow stepped forward, followed by the other prelates and dignitaries who attended him. Mary looked calmly on them as they approached; and when the Bishop was come before her, she gracefully held out her hand, which he kissed, kneeling at the same time. Before he had well recovered his erect position, she stepped a little aside to indicate that his homage was performed, and she again presented her hand, in the same manner, to the Abbot of Kilwinning, next in order. In this manner, without any particular demonstration of preference, she received the Roman clergy.

Immediately after them, almost as it were in their train, a party of the reformed clergy followed. At their head was old Mr. Allison, whom she had so distinguished in the morning, and recollecting his mild. pale, and thoughtful countenance, as well as the personal compliment he had paid to herself, she forgot at the moment the invidious eyes which were then upon her, and smiled with particular graciousness as the old man drew near.

The incident attracted universal attention, and the happiest auguries were drawn from it by the protestants. Immediately, however, behind Mr. Allison, came the dark and austere Dr. Glossar, who also had not been forgotten in her recollection of the morning audience; and, unfortunately, she received him coldly and proudly, and withheld from him the wonted condescension of her hand.

It were needless to descant upon this circumstance. Mr. Allison, though much respected by the multitude, was too meek and temperate in his doctrines and demeanour to be held in any vehement esteem : while Dr. Glossar, a stern, uncompromising, and ambitious zealot, was regarded with awe and veneration. Few of the reformed clergy were, indeed, in the enjoyment of greater reverence; and none exacted a more implicit compliance with his opinions. The effect, therefore, of the marked distinction between the Queen's reception of him and his more amiable though less venerated colleague, was noticed by all present, and audible murmurs of dissatisfaction circled around the apartments. It was thus by yielding to the momentary impulses of her feelings, and forgetting the severe impartiality which royalty prescribes, that the ill-fated Mary disappointed the hopes and loosened the attachment of her subjects, even while design and dissimulation were far from her thoughts.

CHAPTER XXXIX.

"But not a courtier
(Although they wear their faces to the bent
Of the King's look), but hath a heart that is
Glad at the thing they scowl at."
CYMBELINE.

Some time elapsed before the two orders of the clergy had passed the presence, and a short pause ensued before the magistrates of Edinburgh reached the Queen. They partook of the disappointment which her cool reception of Dr. Glossar had occasioned: but as they were men of good sense in the main, though marked by their citizenship with some peculiarities, they approached her in a calm and respectful manner, and she made one step forwards to receive them. It happened, however, that in this motion her hand carelessly threw forwards the train of her robe, in such a manner that it entangled the Provost's feet, and nearly threw him down. The accident was trivial in itself, but it bred some ludicrous confusion, and the gay and youthful Mary could not stifle her risibility.

Although every one near her saw that it was purely an accident, yet those who were at a distance attributed the mirth of the Queen to some feeling of ridicule for the magistrates, and, in consequence, such want of decorum was loudly condemned: she was not, however, even then without partizans, inspired by her rank and her beauty. These instantly stood for her defence, and aggravated the resentment that was felt for the supposed disrespect practised towards the Provost. Saving this little mischance, nothing of any particular moment afterward interrupted the course of the reception, till the well-garnished Laird of Cornylees came forward.

During his passage through the crowd, he had been particularly careful of his velvet clothes; but just as he was advancing to the Queen, the slashes in his doublet caught hold of the hilt of a bystander's sword, and when he bent forward, which he did, not being much accustomed to such ceremony, somewhat rashly, the hilt tore the doublet, and precipitated him on the floor: this was beyond the power of court etiquette or formality to control. A general laugh ensued: and the Queen herself made no effort to restrain her amusement. The Laird scrambled up in a fury, and hastily, as he rushed out of the room, shook the gentleman by the collar, who had been the innocent cause of his disaster. It happened to be the Count Dufroy, whose equanimity was not disturbed by the assault. On the contrary, the Count was as much diverted as the rest. It however had the effect of causing the Queen to break off the Reception while there were still a few gentlemen to come forward—among others Southennan; but Mary, with her characteristic quick-sightedness, saw, among those who had lingered, several whom she would have been pleased to have received; and in consequence, in retiring from the presence-chamber, she ordered Dufroy to bring in such of them to supper as he thought deserving, by their quality or breeding, of the distinction. It thus happened that Southennan was invited, and placed in a position to observe the conduct of Chatelard, of whom rivalry had made him suspicious. But he valued the honour, chiefly, on account of the opportunity it afforded him of addressing himself to Adelaide.

Between the Reception and the supper, some time of necessity elapsed, during which, the Count Dufroy having special duties to perform, Southennan was left among the other invited guests, to pass the interval in the gallery, where many of the crowd still remained. As he was lounging carelessly among them, he happened to pass near the door, when he felt himself suddenly jerked by his cloak, and on turning round discovered his boy among a crowd of other servants, who who were waiting on the landing-place and stairs for their masters.

Southennan was displeased with the familiarity of Hughoc, and roughly inquired what he wanted.

"I hae," said the boy, rising on his tip-toes, and whispering, "a dreadfu' something to tell, and ye maun come down the stair and out to the court, for its a thing o'. awfu' instancy."

All the tidings which Hughoc had brought to him, from the time of their arrival the preceding evening were of an extraordinary kind, although not, perhaps, of that importance which the boy attached to them. This had the effect of inducing him to yield more complacently to the request than he would, probably, otherwise, have done.

Vol. I.—12

"What is it," said, " that you have heard?" when they were come down into the court.

" Just a dreadfu' misdoubt that I hae ta'en o' our Baldy. Odd, sir, I'm thinking he's growing a traitor-man; for when him and me were standing amang the ither flunkies, waiting till it would be needfu' to light our links, bye came a big dark carle, in a friar's gown, through amang us, and he gied Baldy a friendly slap on the shouther. ' Eh!' cried Baldy, ' is this you.' ' Ay,' said the man, ' it's just me,' and wi' a glint o' a flambeau that was gaun past at the time I lookit in the stranger's face, and wha do ye think it was, Laird?—just Friar Michael, that I saw this very morning in a randy's gown and garb crossing the water o' Keith. Odd, sir, a' this masquing and guising disna' came o' honesty!"

"And where," cried Southennan, " is Baldy now?"

" Ye may speer that, Laird! but its mair than I can tell. Awa' they ga'ed, colleaguing thegither, and they hadna' gaen far, for I ga'ed a bit cooke behint them, when they met auld Father Jerome, and ye would hae been confounded if ye had seen what a hearty gude will was amang them at this meeting."

"And is this," said Southennan, " all that you have got to tell me?"

" I'm sure, Laird," replied the boy, " it couldna' be mair awfu',' unless there had been blood and murder in't!"

Southennan did not see the mystery in colours quite so grim, but still it seemed to him singular that there should be so much secret work between Baldy, Friar Michael, or Auchenbrae, as we should rather call him, and Father Jerome. Of the fidelity and worth of Baldy, as a servant, he had no doubt; but this unaccountable plotting and seeming machination discomposed him exceedingly. He, however, affected to make light of the intelligence, and bade Hughoc return home, and come back with Baldy after the Queen's supper. He then returned up stairs into the gallery, where he presently saw the Count Dufroy anxiously looking about. The moment he threw his eyes on Southennan, it was evident that he was the object of his solicitude, for he immediately came eagerly towards him, and taking him by the arm drew him aside.

" Could you imagine," said he, when they were apart from the rest of the company, " that in the midst of so much splendour and joy there should have been malice, I might almost say treason. The ancient clergy are dissatisfied with their reception, and the Bishop of Glasgow and the Abbot of Kilwinning are closeted with the Queen, complaining of the coldness with which she received them. The magistrates of Edinburgh are still more discontented, and the new clergy, with the gaunt dark Dr. Glossar, have declared that atonement is due to them. Heavens! can they think a poor young creature, in the playfulness of her teens, can be such a Machiavelli as to please them all. In a word, Southennan, I see nothing but trouble and distress, unless the young gentry of the kingdom make a party for the Queen, without reference to either clergy."

Southennan was profoundly impressed with the earnestness of the Count's speech, and expressed himself sensible of the necessity of some third party interposing, to protect her Majesty from the importunity of the contending clergy and their partisans. Little more was said at that time, for the sounds of the musicians, preparing for the supper, echoed through the rooms, and prevented farther conversation; soon after the Count was summoned to attend her Majesty, and the guests proceeded to the banqueting-room to receive her.

CHAPTER XL.

"If he love her not,
And be not from his reason fall'n thereon,
Let us be no assistant for a state,
But keep a farm and carters."

HAMLET.

THE personal graces of the Queen of Scots, and the brilliancy of her mind, shone brightest in the midst of the splendour of her Court. Though she affected the privacy of domestic life more than properly belonged to her regal condition, it was not in that sphere she was most distinguished; for she was herself fond of admiration, and conscious of deserving it; and the whole object of her education had been directed to prepare her for distinction in public. Perhaps on no occasion—at least on none within her ancient kingdom—did she appear to more advantage than on the evening we have to commemorate. Sensible that she was then the observed of all observers, every accomplishment she possessed, that could be exhibited to the admiration of her guests and subjects, was ostentatiously displayed, even to the practice of a familiarity that put her dignity more than once to hazard.

Towards the great officers of the realm—ancient men, and celebrated for their energy and wisdom—she practised the most fascinating deference ; acknowledging with smiles the suggestions which momentary circumstances sometimes induced them to make, and delighting them with the acuteness of her remarks, and her intelligence on all topics, especially on matters of state, to which, from her youth, and previous life, it was not supposed she had much attended. Her deportment to the different noble ladies invited to the banquet, was still more the theme of approbation. Endowed by nature with the power of discerning the springs and foibles of character, she discovered with intuitive penetration the weaknesses of her own sex ; and by her condescension, ever varying according to the peculiarities of the personages she addressed, she won from them easy victories to the superiority of her own manners and accomplishments. The influence of her address, elegance, and condescension, diffused a degree of gayety and delight, which the oldest present had no remembrance of having ever witnessed in the Scottish Court: but it was not in her power to repress the impulses of personal feeling. It was evident, that towards some of the old and stern nobles, who accounted themselves not less than the masters and main-springs of the government, her affability was in some degree constrained ; nor, indeed, did it require much of a discerning spirit, to perceive, that her gayety was in some degree rebuked by their austerity. She plainly endeavoured to win their good opinion upon some other principle than that of esteem ; and, in consequence, with them she was less at ease and less delightful, than with those to whom she more freely unbended. But the remark which was most emphatically made to her disadvantage, was invidious and uncharitable.

It was said that she placed herself more with the foreigners than with her own nobility, and that she showed towards them a freedom of manner inconsistent with the reserve and majesty which the Queen of Scotland ought to have maintained. In this, men more experienced in the world would have discovered only the habitude and effect of elder intimacy. But it was construed into an unpatriotic partiality: and thus it happened while every one acknowledged her endeavours to please, the effect was frustrated by the jealousy with which her little apart attention to her private friends was observed and envied.

But gracious and splendid as the Queen appeared to all the assembly, the attention of Southennan was more attracted towards the milder beauty of Adelaide; not only on account of the spell in her loveliness, but by a cast of anxiety and restlessness in her countenance, of which he was not the only observer. Chatelard was present; and it was towards him that the soft eyes of Adelaide were continually wandering; and our hero perceived, that notwithstanding the intensity of the solicitude with which she followed all his movements, he rarely returned a glance towards her; and that even when he did so, it was expressive of apprehension, as if he feared she was too vigilant. His whole mind seemed to be absorbed in the contemplation of the Queen; and there was, at times, an impassioned ardour in his manner, that appeared bold and dangerous considering their relative condition.

On one occasion, when this was particularly remarkable, Southennan noticed, with something like the embarrassment of detection, that he was himself keenly watched by the shrewd and dark sharp eye of Rizzio. The incident, though it surprised him, was unaccountable; but he soon discovered that he formed only one of a group which the subtle Italian was suspiciously studying. Indeed, he was not left long to ruminate on the subject, for Rizzio had perceived that he was watchful of the passionate animation with which Chatelard doated on the Queen, and coming to him said, with affected jocularity—

"Your French friend seems to have more loyalty than he dare show."

" It surprises me," replied Southennan, unguardedly, for it was admitting the fact; " for I have heard him speak in such terms of the young lady on whose arm the Queen is now leaning, that I believed he was enchanted by her alone."

" I thought so too," replied Rizzio; " but he wears a better mask than I gave him credit for. However, let us observe, and say nothing."

At this juncture the Queen, who had some time before left the apartment in which the banquet had been served, and had passed into the other chamber into which the company had withdrawn, seated herself and directed the musicians to be assembled. From some accidental cause, not perhaps susceptible of any satisfactory explanation, the selection of the music was not much to the taste of her Majesty, and in consequence during a pause in the performance, she, without reflecting on the observation it attracted, beckoned on Chatelard, and directed him to play and sing one of his romances. This he was but too happy to execute, and taking a lute from one of the musicians, he began with more than even his own exquisite taste and delicacy.

SONG.

Lie still, lie still, fond fluttering heart!
    Thy trembling pulses throb in vain;
For she that barbs the mystic dart
    Shall never know thy secret pain.

Mine eyes, with rude unconscious gaze,
    Pursue her form through all the dance,
And her's as oft in strange amaze,
    Rebuke my wild unwary glance.

Whene'er the changeful measure brings
    Her gentle hand to meet with mine,
From the soft touch ecstatic springs
    The sparkling sense of love divine.

Lie still, lie still, fond fluttering heart!
    Thy trembling pulses throb in vain;
For she that barbs the mystic dart
    Shall never know thy secret pain.

During this performance the profoundest silence prevailed. Adelaide listened to him with a rapt and entranced delight; and Rizzio watched alternately his imploring look and the countenance with which the Queen listened to him. It was plain, that with whatever enthusiasm he worshipped in his song, the Queen was only interested in the melody. At the conclusion she took off her glove, and presented to him her hand in acknowledgment of the pleasure his performance had given. But both Rizzio and Southennan, as well as Adelaide, observed that he bent over it with such impetuosity that Mary suddenly drew it back, and with a look of surprise awed him to retire. There were, however, cooler heads, and eyes as eager, with whom the incident passed not unnoticed; and the conclusion among some of the elder courtiers and their scrutinizing dames, was not to the Queen's advantage.

CHAPTER XLI.

"Dexterity and sufferance
Are engines the pure politic must work with."
FORD.

For some time after the Reception, a succession of entertainments were given by the city of Edinburgh to her Majesty and the Court. It was, however, remarked, that she appeared but little disposed to cultivate any intimacy with the families of the nobility. She stood too strictly, it was alleged, on her royalty, and even in her court she formed a small circle of familiars around herself, within which few, even of the most accomplished and esteemed of the Scottish gentry, found admission. The fatality of her ancestors had already overtaken her; and scarcely in any one measure of conduct, or of government, did she appear worthy of the reputation she deservedly enjoyed for intelligence, discernment, and judgment.

Within that little exclusive household circle, Southennan was frequently an honoured guest; but while enjoying the sunshine, he could not behold, without alarm, the clouds arising in the horizon. And yet there appeared no deviation from propriety in the behaviour of Mary, as a gentlewoman: he thought her occasionally, perhaps, too familiar; but from any sight inflexion of conduct of this kind, she retained her dignity with so much ease and grace, that the aberration only served to extend her influence among those who were favoured with her private countenance.

The bustle and the banquetings, in which the Court was engaged, prevented leisure for particular remarks on the conduct of those by whom the Queen was surrounded; but, nevertheless, the demeanour of Chatelard, though regulated by extreme caution and delicacy, did not escape the shrewd observation of our hero, to whom it was evident that he lost no opportunity of always appearing in his most attractive colours before her Majesty, while his artificial deference to Adelaide in public was no less manifestly the deliberate effect of systematic study.

It would be to equivocate with the human heart, to say that

Southennan beheld the increasing passion of Chatelard without something like gratification; nor did his loyalty much repine, when he perceived that Mary did not rebuke the rash young man with such decision as would have quenched his hopes, but amused herself with his ardour, even while she evinced something like flirtation, if such a term may be applied to the reciprocities of persons so far apart in their respective spheres.

The effect of Southennan's discovery of Chatelard's presumptuous affection served to nourish his own love for Adelaide. He was persuaded by many incidents, that she also had perceived the ambition of the accomplished Frenchman; but he calculated without a sufficient knowledge of the fond feelings by which she was animated, when he fancied, that the hopelessness of her unrequited attachment would extinguish its ardour. This made him patient. Day after day passed with him in jealous vigilance; but the deportment of Mary was so often seemingly equivocal, though only dictated by the suggestions of feminine gayety and juvenile playfulness, that he could not always repress his persuasion that the Frenchman would ultimately triumph. His confidant was Rizzio.

The ambition of the Italian was piqued by the favour which he thought the Queen evinced for Chatelard: envious in his nature, he dreaded a competitor in the ascendency which he secretly, with all the zeal of an acute and adventurous spirit, was endeavouring to attain. He was thus his unprovoked enemy, and the fear of being frustrated by his influence chafed his jealousy into hatred. Rizzio in his hate, however, was no less subtle than wary in his ambition. He concealed it as carefully and studied its indulgence with equal solicitude.

Acquainted with the depth to which Southennan was enamoured of Adelaide, he darkly discerned that her passion for the Frenchman might be managed so as to render her Scottish lover subservient to his machinations.

It is mournful to reflect on the cabals which infested the palace of the Scottish Queen; by the ingenuousness of youth, and perhaps also of her nature, she was incapable of suspecting the intrigues, personal and political, by which she was environed. She saw in her counsellors, and the great officers of state, men of harsh feelings, and forbidding countenances, who treated her with less homage than the worship to which she had been accustomed in France; and, save her ladies, she had no advisers in those things which most concerned the graces of her character; for her natural brother, the Prior of St. Andrews, partaking of the austere temper of the time, often in his kindest admonitions, breathed more of restraint than accorded with the vivacity in which she delighted, and which was natural to her age and sex.

Of all her ladies, Adelaide enjoyed her confidence the most; but from the time she had observed her attachment to Chatelard, and suspected his devotion to herself, she assumed a slight though obvious degree of ceremony towards her. This did not escape the penetration of Rizzio, but he erred in the construction he put upon it. Knowing the Queen's confidence in Adelaide, and observing that, if not withdrawn, it was suddenly regulated by some occult motive, he ascribed the change to a kindling predilection on the part of Mary for the ill-fated Frenchman.

This apprehension roused his latent energies. The slightest manifestation of affection, on the part of the Queen, he foresaw would be ruin to his anticipations, for he knew that Chatelard stood in some awe of him, and with that sinister wisdom which often overreaches itself, he apprehended, that were Chatelard once possessed of influence enough over the Queen, to move her to any measure, he would not long be allowed to remain in her service. A simple incident soon brought these anxieties into action.

One day as her Majesty was descending the stairs, attended, accidentally, by himself and Chatelard on her right and left, followed by Adelaide and the Lady Mary Livingstone, she slightly stumbled. The Italian instantly offered his arm, but she took hold of the Frenchman's. It was an act of the moment, unpremeditated, and done without intentional favour or distinction, but it seemed not so to the seething spirit of Rizzio. He beheld in it an indication which his adversary would construe into a mark of special favour, as he believed it was intended to be; and from that moment the unhappy fortunes of the Frenchmen were determined.

Rizzio brooded over the incident, as if it had discovered to him something which he had not before suspected. With the ingenious cunning of his nature, like the wounded scorpion, he struck the venom into himself, and writhed with the agonies of his own infliction. Though his apprehensions were, perhaps, not altogether imaginary, they were yet beyond reason, for Chatelard was not envious, and his passion for the Queen was too much of a blaze, shooting up from vanity, to have respect to aught save its own object. He might occasionally be uneasy at observing the vigilance with which the Italian's dark and piercing eye followed him ; but there was a quality in his passion, arising from the direction it had taken, that gave generosity to all his thoughts. The insane fancy of gaining the Queen's affections filled him with vast ideas of liberality and munificence.

CHAPTER XLII.

"Deliver with more openness your answers
To my demands."
SHAKSPEARE.

On the evening after the little incident mentioned inthe last chapter, Rizzio took occasion to throw himself in the way of Southennan, without appearing to have sought him, although the meeting was the result of study and contrivance. In the management of such seeming accidents the sinister Italian was ingeniously expert.

It happened to be Friday, a day which the Queen always passed in a more sequestered manner than any other of the week, save on the high festivals of her religion. Her household circle was not assembled in the evening : only her ladies were admitted to her ; for even her ministers were directed not to disturb her retirement, unless their business was urgent, and could not be postponed without detriment to the state. Her attendants, those of the chosen number, were in consequence at liberty to amuse themselves as they thought fit. Southennan on these nights rarely went to the palace, for Adelaide was generally on them the preferred companion of her royal mistress Rizzio had noticed this, and planned his machination accordingly.

It had been his custom to dine occasionally at the Unicorn with the foreigners by whom the table was frequented, and where he knew our hero was almost a regular daily guest. He went there at the usual hour, and, as if he had no particular wish for conversation with Southennan, he took his place at dinner on the opposite side of the table, and discussed with those around him, in the apparent ease of a disengaged mind, the various topics which chance or remark suggested. Even after dinner, and when several of the guests had departed, he evinced no dispositian to move nearer to Southennan ; but he sometimes particularly addressed him across the table, as it were in reply to some opinion in which he affected to differ from him.

In this apparently unpremediated manner he continued to act, until he perceived a disposition on the part of Southennan to rise, when he dexterously turned the conversation on some one of the many topics of the day by which the minds of all men were then agitated, expressing himself with a degree of confidence on the subject which drew from our hero an equally decided reply. A controversy was the consequence, which Rizzio managed with so much zeal, that although there was not the slightest approximation to a quarrel between them, their conversation was yet so little agreeable to the other gentlemen in the room, that they one by one dropped away, and left the apartment to the disputants.

When Rizzio had thus obtained for themselves exclusive possession of the room, he suddenly paused, and looking suspiciously to the right and left, moved from the place where he sat at dinner, and took a seat beside our hero.

The abruptness of the pause, the jealous vigilance with which he cast his eyes around ; and something singular and emphatic in his manner, were greatly calculated to rouse attention.

" I hope," said the Italian, with a whispering earnestness, " that nothing during dinner nor since, in my manner towards you, has indicated any particular desire for such an opportunity as this, to speak with you in confidence."

Southennan was surprised at the observation, and naturally enough remarked in reply, that he could not imagine a cause or an occasion for so much address to procure an opportunity for a confidential conversation with him ; for the candour of his mind did not allow him to suspect, or rather to understand, that the art of Rizzio's explanation might be the effect of design, and calculated to augment the impression of what he had to communicate.

" I am glad it is so," said Rizzio ; " and I trust that those who last left us are persuaded we were on the eve of a quarrel, or at least were not likely to have had either treason or conspiracy to arrange."

" Treason !" exclaimed Southennan, " to what do you allude ?" and he said this firmly, for he thought the conduct of his companion more curiously ingenious than any thing between them could possibly require.

"Hush! speak lower," murmured Rizzio, raising his hand, and assuming a knotted and significant look; "What we have both feared, and perhaps one of us wished for, is not far off."

"Explain yourself, Rizzio; I am incapable of comprehending the meaning of this mystery."

"Did you not first point out to my attention the sensual ardour of Chatelard's devotion to the Queen?"

"What of that?" inquired Southennan eagerly, with an accent of anxiety, almost of alarm, dreading he might have said too much upon the subject, or been treacherously dealt with; for it was not to the Italian alone that he had spoken of the Frenchman's presumptuous attachment, but to others he had been also jocular; to Rizzio only had he expressed any feeling of interest or apprehension on the subject.

"Let us not talk of it, nor mention names more than may be necessary," rejoined Rizzio; "I have myself noted it, until a conviction has been wrought as perfect as your own. But——" and, in pausing, he again looked eagerly and apprehensively around.

"Well! what would you say?"

"I believe you Southennan, to be an honourable man, and my friend; but there are things which ought only to be spoken of by the eyes. My fortune, my life perhaps, hang upon what I have to tell; cannot you hear my thoughts?"

"Perhaps I do," replied Southennan, a little dryly, displeased at being distrusted; "but speak out. I do not despair that fidelity shall win its reward."

"You have said it," exclaimed Rizzio, with a hollow and suppressed shout, as it were, of triumph.

"You say not so?" said Southennan.

"It were perdition to us both to breathe the mildew and the blight that might be in the infectious answer to your question," said the Italian solemnly; adding, less seriously, "I did not say the love had yet met return,—had yet——"

"It would be cause enough," replied our hero fervently, "to make the chaste of Adelaide quit——"

"Hush! Let not your tongue give utterance to what you have imagined; steal the best pearl from the crown rather than breath such an imputation. I beseech you, Southennan, to ask no better knowledge than you have guessed; but let us consider how it may advantage your own cause.—Nothing, I fear!"

"Unless it can be made known to Adelaide," rejoined Southennan thoughtfully, adding, " how may that be ? She will herself find it out!"

" I fear, Southennan, we both stand in jeopardy : knowing and not to tell. Are not you friendly with the Prior of St. Andrew's ?"

" Would you have me speak to him ?" cried Southennan, starting, " after having so warned me how near akin the thing is to treason. He will call for proof: what have we, but conjecture : and with conjecture only, dare we impeach the honour of the Queen ? This matter is not yet ripe even for talk, Rizzio."

"I said not that it was so," replied the Italian ; " but only thought it might soon be."

Here their conversation was interrupted by the return of some of the gentlemen who had dined with them.

CHAPTER XLIII.

" Thus I take off the shroud in which my cares
Are folded up from view of common eyes."
                                    THE BROKEN HEART.

SOUTHENNAN and Rizzio left the Unicorn together. The Italian went to the palace, and our hero to his own lodgings.

It was by this time late in the afternoon ; the sun had indeed set, and the twilight was advancing. The streets were in consequence thronged as usual in Edinburgh at that time of the day, with handicraftsmen and apprentices.

In passing up the High-street, Southennan, not being much accustomed to thread the mazes of a crowd, felt himself a good deal pushed about, especially near the Cross, where the assemblage was numerous and restless. At the entrance of a narrow closs, where the people were thickest, an old man addressed him by name, and begged he would follow him.

Something in the appearance and voice of the stranger excited at once his attention and curiosity, and he followed him down the closs, and up a Jacob's-ladder ascent of stairs, to

VOL. I.—13

the eleventh story of one of the Babel edifices that overlooked the North Loch.

The appearance of the old man, as he walked before him, seemed to Southennan to be something remarkable. He had evidently been of a stout frame, and his limbs were well formed and firm, but his steps were tottering and unequal, and the bend in his shoulders showed more of a stoop than decrepitude. When they reached the top of the highest stair the stranger opened the door with a key, and through a dark passage conducted him to a small room cheerfully lighted by a window which was open, and which commanded a view of the magnificent landscape that spreads from the city towards the northwest.

When they were in this room, and the door shut, the old man requested Southennan to be seated, and, with a smile, pulled down his beard, and showed the face and features of Knockwinnie.

Our hero laughed at the revelation, and said—

"I could not have thought it possible that one so robust could have assumed so much of the infirm appearance of eild."

"Ah!" replied the Outlaw, "Time will allow us to anticipate his triumphs, but he has put it out of our power ever to imitate youth. I have, however, only time to tell you briefly my voyage. It was but this morning that the vessel in which I returned reached Leith roads, and since then I have been eagerly in quest of you without success. I was returning to these lodgings when I happened to observe you in the crowd; it is fortunate that we have met so soon. Have you been able to supersede my outlawry?"

Southennan did not return a direct answer. He only expressed his satisfaction at seeing Knockwhinnie again so well, and trusted that his inquiries were calculated to appease the disordered feelings with which he had been so long afflicted.

"Then you have not," said the Outlaw, "procured either remission or pardon. What have you done in the business."

Southennan looked confused. He had literally effected nothing; not altogether from neglect, but from a feeling of procrastination, induced by his unsatisfactory mediation with Dufroy, and from a wish to avoid any explanation concerning the reluctance of Dufroy to lend his assistance.

"So!" cried Knockwhinnie; "you have not been able to do any thing for me. Well, it can't be helped! But have you learned any thing likely to mitigate the pain of this disappointment?"

"Tell me first," replied Southennan, "what has been the result of your own visit to Normandy; for you went off at an unlucky hour."

Knockwhinnie looked a little grave at this question, which seemed to him someting like an evasion; but giving his head a slight toss, as if to shake off something disagreeable, he replied, "Perhaps you say justly; for I met with nothing of which I might not have better ascertained the facts here. My wife is dead—some years ago she died; and my child has been brought up in the family of Count Dufroy. Instead of doing me wrong, he has, in kindness to his Adelaide, been my greatest benefactor. By his influence with the late King Francis, the husband of our Mary, he procured my Adelaide to be placed among the honourable attendants of the Queen; and the occasion of his visit is to restore her to the family of her mother. Have you seen her?"

Southennan replied, with emphasis, that he had, and that she had inspired him with the most ardent affection, which he hoped would be approved by her father.

"What says she herself?" exclaimed Knockwhinnie, eagerly, at the same time holding out his hand in token of his satisfaction at the news.

But Southennan again looked exceedingly confused, and was about to make some general reply.

"Deal plainly with me!" cried the Outlaw. "Is there any obstacle on her part to your union?"

The straightforwardness of Knockwhinnie admitted of no equivocation; and, in consequence, our hero found himself constrained to speak of what he had observed in the conduct of Adelaide.

Knockwhinnie listened to him evidently with greedy ears: his eyes were seemingly cast on the ground; but they were abstracted, and took no heed of aught within the scope of their vision. He leaned forward, resting his hands upon his knees, and presented altogether an appearance of intense and anxious attention.

When the recital was finished, he continued for some time in the same posture, and silent. At last he said, half, as it were, in soliloquy, without lifting his eyes, "Dufroy requires atonement from me, before I can hope for his assistance to procure the reversal of my outlawry!"

Southennan, who had been speaking with warmth and tenderness of Adelaide, was surprised at the irrelevancy of her father's remark, and found himself, as it were, constrained to say, "I was speaking of your daughter."

"True—true—I heard you," replied Knockwhinnie; "but something must be done before we talk of that. This Chatelard, of whom you have been telling me, must be got rid of." And, in saying these words, he unconsciously darted a keen look at Southennan, the effect of which on him was such a hurried recollection of the conversation he had so shortly before held with Rizzio, that it touched him with something like alarm; and he exclaimed, with a voice of dread, "How rid of him?"

The Outlaw looked at him sternly. "I think, Southennan, that by this time you should have known that I do not regard the dagger as always the best means."

Southennan saw that he had touched harshly upon a tender string. But the construction whick Knockwhinnie had put upon his words could not be easily obviated, without mentioning the attachment of Chatelard to the Queen.

The Outlaw, seeing his embarrassment, subjoined, "I do not, however, wonder at your question. Only there has not been enough of provocation, even in the feigned affection for my daughter, committed by this Chatelard, to justify an appeal to violent courses. But, as I have said, we cannot yet talk of that, as my esteem for you would prompt me. I therefore have only to beseech you, before any suspicion is entertained of my return, to bring Count Dufroy and myself together. I am his debtor, and must humble myself to obtain an acquittance of the debt. I have done him an injury; it is necessary that I should atone for it. I pray you, for the affection you profess for Adelaide, that you lose no time in this business: let it be done, if possible, to-night. Do go at once, and I shall wait here an answer, or your return."

CHAPTER XLIV.

"I saw a smith stand with his hammer, thus,
The while his iron did on the anvil cool,
With open mouth, swallowing a tailor's news."
SHAKSPEARE.

In proceeding from Knockwhinnie's lodgings, Southennan met his boy.

"Ah! Laird," exclaimed Hughoc, on seeing him : " do ye ken what a come-to-pass has happened? Knockwhinnie's back frae France ; and sic a like sight! ye wouldna' ken him were ye to see him in your spoon."

Our hero was a little startled, apprehensive lest the Outlaw might have been discovered by some other person.

"How came you," said he, " to know of this ? Who told you?"

"Na," replied the boy ; " I'se warrant naebody told me : but ye see, I chanced to ha'e a needcessity about the horses. so I was down at Widow Hutchie's house, and standing at the door, glowering frae me, there came an auld gaberlunzie looking man, wi' a white beard, that would ha'e been creditable to the auldest he-goat in Arran, and leaning on his staff, which was a very pretty ane, and, I daur say, had a sword in its kyte, for it had a silver virl just below the heft lith, he asked me, wi' a kind o' strangulated voice, if I could tell him where young Southennan was to be found. 'I ken but ae Southennan,' quo' I ; and I looked up in his face, and as his mouth was open, I discerned by his teeth that he was na' sae auld as he was like, and hadna' lost mark o' mouth ; so a jealousy fell upon me, and I thought, wha can this guisart be ?"

"Speak to the point," interrupted his master.

"Well," resumed Hughoc, "speaking to the point : I looked a little better at him ; but really his face was sae weel hidden aneath a coat o' paint, that for the leeving soul o' me, I couldna' guess wha it possibly could be ; but it cam' into my head to cry wi' a loud skreigh o' terror, ' Eh ! gudeman, there's a jenny-wi'-the-many-feet crawling on your coat-neck.' ' The deevil there is !' said he, in his natural voice ; and wha's natural voice, think ye, was that, Laird? As sure's death, it was Knockwhinnie's! Seeing he wasna' disposed to be confidential wi' me, I didna let on that I kent him, but just said, that ye were down at the Abbey gallanting wi' the Queen and her leddies."

"Well," replied his master, "you have shown yourself, Hughoc, both shrewd and sharp; but tell nobody what you have discovered."

"Ye needna' counsel that," exclaimed the boy. "Wha would I tell? Ye surely, Laird, dinna' think me so lost to discretion as to speak on sic a kittle point wi' our Baldy, wha, for any thing that I see, is growing to be a monk. Hech! but it's a puir trade now-a-days. He'll no make his plack a bawbee by that."

This information respecting his servant a little molested the tranquillity of Southennan, although it was not altogether new to him. He had remarked something like remissness in the conduct of Baldy from the first day of their arrival in Edinburgh, and he thought him too particular in his attendance on Father Jerome, who he well knew was stirring among the Catholic priesthood; the arrival of the Queen having drawn them in great numbers to the town. Being, however, anxious to complete his mission to Count Dufroy, he ordered Hughoc to attend him to the palace, and, as they went down the Canongate, he inquired his reason for supposing that Baldy was likely to turn a monk.

"Oh! oh!" said the boy: "I didna' mean that he was sic a desperate sneck-drawer as to turn a true monk; I only meant that he was growing ane in a certain sense. But, Laird, I would look weel about me if I were you; for I heard Father Jerome tell a muckle fat painchy priest that he had but sma' expectation o' you, and the utmost it would be in his power to do was, wi' the help o' Baldy, to keep you frae falling into harm's way, which they meant was going to the orthodox kirks!"

Southennan bit his lips at hearing this; the idea of being so circumvented by his servant provoked his indignation, but he only said to the boy in an indifferent tone—

"And how did you overhear this conversation?"

"Ye see, sir, I hae sometimes naething to do, and so whiles I dauner about, and whiles I gang in till Widow Hutchie's room, and lie down on the big kist that stands ahint the door, and make a bit skip frae care into the land of Nod. Nae farther gane than yesterday, being in the humour for a doze of forgetfulness, I lay down on the kist lid, and when I was lying there, in came Father Jerome wi' that haggis-bellied monk, and they were unco couthy and cosy, talking into ane anither's lugs about papistical matters. Now I like, when I see folk sae earnest, to get some notion o' what the're saying, and Baldy just gae's wud whenever he catches me wi' my lug at the keyhole. 'Od, Laird! but the body has turned unco cankery; howsomever, that's nane o' our business even now. But when I saw the twa enter the room, I snored wi' a' my might, and closed my eyne. 'Puir chicken,' said the round-about friar, 'he's tired, let him alone;' for Father Jerome was going to waken me. Then they sat down and they had—Lord Laird! but fat priests are ay dry—they had a chappin o' the Luckie's best, and they spoke, and they better spoke, and ye would hae thought that they had a' the cares o' Scotland on their backs, and the sins o' the warld likewise; sae frae less to mair, they couldna' weel do without haeing a rug at your tail. That's just the way that I overheard them."

The peculiarities of Hughoc and his natural shrewdness had often amused his master, who began to think that he had been progressing since they had come to Edinburgh; and this, as they walked along, induced him to inquire what the boy thought of the town and people.

"The town," said Hughoc, "is weel enough, for I fancy a' towns are naturally dirty; but as for the folk, I dinna think they're right folk at a'. In the country, if ye're weary, or dry, or hungry, ye may gang into a neighbour's house, and rest yoursel', or seek a drink o' milk or a bite o' bread. 'Od, sir! this is a faminous place; and then the're a' sae wise; Gude keep us, but the folk o' Embro' are wise folk, considering their ignorance!"

"However, Hughoc, no doubt you find them very civil?"

"Ceevil!' od, Laird, they ken na emair o' ceevility than stupit stots. There was twa' o' them; ane a man wi' a bailie's belly, and anither wi' his hosen up o'er his breek knees, wi' a green apron and a red nightcap, threads about his neck, swatches in the ae hand, and a pair o' muckle shears in the ither, holding a discourse concerning the Queen's Majesty; and the tailoring man, that was him wi' the shears, said to the other that he was mista'en if he supposed a papistical princess like the Queen, could be any better than a malefactoring nun amang friars. Hearing this, I stopped and turned up my lug to kep what they were saying. Weel, it's dreadfu' how they daur't to touch me! but the lean man wi' the nightcap and the shears, gied me sic a pelt on the head that he dunkeled my hernpan, and the man that was sae big wi' belly lifted up his foot, and—"

"What did he do?" inquired our hero; for Hughoc paused, as if suddenly afraid to tell more, but encouraged by the question, he cried,

"Do! I just took haud o' him by the leg, and he was down on the breadth o' his back on the causey stanes without conoversy."

"You will get yourself into trouble, if you dare to do such things," said his master, laughing.

"'Deed, Laird, that's as true as the reformed gospel."

"How?" exclaimed Southenan; "what do you know of the reformed or unreformed gospel?"

"Weel, Laird, if ye'll no be angry, I'll tell you the truth; it was ordained that I should go by Giles's kirk last Sabbath."

"Ordained, and Sabbath!" ejaculated Southennan.

"Just sae, Laird, and nae harm in't. Sae going past the kirk door, I heard a bum-bizzing within, and could do nae less than look in; and there I beheld a divine, hallooing at a dreadfu' rate against what he called—'Od! I doubt he'll get his fairing for't hereafter—the idolatry o' the mass. But ae thing he made plain to me, that it couldna' be an idolatry; for by the eyne he convinced everybody bread and wine wasna' flesh and bluid;—now, Laird, I'm o' that way o' thinking. And he told us that unless we made use o' our senses, the scales could never be removed from off the eyes o' the understanding. But when I got hame, and told Baldy what I had heard, he loupit like a blackbird, and gied me sic a skelp o' persecution on the haffit, that I think it did weel to reform me."

By this time they had crossed the gutter that marked the boundary of the sanctuary of the palace, within which a considerable crowd was assembled round a tall, strapping, randy-looking woman.

"Eh! pater-noster!" exclaimed Hughoc, "it's Friar Michael."

CHAPTER XLV.

"Thus I talk wisely, and to purpose."
THE LOVER'S MELANCHOLY.

SOUTHENNAN, enjoining Hughoc to remain for him at the portal, went into the Palace; but it would have been a strong injunction indeed which, on such an occasion, would have curtailed the freedom of that boy's will. The transformation of Auchenbrae had deeply interested his curiosity; and he mingled with the crowd, around the apparent termagant.

The appearance of Auchenbrae at that time, and in that disguise so near the Palace, was not altogether voluntary. He had been out on some of his wild rambles, beyond the water of Leith, and in returning across the ferry, had been recognised by Johnnie Gaff and one of his compeers, who happened to be present, and who attempted to seize him. But he rescued himself, and, gathering up the petticoats of his disguise, ran from them across the Links to the sanctuary of Holyrood Chapel.

Being the first who had taken refuge there since the purification of the church, the crowd were in doubt whether he could be taken without the bounds, and carried before the magistrates, and one among them maintained the legal impracticability of violating the Sanctuary; but Johnnie Gaff, who was the Orator of the human race on the occasion, with his lips quivering, his face pale with passion, and his eyes as if they would have kindled candles, holding the delinquent by the throat, denied the doctrine as a papistical abomination.

"I will prove it," exclaimed Johnnie; "and I call in the Queen's name for the *Posse Com-a-to-us* to implement the caption. This is a case o' reestment *jurisdictiony fundandy*, and no question *quoad privilegy* can be raised on it."

In the midst, however, of Johnnie's oration, the disturbance had roused the Palace-guard; which, without respect of persons, laid hold of Auchenbrae as well as the orators, and dragged them to the guard-house. In vain did Johnnie plead his privilege as a halberdier of the Lord Provost: the soldiers only laughed at him. Auchenbrae, who in the mean time, had all his eyes about him, was eagerly looking for an opportunity to escape; and having been much incommoded by his female garment, he was quietly untying his petticoats, the easier to shoot out from among them.

Johnnie Gaff, in the mean time, was waxing more and more wroth at the irreverence of the soldiers, and threatening them with all sorts of pains and penalties, for the indignity with which, in his person, they treated the authority and jurisdiction of the Provost, Bailies, and Council of Edinburgh. His menaces only served to increase their derision; in the midst of which, the door being accidentally left open, the culprit dropped his petticoats, and was off like an arrow from the bow.

"Gude guide us," exclaimed Johnnie, cooled in an instant, "he's *fugæ* again, wi' neither kilt nor breeks!"

This new escape had the effect of instantly clearing the guard-house: but none of the soldiers followed. Johnnie Gaff, however, as if he had been booted in seven-league boots, rushed after the fugitive like the nucleus of a comet, with a spreading train of children, huzzaing and cheering him forwards.

The condition of Auchenbrae deterred him from running far into the town. He ascended the first outside stair, and darted into a room where an elderly female was spinning on a distaff, and singing, at the open window. Without leave asked, he bounded into a bed which stood in a corner, and drew the coverlet over him.

Scarcely was he in this asylum, when the noise of his pursuers rose loud in the street, by which the industrious housewife was moved to look out, and, on seeing them, to call aloud—

"Hey gudeman!" and, licking her fingers, she twirled her whorl, and cried still louder, "Hey, Johnnie Gaff, there's a wud woman in our bed! Come and tak' her out immediately."

But Johnnie flew still onward, regardless of the cool cry of his wife. Auchenbrae heard what she said, and called to her for goodness' sake to make no noise, but to come in and lend him a petticoat, for which he would reward her. On hearing his hoarse masculine voice, she was so startled, that she flung her distaff from her, and ran down the stair, crying "Robbery and murder!" At the same moment, Auchenbrae chanced to observe Johnnie's best breeches, and all the paraphernalia of the full dress in which he attended the magistrates to church on Sundays, hanging behind the door. His case admitted of no delay: he sprung from the bed, tore off the remainder of his female vestments, and was soon closed in the garb of the Provost's chief halberdier.

By this time Lucky Gaff had roused the neighbourhood; the men and children had followed the chase, but the wives joined her: and, just as she was leading this army of auxiliaries to the stair-foot, Auchenbrae made his appearance on the top, dressed as her husband.

"Eh! it's my gudeman's wraith," cried she, and fell back with the terror of astonishment into the arms of one of her kimmers; while Auchenbrae, dashing boldly through them, was again free.

Meanwhile, Hughoc, in total oblivion of his master's orders, was one of the most forward and eager of the hounds in the hunt; but his sagacity had soon apprized him that they had lost the scent, and that the fox was earthed. Anxious to tell Johnnie this, he kept crying aloud behind him, "Stop, stop, stop him!" At this juncture, Knockwhinnie, unable to repress his anxiety to meet our hero, was coming down the street in his disguise, crippling slowly, in the twilight. The sound struck his ear; and, being instantly alarmed, he forgot his assumed infirmities, and ran with the speed and agility so necessary to an Outlaw. The chase was turned. Johnnie, on seeing the new game, rushed upon Knockwhinnie, and, seizing him by the collar, held him fast. Among the foremost of the crowd, by whom they were instantly surrounded, was Hughoc, who exclaimed, on seeing who was taken,

"Eh, what a pity!" and darted away, while the Outlaw was conducted to the Council Chamber.

In the meantime, Southennan had ascended the palace-stairs, and was waiting in the gallery for the Count Dufroy, who was then engaged with the Queen; and, as he was standing there Adelaide came from her own apartment.

"I have great news for you," said he, addressing her. "This morning, your father returned from France. We must, without delay, endeavour to procure his pardon. Though the Count refuses to assist, I trust he will do nothing to mar our application."

The news, and the abruptness of the communication, so affected her, that she was for some time unable to speak, until relieved by a burst of tears.

"Where is he?" was her first exclamation. "Let me but see him—take me to him!"

Southennan replied, it could not be that night; "for," said he, "although it might facilitate what we so earnestly desire, were he taken, yet a reasonable doubt hangs upon it. If taken, he will be brought to trial, and the Queen, so soon after her arrival, will hesitate to interfere until his trial shall have been completed. And should he be found"——

"Oh!" cried Adelaide; "say not the dreadful possibility. I will this night myself supplicate the Queen."

More she would have said; but Chatelard and Rizzio came into the gallery. And at their appearance Southennan softly cried, "Hush!" and made a signal for her to be silent.

CHAPTER XLVI.

"Now came still evening on, and twilight gray
Had in her sober livery all things clad."
MILTON.

THE twilight was almost faded when Auchenbrae escaped in the habiliments of Johnnie Gaff. As he could hardly expect to pass up into the town unremarked, he directed his flight across the King's Park, and ascended the road which led to the chapel of St. Anthony, to wait on the mountain until the darkness of the night would allow him to return in safety to his lodgings.

The original character of this profligate man was not without qualities which might have been improved into virtues. He possessed, besides an impassioned admiration of female beauty, extreme sensibility of the charms of external nature. In the midst of his wildness there was much of poesy, and in consequence the contrition which he sometimes felt for his licentiousness was often blended with an elegance of sentiment, strangely, as it seemed by its sadness, at variance with the tenor of his life. His excursion across the water of Leith had been one of those loose and low enterprises in which he sometimes recklessly indulged; but the humiliation to which he had been exposed at the Palace Gate, so derogatory to his birth, deeply moved him when alone on the solitude of Arthur's seat.

He continued to ascend the hill until he reached the summit, and sat down looking towards the west, where a faint amber tinge still glowed along the horizon. It was just enough to show the contour of the Highland mountains, and the brighter and darker masses of the rising grounds and the hollows between. All the dome of the heavens was unclouded, pure azure, in which the stars were numerously kindling. But where the twilight lingered, horizontal streaks of black vapour recalled gloomy associations of the free day, as seen from within through the bars and gratings of a prison window.

The sullied fancies of Auchenbrae yielded to the influences of the scene. The memory of youthful times and sunny days and purer thoughts returned, and with a feeling of disgust at himself, he courted, as it were in revenge of his own folly, sullen resolutions, not of amendment, but to hasten the conclusion of his dishonourable career.

As he sat in [this desolate mood, leaning forwards with his chin resting upon his hand, his abstraction was broken by the sudden apparition of a splendid meteor, trailing its golden fires in a beautiful arch across the heavens. His eyes eagerly followed its course, until it was suddenly shattered into momentary stars, and extinguished. He viewed it as an emblem of his life, a brilliant promise, ending without fulfilling one hope of the admiration that had attended his outset.

In these gloomy ruminations the recollection of the injury he had done to Knockwhinnie was one of the keenest and the deepest. It was the molten fire of the remorse of the moment, and its lurid gleam changed the hue of his reflections. The anguish of its intensity became as it were an impulse, rather than a motive, to redeem the past; and he arose with the intention of proceeding at once to the magistrates, to acknowledge the extent of his aggression, and afterward to return to Kilwinning, where he had, from the time of the outrage, assumed the garb of the Cistertian order, and where, although the great edifice of the monastery had been destroyed by the Reformers, many of the brotherhood continued to reside in the village. But this determination was, like all the promptings of his feeling, an evanescent flesh. Throughout the kingdom there was no longer a religious house remaining in which piety or penitence could find refuge. His mind was thus turned to consider the state and circumstances of the times, and he resumed his seat to reflect in what way by them he might retrieve in some degree his long abandoned ambition for fame. But even this flickering of virtue was soon over; the tainted habitude of his thoughts gradually returned, and the

Vol. I.—14

spirit of the solitary mountain and the solemn hour departed. The moral inspiration of the scene passed away ; and with the cold contemplation of an artist's eye, he looked only at the forms and outlines of the material things before him ; among which, the dark masses and huge lineaments of the city, sprinkled all over with lights, interested his imagination the most. He traced fantastical resemblances in them to the unreal creations of necromancy ; but still, as often as he embodied these dreamy images, something haunted him of a melancholy cast. The emotion he had felt was, it is true, at rest, but it was like the calm of the sea, which reflects all objects above and around it. Above and around him were the solemnities of the heavens and the earth, the ocean and the murmurings of a great city, all in the shadows and mysteries of night.

By this time the glow in the west was entirely faded, and he was admonished by a faint brightening in the eastern horizon that he ought to seek his lodging before the moon rose, and while there was yet darkness in the streets to conceal his disguise. He accordingly returned down from the brow of the hill, and hastened by all the crooked wynds in which he was least exposed to observation, to the house of his kinswoman, which he reached unmolested. But just as he was on the point of entering to ascend the stair, he was met by Johnnie Gaff and Hughoc, and Southennan himself, all proceeding to the Council chamber.

The boy was the first who observed him, and exclaimed,

" Oh Laird, here's anither officer !"

With an instinctive grasp, Johnnie Gaff instantly seized the fugitive with both his hands. Auchenbrae, being a more powerful man, might easily have disentangled himself from the tall and meagre halberdier, but his good genius was at that time hovering at hand, and he submitted to be taken prisoner without an effort.

" Who is it ?" exclaimed Southennan.

" Oh, Chirstal ! it's Friar Michael," replied Hughoc.

" It's the deevil incarnate in *pro. per.* and my best breeks and coat," exclaimed Johnnie Gaff; for his wife had in the mean time informed him of the robbery ; " but Clootie hae his will o' me if he slips through my fingers afore I hae him forenent the Provost, Bailies, and Council of the Burgh o' Embro, to answer in *foro*, for haimsucken in the house o' Kinlochie and stouthrief in mine. My word, but ye're braw in your barrow't feathers ! but ye shall mak a *cessy bonorum*, before the night be an hour aulder."

Auchenbrae was not acquainted with Southennan, but discerning, by the light of one of the bowets which had been recently put up in the streets for lamps, his gentlemanly bearing and garb, said,

"Sir, by your appearance I am emboldened to claim your protection. I beg you will, therefore, request this rude fellow to remove his hands: I give you my honour to follow him quietly; but I will not submit to be treated as a common sorner. I am a gentleman."

Against this appeal Johnnie clamorously remonstrated, venting a tirade of maledictions and accusations interlarded with Latin, so extravagant, that even Auchenbrae himself could not preserve the gravity suitable to his situation. Southennan laughed heartily, and told Johnnie that he would be answerable for the quiet attendance of his prisoner.

"Weel, sir," replied Johnnie, a little softened by the manner of Southennan, "since ye'll no be an *amicus coqrie*, and help me, ye maun gie me caution *judicy sisty*, afore I can part wi' him; and a consideration as a *solatium*, for the damage and detriment done to my breeks."

Southennan drew his purse, and presented Johnnie with a piece of money; at the sight of which Hughoc exclaimed,

"Oh man, but ye hae your ain luck!"

"Hush!" said his master, "take no notice of what I do."

"Steek you eyne, ye deevil's buckie," said Johnnie, soothed by the liberality of Southennan, adding jocularly, "it's an unco thing that a man canna earn an honest penny in this world, without stirring up an *animus injurandy*."

Matters being thus accommodated, the party proceeded to the Council Chamber, and as Auchenbrae walked with Johnnie, the children remarked as they passed along, "Eh! hasna' the town gotten a new Johnnie Gaff?"

CHAPTER XLVII.

"Courts can give nothing to the wise and good
But scorn of pomp and love of solitude."
YOUNG.

IT is now necessary to explain what had come to pass in the mean time, after Hughoc had seen the arrest of Knockwhinnie. His own neglect of his master's injunctions was recollected with alarm, and he ran back to the Palace, in case he should have been missed. He was there, however, long before his master made his appearance at the portal.

Southennan had been detained by Count Dufroy, who almost immediately after Chatelard and Rizzio had joined Adelaide and him in the gallery, came from his audience with the Queen. The Count, on approaching them, discovered something embarrassed in the appearance of Adelaide and our hero, and rightly conjectured that the other two had come upon them unexpectedly. Being a clear-sighted man of the world, he perceived that it would not be fit, before the intruders, as he deemed them, to inquire the cause of the perplexity, which was, indeed, as obvious to them as to himself. He accordingly said to Adelaide, that the Queen was alone, and he would conduct her to her Majesty, giving, at the same time, a significant look to Southennan, to intimate that he would return to him. He then took Adelaide by the hand to lead her away, and was followed to the door by Chatelard, who evidently intended to go in with them; but the Count stopped before opening it, and, turning round, said, with a countenance of cool dignity,

" The Queen has given directions respecting the hours when she will receive her private company. I have not had time to make her commands known to the household; but you will have the goodness, in the mean time, to obey them."

Chatelard returned in considerable confusion towards our hero and Rizzio, but did not remain long with them. On some pretence of business to be done before supper, he retired to his own apartment.

During this short scene, Rizzio, in a look which he gave to our hero, disclosed a degree of exultation of which the cause was not apparent; but as soon as Chatelard quitted the gallery, the Italian took hold of Southennan by the arm, and led him into the bay of one of the remotest windows.

" This," said he, alluding to the communication which the Count Dufroy had made to Chatelard, " was becoming necessary."

" Why? how necessary?"

Rizzio then told him, that he had deemed it his duty to acquaint Dufroy of what he had observed in the freedom with which Chatelard often regarded the Queen; and that that just and correct noblemen had expressed to him a determination to speak to her Majesty on the subject.

" He has done so, I doubt not," said Southennan; " and the order he has received is the fruit."

"I think so too," replied Rizzio; " and it shows that her Majesty may be advised, even in her passions."

" It does more, in my opinion," said Southennan; " it shows that she does not entertain that attachment which you suspected."

" Do you think so?" inquired Rizzio, with one of his dark, sinister, keen, piercing looks.

"What else should I think?"

Rizzio at once assumed his more usual mask of gayety, and replied, with a disengaged smile,

"I should have thought, Southennan, that you had known more of woman. May not this very order of the Queen have been given only to lull the suspicions of the Count, and to prevent her partiality from being discovered. It is not so difficult to arrange an intercourse that may not be observed, and at the same time to keep this assurance of decorum to the eye."

" You judge too suspiciously of the sex," was Southennan's answer, expressed in a tone of reserve; for there was something in the address which Rizzio had displayed in the affair, so very like design, that he did not much like it. It had been his resolution to keep aloof from all court intrigue, and he was a little troubled to find himself so near the hazard of being involved in one of the deepest, perhaps most dangerous.

" But, Southennan, let me ask you one question," said Rizzio. " You have told me of your attachment to Adelaide, and its hopelessness while hers, so manifest for Chatelard, continues; and yet, when we came in upon you just now, there were tears and confidence, and other very lover-like symptoms between you: what was the cause?"

Southennan had preserved, with all but the Count and Adelaide, a studied silence with respect to Knockwhinnie, although, once or twice, he had almost resolved to take the advice of Rizzio, for whose remarkable discernment and dexterity of management he had a high opinion. This question decided him, and he laid the whole case before the Italian.

Rizzio listened with great attention. He made no observation while Southennan was speaking; but when our hero expressed his wonder at the reluctance evinced by Count Dufroy to interfere with the outlawry, he once or twice looked eagerly, as if something was passing in his mind; and a smile, not expressive of any satisfaction, but of some intellectual conception, mantled on his features. It indicated no pleasure; it betrayed no mirth, nor the anticipation of any enjoyment; but

14*

it evinced a profound feeling of satisfaction; for the countenance of this gifted adventurer was transparent to the movements of his mind; and, although few young men were possessed of equal self command, yet, when his reflections were animated, his countenance could not hide their complexion and character.

After Southennan had concluded the story, there was a short pause, during which Rizzio appeared thoughtful. At last he said slowly, but without hesitation,

"This Count Dufroy is incomprehensible; he hath notions unlike those of other men; he is governed by motives that I cannot understand. He is apt as most men to the frailties of our nature, and yet his mind is not accessible by the influence of any object to which at any time he seems attached. There is about him an unimpressible probity. He has the ear and the confidence of the Queen: he was the very master of her late husband, Francis. Altogether, he is not a man to be dealt with like others about the Court; for in his courtiership he hath rather impaired than enlarged his estate: and since he came to Scotland, he hath made no endeavour to obtain power, contenting himself with being the friend and personal counsellor of the Queen, in matters purely of private conduct."

"You have given," rejoined Southennan, "a vivid picture of a good great man."

"He is so," said Rizzio; "but I cannot imagine the existence of a man who has not his weaknesses, although I have not yet been able to discover in which of his heels the Count Dufroy is vulnerable."

Southennan looked inquisitively at Rizzio. It struck him as something wonderful, that one who could claim nothing for parentage, and but little for advantage of person, should speak of the most accomplished man of the age, and who was no less able than honourable, as if he contemplated the possibility of reducing him into an agent. He repressed, however, the suprise with which he was so affected, and inquired what Rizzio thought the cause might be, which rendered Dufroy so averse to any mitigation in the unhappy circumstances of Knockwhinnie.

"If," replied Rizzio, "he were a man much addicted to the pageantries of the church, I would say religion: but, being, as he is, a gentleman of free carriage, I must call it honour. Had Knockwhinnie challenged him to open combat, and done him ten times the injury in the lists, it would have been generously forgiven; but the clandestine dagger, is, I suspect, the cause that hath made the attack base in his opinion. He accounts, or I am very wrong in my guessing, Knockwhinnie a man naturally prone to take unfair advantages. I have met with some few men like the Count, both in France and Italy, who have stoutly set themselves against self-redressers, and who stand resolutely for the restoration of jurisprudence, which hath so long been hidden in the sepulchres of imperial Rome.

These are the leaders of the age, and are doing that for manners, which your Knoxes and your Luthers and your Calvins, have done, and are doing, for religion."

Southennan started at hearing this : he conceived it was impossible that one trusted with the private correspondence of the Queen, herself so firm in her adherence to the Pope, should hold opinions so pernicious to the cause of the church. But he had no opportunity of making any answer ; for at that moment the Count returned from the Queen's apartment.

CHAPTER XLVIII.

"Know thy own point : this kind, this due degree
Of blindness, weakness, Heaven bestows on thee."

POPE.

Rizzio had observed the effect which his free thought had produced on Southennan, but the Count's entrance deprived him of an opportunity then of extenuating or explaining the sentiments he had expressed. He was conscious that he had said a little more than our hero was ripe for, and that it would be necessary to take some step to regain the ground which he had so inadvertently lost in his good opinion. This induced him somewhat abruptly to retire.

"I have observed of late, Southennan," said Dufroy, as he came towards him, " that Rizzio and you have become great friends. If you can keep your mind independent, and use your ears and eyes well with him, he will prove a valuable confidant : but take care of yourself."

"How, my Lord? In what way should I take care of myself?"

"Oh!" replied the Count carelessly, "I have perhaps used a wrong term. I only meant to imply that Rizzio is a clever ambitious adventurer, and may be a little lefthanded in his ways of working, by which your natural ingenuousness may be brought into trouble. You were never intended to thrive by Court intrigues."

Southennan replied : " It is odd that Rizzio has just been giving me a description of your Lordship's character, and it was something more flattering than what you have said of him. But I must not tell you, though I account it no breach of confidence to speak of the good opinion one holds of another."

" Then I am honoured," said the Count, " with the good opinion of Rizzio. Verily, if he spoke his true sentiments, it is something to be proud of, for I have never seen a man possessed of such acute perception of character as that Italian. He enjoys great gifts : his only weakness, and it is one not uncommon to persons of low origin, is to be too sensitive to slights from superiors. This Scottish Court requires a different temperament. The sovereign herself is here not safe from rudeness, and these old Barons, with their wide heaths and long pedigrees, are not likely to spare Rizzio from the inflictions of their pride. Be you therefore watchful how you become interwoven with his affairs ; for depend upon it, he is a man who will make difficulties for himself." And without pausing he added ; " and so Knockwhinnie has come again. I have left Adelaide with the Queen, entreating the remission of his outlawry."

" I hope," said Southennan more simply than accorded with his general intelligence, " that your Lordship will not interpose your influence against her suit."

The Count stepped a pace or two backwards, and for the space of a minute or so, looked at Southennan with a proud and somewhat stern aspect. Our hero was unconscious of the offence his words were calculated to give, and appeared in consequence astonished at the effect they had produced. But Dufroy observing him, saw that no offence was intended, and said emphatically,

" He is her father, and I am one of those who hold the ties of nature to be indissoluble even by crime."

" I would she had your advocacy to help her," said Southennan ; " the worst deed of Knockwhinnie was his attempt on your life, and it sprung from the offended feelings of a true and loving nature."

" Do you think," said the Count, with some severity, " that I am actuated by a resentful remembrance of his attempt."

"How may I answer that, my Lord : it is known only to God and yourself. But, and I trust my frankness will not offend, I have thought your reluctance to mediate for his pardon might be dictated by some sentiment made up of resentment and a sense of wrong."

"I honour your candour, and I trust you will cherish it as the best quality in the mind of a man in your station," replied the Count. "But I fear Knockwhinnie is one of those violent men who have survived a turbulent age, and are only to be treated as unfit to share in the reciprocities of a better-ordered society. Towards Knockwhinnie, how should it be thought of me that I am ruled by resentment ? Have I not made his child my own, when his own rashness caused the forfeiture of his station in the world, and deprived him of the power of protecting her ? Had his lady lived, she too could have borne witness how greatly I have endeavoured to appease the anger of her father, who considered her as a deserted wife. Had I been the brother of Knockwhinnie, more I could not have done to disarm the sufferings of those who were dearest to him. But had he been my brother, I would not have looked with less austerity on the contempt of honour and justice, that was in the base guilt of assassination. His attempt, though it failed, was not the less criminal."

The Count delivered these few sentences so earnestly, that Southennan did not venture to make him any answer, but only acknowledged the high-mindedness of the speaker by a profound and respectful bow. He perceived that the mind of the Count was as Rizzio had described it, inaccessible, at least by the means of ordinary persuasion, and he refrained from farther solicitation. He thought, indeed, that it was useless to communicate to a man so lofty and firm of purpose, the wish of Knockwhinnie to be admitted to an interview ; and accordingly, after a few short general remarks on indifferent topics, he wished Dufroy good night, and left the Palace.

Southennan had scarcely quitted the gallery, when Chatelard made his appearance. On observing the Count he hesitated to advance, and was on the point of retiring, when several other gentlemen of the household entered, and relieved him from the embarrassment he felt at encountering him alone. Their presence, indeed, so far emboldened him, that he advanced towards Dufroy with as much of his former ease as he could assume; for the rebuff he had met with at the door of the Queen's apartment had apprized him that his behaviour towards her Majesty had been noticed, and the consciousness of this perplexed him with a diffidence unusual to his character.

The Count, however, received him with his customary urbanity, and adverting to the command which he had been ordered to communicate to those who enjoyed the honour of the Queen's private suppers, led him aside, and with a tone of friendly anxiety, told him, that the order had been given in consequence of his indiscretion.

"It is not," said Dufroy, "commendable in those who receive instances of royal condescension to presume upon them. The favours of princes must not be familiarly accepted; and for a worthy reason, they can only be conferred on a few, and are thereby rare and honourable. Her Majesty's gracious nature, like the light of the day, and the dews of the evening, hath in it an impartial beneficence, an universal quality, that is marred by those who would engross more than their due proportion. I beseech you, Chatelard, to look well to this; for the bird is often dazzled that flies too much in the sun."

The passion by which the young Frenchman was animated had in it more of desire and ambition than of tenderness. Its promptings were bold and courageous, but the detection of it disturbed his self-possession; still the token he had received of Mary's preference, as he believed it, threw him off his guard, and almost precipitated him, notwithstanding the kindness of the admonishment, to answer the Count frowardly, who, however, before he had time to make any reply, added—

"I see you do not relish my counsel; I can, therefore, only bid you beware. Recollect you are observed, and a rebuke from her Majesty will destroy you."

With these words Dufroy retired, and Chatelard, eyeing him superciliously as he walked towards the door of the gallery, muttered to himself with a sneer of scornful bravery—

"Yes; if she does rebuke me!" So much was he already infatuated.

CHAPTER XLIX.

"Thou shalt be punished for thus frighting me;
For I am sick, and capable of fears;
Oppress'd with wrongs, and therefore full of fears;
A widow, husbandless, subject to fears;
A woman, naturally born to fears."
SHAKSPEARE.

In the mean time Adelaide had been entreating the Queen for the pardon of her father, with all the earnestness of affection and anxiety. Mary had heard something of his story, and with the gentle compassion of the female heart, she saw not the attempted assassination in those dark hues of guilt with which it appeared to the high and masculine mind of the Count; she was, in consequence, on the point of promising her consent to the reversal of the outlawry, when Dufroy again appeared in her presence.

"This is a sad tale which my poor Adelaide has been telling," said her Majesty to him; "but as the intention failed, it cannot be consistent with justice to let the law always endure in its rigour against her unfortunate father. What think you?"

"If the Queen," replied the Count, "desires my opinion, simply, as a man, perhaps I should acknowledge the mercifulness of your Majesty's sentiments, especially as I bear no malice against Knockwhinnie; on the contrary, I feel all manner of Christian pity for him. But I have crossed the seas with better purposes than to counsel the remission of offences, which cannot be suffered with impunity, without damaging the frame and cement of society."

Adelaide heard him with sorrow, and clasping her hands, looked imploringly at the Queen, who pensively regarded her for a moment, and then addressed the Count—

"Is not mercy consistent with justice, when the guilty intent has not been performed?"

Dufroy replied with more than his wonted deference, but with firmness—

"Your Majesty may pardon; and I doubt not the prerogative of mercy is too delicious in its exercise to your royal nature, to be foregone for the harshness of justice."

Mary regarded him for some time with visible emotion and surprise.

"You then think," said she, "that there may be error in mercy in this case?"

"I do."

The Queen turned her eyes, filled with tears, towards Adelaide, and said, with the softest accents of commiseration,

"Alas! here is a wise and just man, long renowned for his equity and honour: he thinks I may not unblamed comply with your becoming solicitation! Hath not," addressing the Count again, she tenderly subjoined, "Mercy, my Lord, been ever esteemed the gracefullest sister of the virtues? but, if she may not always sit in royal councils, can she be indeed a virtue? This matter touches me with the anguish of exceeding grief. What is the recompense of my abstracted condition, if all show of warmth from others must be rejected, and all kind inclinations repressed in my own bosom? Truly the sovereign of this stormy and inclement realm hath but cold encouragement to rule with gentleness. But a few minutes have elapsed since you exhorted me to rebuke the ardour of Chatelard; and what was his offence? He loved not wisely! As if such love were not for its hopelessness more entitled to the charity of pardon, than to be cast into the peril of punishment."

The mildness and the tone of regret with which the Queen expressed herself, alarmed the jealousy of Adelaide, who, in the emotion of the moment, forgot her father. The Count also was surprised; for her Majesty had professed to himself her vexation at the obtrusive freedom with which the infatuated Frenchman sometimes dared to approach her, and had readily assented to the regulation for restricting the admission too freely allowed to her domestic apartments.

"How capricious is woman!" thought he. "Is it possible that the restriction which prudence and dignity equally required, can have produced any interest for that audacity which is too weakly indulged by permitting Chatelard to remain in her service."

But before he could reply the Prior of St. Andrew's was announced, whose staid demeanour and sober courtesies had always a serious effect on the Queen; for, although he was a person of many virtues, there was yet a collected method in his manner, which, notwithstanding the decided esteem which he was held in by her Majesty, checked the freedom which she allowed to herself with Dufroy and many others. His genius, notwithstanding the defect of his bastardy, awed Mary; and in his presence she felt, as it were, a shadow upon her gayety. At this particular time, her mind was more moved to melancholy than to mirth: but still his appearance had a saddening and repressing effect, especially when, after stating to her his wish for a private audience, (upon which Dufroy and Adelaide retired) he mentioned with solemnity that he had been requested by the leading Protestant divines, to solicit her Majesty to cause a stricter observance of decorum to be enforced among her household.

"Unseemly brawls," said the Prior, "have taken place at the very portal of the Palace; and the town is amazed that such tumults should, by any accident, be permitted. During the lifetime of her late Majesty, your royal mother, it was otherwise managed: she was a lady of sedate manners, and, although a stern adversary of the Reformation, yet no one could impute the blemish of any lightness to her deportment. She did more for her faith, by the purity and temperance of her conduct, than by her armies and the arms of France."

The Queen appeared greatly affected, even to distress, by this communication. Tears rushed into her eyes, and she exclaimed, in a tone that partook more of indignation than of sorrow,

"Ah, me! what shall I do? I can stifle and sacrifice my own wishes; but how can I satisfy a people that claim from me a severity which Heaven has been pleased to deny me the power of exercising. In my house there has been no irregularity."

"Alas!" said the Prior, "I beseech you not to deceive yourself with such flattery, for it is rumoured that you evince a favour for the Frenchman Chatelard, that assorteth not well with your royalty."

"Is it come to that?" cried Mary, roused by an accusation of which her heart acquitted her; "has the young man already made himself such enemies that they so openly desire his ruin?"

"It is not so. It is only your Majesty that is blamed for a carriage towards him unsuitable to your dignity."

The freedom of this speech offended her; her lips became pale, her colour fled, and her eyes sparkled with anger, as she replied,

"James Stuart, forget not the carriage that belongs to yourself! To change in any respect the wonted customs of my

VOL. I.—15

house would be to acknowledge they had not been innocent: go and tell those who sent you to rebuke me so, that I will, without their counsel, uphold my dignity; and let them show me more of their duty. Here hath been a poor maiden supplicating a grace for her father, who but only attempted an offence, and I am warned that there may be guilt in granting her petition; then this same Frenchman of whom you speak hath but offended by excess of loyalty, and I must forsooth, for to that end such counselling tends, drive him from my service, and put myself under the restraints of a gloomy captivity. Call you this royalty? Tell me wherein I am a Queen? Oh! wherefore did I come to this bleak land of rocks and harder hearts?"

"Hear me, madam," replied the Prior, respectfully; "by duty, and the dearer claim of blood, I entreat your Majesty not to let such words escape you, even in the hearing of these walls!"

"God help me!" cried the Queen, bursting into a flood of tears; "what shall I do? An orphan! a widow! while yet too young to be a wife, almost without a friend! But I will not thus be schooled; I have not been the worshipped Queen of France, to bear the unmannerly demands of those that should obey me. That is my answer;" and with these words she abruptly retired into an inner chamber.

CHAPTER L.

"O place and greatness, millions of false eyes
Are stuck upon thee! volumes of report
Run with these false and most contrarious guesses
Upon thy doings! thousand 'scapes of wit
Make thee the father of their idle dream,
And rack thee in their fancies."

SHAKSPEARE.

The Prior of St. Andrew's had not long retired, when the Abbot of Kilwinning, attended by Father Jerome, came to beg an audience of the Queen, and were at once admitted. It was evident to them, that she had been recently agitated; the traces of distress were visible on her countenance, and there was an air of dejection in her appearance, which rendered her more interesting than when her beauty was unclouded.

"Madam," said the Abbot, approaching towards her, "I fear the errand I am come upon will not be acceptable to your Majesty."

"Then," replied the Queen, dejectedly, "come with it to-morrow; for in truth, I am very sad. I have had enough of such errands to-night. But I must endure my lot. Alas! it promised once to be a brighter and happier."

Father Jerome softly whispered to the Abbot, reminding him that their business was urgent, and the Queen, partly overhearing him, subjoined,

"But if the matter presses, I am ready to hear it"

The Abbot then briefly recapitulated Knockwhinnie's story, which had been so recently related to her, and she exclaimed impatiently,

"All this I know; but what can I do in it?"

"The unhappy man has been this evening taken," said the Abbot, "and is now in the custody of the city officers: his offence is less than it seemed, for the blow which he aimed at the Count Dulroy was intended for another."

"How doth that lighten his guilt? It rather magnifies it; seeing that in his rashness he attempted the life of one that was blameless."

"Even so," replied the Abbot; "but he had such provocation that justice almost warranted his intention. The man who did him the wrong is also in custody, and hath acknowledged his guilt."

"But Father Abbot, how comes it that you are moving in this business?"

The Abbot in reply informed the Queen, that Southennan had urged him on behalf of Knockwhinnie, to solicit the reversal of the outlawry.

"My aged brother here," said he, "is of his household, and your Majesty hath not in all the west country a better subject than Southennan; nor the Church a truer son. He sent at this late hour to beg my mediation, with strong assurances of faithful service could the boon be obtained."

"Southennan!" said the Queen; "is it the same that is so often here? Ah, now I know the motive of his visits, Adelaide. Good Father Abbot, I am much inclined to compassionate the unfortunate Knockwhinnie: but I fear he must go first to trial. I may not unblamed, until he hath passed the ordeal, grant him grace. I am still too young in this land to venture on any measure which may not accord with the rude temper of the people. There has been much preaching among them of late, as I am told, concerning the impunity allowed to breaches of the law, and the self-revenging of private wrongs. It hath scared the mercy-dove from off the sceptre. But what I may do without offending justice, shall be done, were it only to help the suit of Southennan with my gentle Adelaide, and win from her for him some portion of that regard which she throws away on Chatelard."

The Abbot and Father Jerome at these words exchanged significant looks, which the Queen sharply observing, said, " And has the story spread to you ?"

" I crave pardon, Madam," said the Abbot, " but it is my duty to report, that this night it has been said that Chatelard was distinguished by some signal act of your royal favour."

" 'Tis false."

" We," said the Abbot, thoughtfully, " the true and ancient brethren of the church, account it an invention of the heretics to blemish your Majesty in the eyes of your people, whom they drive and devour as they list, like wolves among sheep "

" It argues," replied the Queen, with emphasis, " more honour in the professors of our faith to discredit such baleful slanders. There can be no rectitude in the minds of those who propagate such injuries. It is to them I owe the malice that hath environed my throne with so many fears and menaces."

" Your Majesty speaks great truth," replied the Abbot; " but things so troubled as they are at present cannot long remain so. The divisions that were among us are healing, and by your countenance we hope to see the Church again uplift her banner in Scotland as high as it ever waved before. She is but as the sun labouring with eclipse ; the darkness which intercepts her light must soon pass."

" Would it may be so," said the Queen ; " but those unhozzled spirits, that work in darkness, grow daily bolder ; and all the signs of the times augur success to them."

" It must be so, while there is no manly will to govern our endeavours. The Prior of St. Andrew's, who is so near of kin to your Majesty, hath openly espoused the cause of the schismatics, and they reckon on his favour with your Majesty, for great things."

" They shall be taught better ; they meddle too much with what concerns me. But I am only a weak and inexperienced woman !" said the Queen.

"Yes;" replied the Abbot, echoing the sadness in the tone of her last expression, "and therein we plainly discern where our cause is most infirm. Would I might venture to ell your Majesty freely what we dread and what we think?"

"Let me hear it," cried the Queen; "my heart is open to all petitions, and my ears are greedy of advice."

The Abbot, after a short pause, said with great apparent humility,

"It hath been a suggestion among us, to pray your Majesty to lighten your cares by dividing them with a consort."

"Verily," said the Queen, with a smile, "this is not the season for match-making. We are still too much in the blast and shower: the mating time is only in the spring days, when boughs are budding and meadows green. But the night is far advanced; I pray you, therefore, Father Abbot, to come betimes in the morning, and the matter of your errand shall then be duly considered; meantime, let me be remembered in your orisons."

The Abbot and Father Jerome retired, and as they were passing down the gallery, Rizzio met them. The Abbot waved his hand to Father Jerome, who walked on to the stairs, where Baldy was waiting to assist him home. It was evident that some recent intercourse had taken place between the Abbot and Rizzio; who addressed him with a degree of freedom, as if he felt himself on some equality with that dignitary.

"Well," said Rizzio, "what success, my Lord?"

"She is in some distress; and hath already, contrary to her inclination, been tampered with against Knockwhinnie."

"But," said Rizzio, "did you hint what is said of Chatelard?"

"As much as was becoming. She had been fretted by it before our audience; but something in her humour, which was ready to flame up, indicated that whatever had been told her, had only served to kindle her resentment."

"Indeed!" said Rizzio, thoughtfully; "did you allude to marriage?"

"I did but allude. She was not in a mood to listen to me; she spoke dejectedly of the unhappy condition of the kingdom."

"Will she, think you," inquired Rizzio, "still retain Chatelard, after being so much admonished for the distinction

with which she has treated him, and on which he so much presumes."

"Have others then," said the Abbot, "been counselling her on his imprudence; there must have been. But if her will be in it, admonition may be spared; she hath the headiness of her race, and will take her own way. I am, however, to be again with her in the morning, when I pray St. Mary's help that she may be in a more composed frame!"

The Abbot then parted from him, and Rizzio walked slowly up the gallery. At the farther end he paused for a short time, and then turning round advanced two or three paces, when he halted, and fixing his eyes on the ground, ruminated to the following effect:—

"I am like Cæsar when he passed the Rubicon—the report of her favour shown to Chatelard, has determined my course and fate—the tale cannot be recalled—it has had wings —it has spread like an epidemic. I am alarmed at the speed with which it has infected all sorts of the world, the reformed and the unreformed—the good, the bad, the foolish, and the wise—all cry out at her unworthy condescension. Some say there is no bar in the law of Scotland, by which she may not raise him even to sit beside her;—he has been of late reserved —averse to me, as if he feared some hinderance from me; and he shall too. A shallow talking Frenchman, that hath as little matter in his mind, as there is substance in the rainbow! but I must be wary. The quick infection with which the story hath rushed all abroad, warns me to be wary. Yes; the marriage is the thing. Where shall a fool be found, ductile enough to bend to those who may promote him; fool, indeed, must the husband be of this Queen of rebels, for no better are these irascible Scots. That is, however, a thing not ripe for action —something bolder on the part of Chatelard must yet be done, and to help it forward be my first business."

CHAPTER LI.

"Oh, how wretched!
Is the poor man that hangs on princes' favours;
There is between that smile we would aspire to,
That sweet aspect of princes, and their ruin,
More pangs and fears than wars or women have."
HENRY VIII.

WE hope our worthy readers have sagacity enough to discern, that during the transactions in Holyrood House, Knockwhinnie had been taken before the magistrates, where he had given such an account of himself, that it had been deemed necessary to call Southennan before them, and that, as we have described, Auchenbrae was carried with him and surrendered.

The delinquents were both ordered to be held in custody for trial; and our hero, seeing no other way of assisting the father of Adelaide, determined, in consequence, to seek the mediation of some of the ecclesiastical dignitaries with the Queen. He accordingly returned to his lodgings, and despatched Father Jerome to entreat the good offices of the Abbot of Kilwinning. The result has been related.

Early next morning Southennan went to the Palace, for the purpose of again trying his influence with the Count Dufroy and also of consulting Rizzio. On approaching the portal he met Chatelard, and recollecting what Rizzio had told him of the disposition which the Queen had evinced towards him, he resolved to try what agency he might obtain in him, to second the solicitation for the pardon of Knockwhinnie.

Chatelard was at the time walking towards the gardens; Southennan immediately joined him, and after the compliments of the morning, opened his business, by saying—

"It has been observed by all the Court, Chatelard—indeed, you have made no secret of it yourself—how much you are attached to Adelaide."

"Whether there was any thing intentionally ironical in this manner, with which our hero expressed himself, or that Chatelard, conscious of his artifice, felt it as such, is not for me to determine ; but he reddened and appeared disturbed, which Southennan observing, quieted his apprehensions by adding—

" But whatever may be your sentiments respecting Adelaide, I have to entreat your aid and service in a matter that deeply concerns her peace of mind, and is very interesting to myself. You are aware of the unfortunate condition of her father ?"

Chatelard, having by this time recovered his self-possession vehemently declared how happy he should be to render even the smallest service to the lady, and his desire to be useful in any degree to one whom he so much esteemed as Southennan.

" I doubt not your good-will," replied our hero ; " had I not indeed had confidence in it, I should not have ventured to solicit the favour I now wish you to do for both. The Count Dufroy has, in a manner which prevents me from applying to him again, declined to entreat the Queen on behalf of Knockwhinnie, and last night, at my earnest suit the Lord Abbot of Kilwinning undertook, without success, to move the Queen's grace to grant a pardon."

" And would you," said Chatelard, with a smile, and something like exultation in his manner, " expect me to succeed, where Dufroy deems his interference would be in vain, and so great a man as the Lord Abbot has failed ?"

"It has not been exactly so." said Southennan. " The Count refuses, not from any question as to the efficacy of his influence, but because he regards the offence of Knockwhinnie as one of those which, for the public safety, should be punished. Moreover, I am informed by my chaplain, who went with the Abbot to the Queen, that her Majesty hath not absolutely denied the pardon. I have therefore thought, as she permits to you the privilege of addressing her more freely, than any other of her attendants, you might find an opportunity of seconding the application of Adelaide."

" I can with sincerity promise you to do all that I may have it in my power to do ; but you are aware, from what took place last night, that the Queen is hereafter only to be accessible upon request or summons. Now I doubt if it might not be to offend men of such weight as the Count and the Abbot, were I openly to work in this business."

" Nay," said Southennan, " it matters not how you work after your promise ; and surely it can never be deemed culpable to be a little zealous in the cause of humanity."

Chatelard appeared for a few seconds to ruminate, and then

he asked, if Adelaide could not obtain a private interview for him with the Queen.

The inquiry startled Southennan: it implied a degree of boldness which seemed to provoke hazard. It was an intrigue of so delicate a kind, that he said—

"Would it not seem more consistent with your attachment to Adelaide to offer your service, and by that obtain her assistance. I stand not so fair in her opinion as to offer a suggestion which would come with so much more grace and effect from you. Can you doubt that, showing so much interest for her father, you will not recommend yourself to her affection." This again touched the tender secret of Chatelard, and he blushed, and was confused; but, recovering himself, he rejoined briskly.

"In sooth, Southennan, I will do my best in the business; but when, or how, must depend upon fortune."

While they were holding this conversation, the Abbot of Kilwinning, agreeably to his appointment, was admitted to an audience of the Queen; whom he found, as he had anticipated, in a more serene mood than that in which he had left her the preceding evening.

"I have," said her Majesty, "thought well of your application, and I have consulted the Chancellor. who speaks wisely, as I think, on the matter. We shall let Knockwhinnie abide his trial; he may be acquitted on it: but should the result be otherwise. then, without detriment to the motives of our royal mercy, a pardon may be extended, and reason shown wherefore it is granted."

The Abbot commended the discretion of her Majesty; observing, however, that there might be more risk in the consequences of such proceedings on the opinion of the people, than were the affair quietly passed over; "For," said he, "Knockwhinnie is firm to his faith. and should he be found guilty, and afterward pardoned, there are not wanting tongues who will despitefully impugn the motives of your Majesty's leniency."

Mary acknowledged that she saw the difficulties and the hardships to which she was exposed, and said,

"Would I had not consulted the Chancellor! because, having assented to his advice, I cannot unblamed recede."

"And yet," replied the Abbot, "there cannot be much wrong in doing so; for the Chancellor in substance agrees with the merciful inclinations of your Majesty. In the diseased condition of the time, it were better to pursue the expedient rather than the legal course. The offence of Knockwhinnie happened years ago; it is almost forgotten, but a trial will revive the popular resentment which the deed at first excited. Your Majesty cannot afford to tantalize the rabid public."

"There is good counsel, Father Abbot," replied the Queen pensively, "in what you say. And will it not be thought that my poor Adelaide has obtained from me the pardon?"

"The people may be so taught," said the Abbot.

The Queen made no answer for some time; at last she said, "Might it not be as well for me to consult the Prior of St. Andrew's? He hath always shown himself most anxious to save me from the peril of doing wrong."

"In that," replied the Abbot, "I would not presume to control your Majesty's inclinations; but he hath leagued himself with the enemies of our holy cause."

The Queen relapsed into her rumination, and after a considerable pause, during which she played with the fingers of her right hand on the table as on a virginal, and her eyes were vacant and abstracted, she rose, and with a graceful and benign smile, said,

"I do not promise to take your advice: but I will think of it, with the wish that mercy may be reconciled with justice in adopting it. This matter, my Lord Abbot, hath within a short time given me much trouble. If by granting the pardon the vexations can be ended, be assured I lack no counselling to quench them. Rest with this assurance; and in the course of the day you shall hear of what I can do."

The Abbot, bowing over her hand, retired without making any reply.

CHAPTER LII.

"——Well! Heaven's above all; and there be souls that must be saved, and there be souls must not be saved."
OTHELLO.

The news of Knockwhinnie's arrest and of Auchenbrae's surrender were the topics of the morning among the guests of the Unicorn.—Cornylees had, for some cause or another, been the previous night sorning about the wynds and closses in the neighbourhood of the Cowgate, according to the use and wont of the west country Lairds when they visit Edinburgh ; and in the course of his nocturnal adventures had heard of the hunt of Auchenbrae by Johnnie Gaff, and the other adventures of the night. These he was reporting with his accustomed glee to the guests at the breakfast-table, and the Maister Balwham, who was in attendance, hearing that Knockwhinnie had been taken, flung his towel over his shoulder, and putting in his little round head from behind to the ear of Cornylees, said, in a whisper,

"Oh, dear! but that's sair news ; when ye hae done wi' your bit kipper, I would treat you wi' a stoup o' the best o't in my ain cham'er. Puir Knockwhinnie was, in the days of his rectitude, often a gude customer to the Unicorn, and it behooves me, as the host and maister thereof, to lighten his captivity. And I dinna ken, when a man's back's to the wa', ane mair able to help him than yoursel', Cornylees."

The promise of the stoup of wine spurred the appetite of the Laird, and he made more than common speed with his kipper ; and then, wiping his mouth and hands, rose from table. The Maister Balwham at the same time, laying down his towel and taking off his apron, as he always did on occasions when he gave what he called " a gratis" to a friend, walked with Cornylees into his own room.

" Now," said he, " sit ye down, Laird, and bide till I get a candle to look in the far neuk o' the cellar, where I'll maybe be able to muddle out a flask o' the right sort."

" Atweel, gudeman, I'se warrant I ha'e been guilty o' waur in my time, in course now."

The Maister Balwham then left him, and presently returned with a flask and two Venetian goblets, which he placed on the table, and seated himself at it opposite to Cornylees. He then untied the bit of leather from the mouth of the flask —in those days the substitutes for corks—and filling the two goblets, said,

" Now, Laird, before I speak my mind, here's as gude a bribe for gude-will as ever was slippit in the shape o' gold into the loof o' a Lord o' the Parliament. Pree 't ; isna' that prime ? Many's the time that Knockwhinnie—hech, but he was a blithe lad !—has called this nectar ; aye, and tried to gi'e 't even a better name, when his tongue had lost the power o' utterance. Puir man ! dinna' ye think that it would be a comfort to his cauld heart, in yon gruesome cage o' bolts and bars, if he had a tasting o't ?"

Cornylees having drank off his glass, and smacked his lips, gave his host a knowing wink, and said,

"Balwham, that'll do! Weel I maun allow that Knockwhinnie is a gude judge o' wine, in course now. Really this is *rosa solus!*" And he held out his glass to be filled again.

Balwham, in filling the glass said,

"I wonder if there's a possibility o' doing a service to the disjasket gentleman. I would gi'e you, Cornylees, a flask o' this to your dinner free gratis, if ye could help me in a kind matter."

The Laird professed his willingness to do any thing for any gentleman in straights, even without reward: "But really, Balwham," said he, "the very smell o' this cordial, in course now, would prick a man on to an adventure better than the rowels o' his spurs. What would ye ha'e me to do?"

"Weel, Laird," replied Balwham, "I'll no' be blate. I saw, frae the first day ye dieted in the Unicorn, that ye were o' a generous nature, and fond o' gude drink, sae I'll speak out. Could ye, in a sympatheezing manner, gang up to the Tolbooth, and speer for ane Johnnie Gaff, a decent bodie, that speaks Latin, and get him by hook or crook; even ye may gang the length o' a palmy wi' him, and I'll thole the cost—to let you see your auld frien', ye understand, Knockwhinnie!— and tell the winsom gentleman how I'm ready to do a turn for him, and that the best in a' the Unicorn is at his command."

"In course now, I'll willingly do that; but this wine, I see, will no' bide in the bicker."

Balwham poured out another bumper to the Laird; but having the fear of his business before his eyes, he only gave himself a small drop, which Cornylees saw with delight, as it was an assurance that the remainder of the flask was destined for him.

"In course now, Unicorn, I'll no' be backward in my errand; but dinna' ye think it would be kindly if I took a flask or twa up in my pouch? Ye ken, if I get na' a visibility o' the prisoner, in course now, Johnnie Gaff can tak' the wine in til him."

"'Deed," replied the Maister Balwham, "that's a friendly thought; and surely I'll no' let you gang toom-handed to yon dungeon o' dolorosity."

The Laird, taking hold of the flask by the neck, said,

"In course now, Balwham, ye're at your last dribble, but

I'll no' let this wine grow dead; it's o'er gude to be lost. In course now, being auld, it canna' be strong."

" I wouldna' trust it, Laird; but you west country folk ha'e baith big bellies and strong heads; sae ye may take your will o't."

" In course now," replied the Laird, beginning to give ocular demonstration in contradiction of his own axiom, " that age did not always imply the lack of strength, especially in wine."

" But, Laird," said the host of the Unicorn, " dinna' ye think it would be as weel to leave what's in the flask, till ye come back, for it's a stay brae frae this to the Tolbooth, and ye'll be nane the waur o' a drappie when ye come back."

" By my Lord, auld Unicorn! we'll ha'e then a fresh bottle. In course now,"—taking another glass—" here's leil hearts and gude wine."

" Weel, weel, that's a blithe Laird! Just gang awa', for ye ken my business disna' allow me to clishmaclaver. I hear customers in the house. Coming, gentlemen," and with these words he whisked out of the room; and Cornylees, with a blouzy countenance, made the best of his way towards the Tolbooth, where he had no difficulty in finding Johnnie Gaff.

Johnnie looked at him somewhat suspiciously, and turning round to one of the other halberdiers, touched his own forehead to signify that he was aware of the Laird's condition, and added—" But, *in vino veritas,* he can do nae harm."

Then addressing the Laird, he inquired whom he wanted; and Cornylees made him understand that he had brought a flask of wine from the Unicorn for a friend of the host's.

" Weel, I'll do any thing in a ceevil way to oblige the Maister Balwham, for there's no' a publican in the burgh o' Embro' that has sic a *ne plus ultra* o' discretion. Ye see what it is to ha'e a frien' in Court, sir."

" By my Lord!" exclaimed the Laird, putting his hand in his pocket, and giving Johnnie a piece of money from his purse, he added, as well as his subsiding intelligibility would allow him—" Ye're an honest fellow, in course now, and kens what's what?"

Johnnie, putting the money into his pocket, took him under the arm, and helped him to the foot of the stair, where calling for Lockie, he desired him to allow the gentleman, " as he has been discreet, to ha'e twa words with ane o' the prisoners."

Vol. I.—16

The Laird, as he clambered up the stair behind the jailer, said,—

"In course now, amang your blackbirds ye ha'e gotten my auld friend, Montgomery o' Auchenbrae, in your cage yestreen. Hech, but it's pitifu' to think o' the changes that befa' gude auld families. His father was a worthy man, left twa bolls, twa firlots, twa pecks, and twa lippies yearly frae the lands o' Capelrig to the monks o' the Abbacy o' Paisley for his soul's health!"

Here the remembrance of such benevolence and piety came softly over the Laird's heart and he began to weep.

"Ah!" continued he, "but sic things are a' gane by now; souls and bodies are laid in the kirkyard as if they were clods o' the valley. Oh, what'll become o' us, if, after a' this stramash that has been in the land, there should be a purgatory!"

Led by this to suppose it was Auchenbrae whom the Laird desired to see, and being come to the room where he was confined, Lockie opened the door, gave him admission, and having locked him in, went down to the ward-room, where the halberdiers were sitting.

"*Tempus fugy!*" cried Johnnie, starting up as he saw him. "I'll break the back o' this groat amang us. Marion Bickers has had a noble browst. Come, it'll just gi'e ilk a chappin and leave a bodle to the lassie."

Johnnie, accordingly, leading the way, followed by the other halberdiers, "all being forefoughten and exhoust," adjourned to the kitchen of Marion Bickers, where a tappit hen was ordered of her last brewing, "*pro bono publico.*"

CHAPTER LIII.

"For well you know this is a pitiful case."
SHAKSPEARE.

PUNISHMENT, whether well or ill-deserved, has always an unpleasant effect on the mind and temper of those who are obliged to endure it. Auchenbrae had scarcely been taken before the magistrates when his virtuous resolutions began to supple, and his high-mindedness to ebb. Before he was a couple of hours locked up in his dungeon, nothing remained of all the regrets and griefs which had hovered in his spirit as he sat alone in the twilight on the top of Arthur's Seat. Like the golden clouds of the evening, they had melted away, and were succeeded by the gloom of guilty desires, and he almost gnawed his hands with rage at his own folly in giving himself up so weakly to justice. But he still trusted by the powerful influence of his family he would be allowed to commute the penalties of the law. Instead, therefore, of being in any thing like a penitential mood when Cornylees broke in upon him, his mind was writhing with the spasms of vindictive thought. Not conceiving that his solitude was to be disturbed by a companion, and believing Cornylees to be another prisoner, he rushed upon him fiercely before he was well within the door, and shook him, as it were with the wrath and worrying of a mastiff, demanding to know why he was so obtruded upon.

The Laird recognised his voice, and still continuing his maudlin interjections, said—

" Hech! Auchenbrae; but I'm wae for you; I'm very wae, in course now; I'm wae for your father's son: oh, but I'm wae!

Auchenbrae knew his voice and flung him off, saying—

" And what the devil has brought you here, Cornylees?"

" In course now, I'll tell you: but oh, this is a black job. Alack! alack! in course now, I canna' help greeting: but it wasna' you, Auchenbrae, that I came to sing wally-wally wi'!" and stumbling along the floor he fell upon the truckle-bed in the corner.

Auchenbrae regarded him with something of disgust when he saw how utterly incapable he was of assisting himself, and returned towards the narrow grated window which looked up towards the castle.

" But in course now, I forgot the wine," said Cornylees; and he laughed, or rather yelled, at his negligence, as he lay on the bed. Then he cried, resuming his maudlin tone, " Puir Auchenbrae, the puir birdie that was catched in a girn, and is now in a cage!"

By these exclamations the prisoner discovered that he was only a visiter, and seeing his helpless condition, at once determined to turn it to his own advantage. Accordingly, he immediately began to pull off his jerkin, and to say that he was grieved to see his old friend so very unwell, advising him to undress, as he would be much better in bed. Cornylees dolorously assented to all that was proposed, and was presently stripped of his apparel, and before the operation was completed he was fast asleep. Auchenbrae lost no time in doffing his own and donning the garb of his friend, determined to watch the return of the gaoler ; for which purpose he armed himself with a bar wrenched from the grate.

In due time Robin Lockie returned, considerably elated by his share of the potations ; indeed he was in such a wavering condition when he looked in to bid the visiter come forth, that Auchenbrae had no occasion to use his weapon : on the contrary, he only pulled him in and threw him down beside the Laird, springing out at the same moment, and turning the key. He then stepped softly down the stair, lest any of the halberdiers should be on guard at the foot : nor was this a weak fear, for Johnnie Gaff was there, *in propria persona*, holding firmly by his halberd, and swinging to and fro, like a tree in the wind, with the effects of Cornylees' largess.

Auchenbrae paused to consider what he ought to do in such jeopardy, when he heard a rustling above, and the voice of Robin Lockie, crying to get out. Not a moment was to be lost. Johnnie Gaff too heard the alarm, and was turning round as well as he could, when the fugitive pushed him down with his strength, and leaped over him as he lay sprawling in the street.

The land, in which Mistress Marjory's house was the ninth story, stood in one of the wynds near to the Luckenbooths, and Auchenbrae escaped into it undiscovered. He ascended the nine stairs with more than his wonted agility, and beat on the door for admission, a peal that would have deafened the knocking of the biggest iron knocker that hangs from the mouth of the fiercest lion's head that frowns on a footman.

Hughoc heard the sound, and being the nimblest in the house, opened the door. Auchenbrae bolted in, and without saying a word, rushed into Mistress Marjory's bed-chamber, where he instantly began to denude himself of Cornylees' habiliments. The boy recognised him at once, and the uproar in the house at such an invasion was shrill and hoarse and vehement. Baldy, Father Jerome, Mistress Marjory, and her hand-maid, came forth to see the cause and occasion of the disturbance. Hughoc did not mingle in the fray ; but knowing it was near the time when his master would expect him at the Unicorn, where he regularly dined, ran off, primed with the news of this new adventure.

In the mean time the noise of the imprisoned jailor had continued with unabated violence, and had awakened Cornylees, while the fumes of the sherries were still clouding his brain. "In what direction has he fled?" was the universal cry; and in all directions the halberdiers ran for a short time in pursuit of the fugitive: it was in vain.

In the interim our host of the Unicorn had become uneasy; he knew the magic that was in his wine, and had seen it taking effect. He feared that it would master the discretion of Cornylees, and that he would himself be brought into trouble. This induced him to come up, in the short interval while his dinner guests were assembling, from the Canongate, to see what had happened at the Tolbooth, and he reached the door of the ward-room in the moment of alarm.

Johnny Gaff, on seeing him, pounced upon him like a hawk upon its quarry, crying,

"Here's a *soshy criminy!* Ye scoundrel Balwham, would ye take the bread out o' my mouth?"

"Whist, whist, Johnnie! there's been a mistake! Hech! but I'm in a flurry, and our gentlemen will be wud if I'm no at my post. Just, Johnnie my man, slip in wi' me, and I'll tell you a' about it. Ae Laird is just as good for a prisoner as anither!"

Johnnie holding him by the lapel of his jerkin, took him into the ward-house, and said—

"If I didna ken, Balwham, that ye were an honest man, I would make an example o' you *in modum peny.*"

"Hout, tout, Johnnie! speak mair like yoursel'! Knockwhinnie ye ken, your auld maister, was a true friend o' mine. I'm sure ye canna' hae forgotten the sprees he used to hae in the Unicorn, before he first gaed to France; could I hear o' his being in a dolefu' prison, and no do something to cheer him? Sae thinking that Cornylees was just the man to do the turn for me, I solaced him wi' a flask o' our best, to gang and see Knockwhinnie; but the wine proving right stuff, it ran awa' wi' the heels o' his understanding: and that's the even-down truth. But, if ye'll tak my advice, ye'll keep your thumb on the whole affair, and ne'er let on, but that Auchenbrae is still in the Tolbooth. It can mak nae difference to the likes o' Cornylees to keep him safe for twa or three days!"

"Wrangeous imprisonment, Mr. Balwham, what may come o'er me for that?"

"Poh! poh! my man Johnnie, we'll souther a' right wi' anither flask. At any rate thraw the key upon him for this day; and come ye down to the house belyve in the gloaming, and

I'll gie you sic a caulker o' Nantz as will gar your eyne stand wet-shod in your head!"

Johnnie who was still in the mists of Luckie Bicker's brewing, thought the proposition not unreasonable: so, after some farther discourse, the host of the Unicorn was permitted to return in time to give his wonted tendance on his guests.

CHAPTER LIV.

"Be it as you shall privately determine.
Th' affair cries haste, and speed must answer."
OTHELLO.

The agitation which intentions of guilt produce in their conception, comes of the rough handling with which the Devil eagerly grasps the chain of destiny, to drag the fated to their doom. It was so with Rizzio, who, after his interview with the Abbot of Kilwinning, when he had retired from the gallery to his own chamber for the night, was overwhelmed with compunctuous self-remonstrances. Alas! they only showed how firmly the adversary had made good his hold. For he deplored not the dangers to which his machinations would expose Chatelard; his prophetic remorse was all of the hazards that might involve himself; and the occasional fits of resolution to proceed no farther in the business partook, in consequence, more of dread than of contrition. But in the morning this qualm of morality had left him, and he resumed the intents and purposes of ambition with refreshed courage.

He knew that Chatelard regularly walked early in the gardens, to which he himself occasionally resorted at the same hour: but it was not with him so much a custom; nor indeed did method often appear in his actions, for it was a part of his system to be seemingly actuated by impulses, in order to obtain impunity from remark when he might happen to require it.

It were needless, therefore, to conjecture whether from design or purpose he chanced this morning to be in the gardens first but he was there some time before the young Frenchman made his appearance: other gallants of the Court were, however, walking in the parterre, but he avoided them. The weather indeed, was dull and anti-social in all its influences. A heavy gray mist rested on Arthur's Seat, and hung in masses along the front of Salisbury Craigs. The air was calm, and the smoke of the city stood erect on the chimney tops, like trees incrusted with hoar frost among the huge rocks of shattered mountains. The shrubs in the gardens were depressed with the last dews of summer; for the bright season was now over, and the dejected flowers were weeping to overflowing, as if affected with some moral sentiment of sorrow; not a chirp of bird or insect was heard save the hum of the bee, and it was sympathetic to yawning; a number of maidens were bleaching their new-washed clothes on the margin of the rill that flows in the meadow; but neither lilt nor laugh was heard from them; nor was jest or good-morrow exchanged with the briskest galliard that passed on the footpath beside them. The slow spirit of a soberness almost sullen touched as it were with torpor the springs of thought, and obscured the vision of the mind.

The effect on Rizzio, knit up as he was with stern purposes, was something like induration, insomuch that when Chatelard joined him he seemed almost repulsive.

"You look," said the Frenchman approaching, "as if this gray-mantled morning had displeased you."

"It must be so," was the reply; "and yet I have some cause for heaviness. I would, for the Queen's sake, this affair of Knockwhinnie was quietly disposed of; considering your openly professed affection for Adelaide, it surprises many that you take so little interest in it. Be assured, Chatelard, that such remissness makes some suspect the sincerity of your professions."

The Italian, in saying so, threw at him one of those deep-searching glances of his vivid eye which few could withstand, and perceiving that Chatelard felt the whole force of the insinuation, he added, with well-assumed carelessness, but with another look that proved how little it was so—

"It has been expected that by this time you would have employed your influence with the Queen."

"Influence! what influence can I have with her Majesty; yesterday Southennan talked to the same effect. How is it supposed that I have any influence?"

Rizzio darted at him one of his most penetrating glances, and hastily looking around to see that no one was near, said in a low impressive voice—

"It has been observed that the Queen, of late, takes much

pleasure in your music, and honours you with particular condescension."

"I am not conscious of receiving such favour," replied Chatelard, blushing, and turning aside to conceal his emotion.

"Come, come, my friend," rejoined the dark discerning Italian, in a free confidential manner. "It is not to be disguised; the whole Court have observed it:" and sinking his voice, he said significantly, "some bright change is expected."

"What change?" inquired Chatelard, with a throbbing heart.

"That the aurelia, still so insensible, shall soon be in motion, moving upwards; and anon on wing, and happy in the radiance of the sun."

"Would you have me swallow such a philter! I thought, Rizzio, you had a better opinion of my understanding."

"Nay, I did not say you were so weak as to love beyond loyalty; moreover, your heart is pledged to Adelaide, so you have freely confessed, no doubt to warn all of the Court from rivalry. Nor can it be imputed to you as a fault if the Queen——it would be too bold to say what I might, but there are few so likely as yourself to win favour in a lady's eye."

The agitation and confusion of Chatelard were extreme during this speech, which was delivered with all the craft of Rizzio, and with such illustrations in his looks and accents as would have left no cloud upon its meaning had it been less plainly expressed.

"Had this been said, Rizzio," replied Chatelard, recovering his self-possession, "at a drenched table, and in the presence of boon companions and flowing flasks, I might have answered you in a strain befitting the vanity of your suggestions; but here, in this cool morning, amid the universal freshness of flowers and dewy leaves, it is so much at variance with propriety that I am puzzled how it should be considered."

"Be wary," replied the Italian, calmly and collectedly; "we are in this country both strangers, something we have known of each other, and that good fortune is the patron on whom we both chiefly rely.. I pray you, therefore, to have some confidence in me. I do not ask you to tell me what it may be prudent to conceal, but by your conduct I shall guess if you understand me. It is manifest, though it may not be seen nor be thought of by those whom you have taken such pains to persuade you are enamoured of Adelaide, that——"

"What?" exclaimed Chatelard, panting with emotion.

"You love her not, not more than you do one of those roses which blush in your admiration! Chatelard, whether you give or refuse me your confidence, I will tell you that your loquacious fondness—as if love were ever else than dreamy, still, and meditative!—has not deceived me. It is a mask. In the name of friendship be not offended with my frankness; but leaving that and all other controversies, it may serve you to intercede for the father of Adelaide with the Queen. It hath already caused surprise that you take no part in a suit which all the household are so earnest in. Come what may of it, whether to gain thanks from Adelaide, or from Adelaide's father, or, let me say in your ear, to sound the Queen's bosom, it is a task that may not be delayed."

And so saying, without waiting for an answer, he parted from him, and returned into the Palace.

CHAPTER LV.

" For 'tis most easy
The inclining Desdemona to subdue
In any honest suit."

OTHELLO.

The Queen, after her interview with the Abbot of Kilwinning, passed an ill-omened night. The demon of the troubled time visited both her waking thoughts and her dreams. She was also grieved for Adelaide, and felt an obscure boding of sorrow coming to herself. Her couch was in consequence uneasy; and when the gray morning looked in at her lattice, it seemed like the visage of a widow. The day was indeed widowed of the sun.

She rose at an unwonted hour, unrefreshed and dejected, with an intention of sending for Adelaide to accompany her into the gardens; but the unhappy night which she had herself spent induced her to prefer, on this occasion, the Lady Mary Livingstone, who was of a gayer nature, and much better calculated to dissipate the hazy griefs which dimmed her spirit.

They descended into the garden soon after Rizzio had left

it; and while Chatelard was musing on the advice, which even to him appeared bold and strange, they approached towards the walk along which he was slowly and musingly moving.

Mary Livingstone directed the Queen's attention towards him, and remarked that he too seemed to have been molested in his sleep; adding, " Doubtless, partly from the same cause which darkened your Majesty's dreams. In sooth, I should account his love but light, if he felt not for me, were I Adelaide."

" Ah !" replied the Queen, " is it not truly so ? Alas, poor Adelaide! I doubt the love burns but in one heart. It has sometimes seemed to me as if he felt peevishly under the beam of her too evident attachment."

" He is a froward and unsteady varlet," replied Mary Livingstone. " Beshrew me! were Adelaide to take my counsel, he should feel that I could resent it ; especially as Southennan, who is the properest man of the two, would lay his neck under her heel for the tithe of half the beneficence she is wasting on that effigy of a lover—reality he cannot be, to talk so loudly of his love, and yet never vouchsafe one private whisper to warrant its sincerity."

" Yet," said the Queen, "he is not one of those blushing youths that would die at a frown. I think in all my experience, even in France, where men are not too much afflicted with bashfulness, I have not met a gallant with more levity in his eye: he often disturbs me. Verily, I must find out a way to repress his bravery, or lose his servitude, which I cannot well spare, both on account of his clerkship and his music. He is truly exquisite on the lute ; and I would have him oftener when my spirits are sad, and need soothing, but that he grows too bold and familiar."

" Your Majesty has a lively discernment: we simple maidens of the anti-chamber have not however, detected such ventures about him. He is as docile as grimalkin, and as capricious as a poodle. I would as leif hold discourse with a popinjay, as seek to draw out his wits; and I doubt what he has, are not often at home. He is so absent and thoughtful ; and yet there is not that gentleness in his pensive humour, especially to us ladies, that should come of one that knows his love would be acceptable. What his clerkship may be to your Majesty's comfort, I know not ; but truly he is like one of the supporters of your Majesty's arms, the unicorn: it hath but one born, and he but one faculty, his music! It is a poor thing for so goodly a person to be able only to sing."

"Go to, Livingstone," said the Queen; "thou art letting thy tongue run away with thy discretion, he may have other cares than thou hast guessed at. We prove in ourself that there may be vexations enow in Scotland, without the anxieties of love."

By this time they had come almost close up to Chatelard, who, absorbed in his own meditations, was not aware of their approach till he turned to walk back. The Queen, at the moment, was not disposed to notice him farther, and the etiquette observed among her ladies, while in her presence, deterred Mary Livingstone from addressing him with more than a silent smile of recognition; but before they could move away he was on his knees, and supplicated the Queen with great fervour to pardon the father of Adelaide.

"I thought it was so, Livingstone," said the Queen. "But rise, Chatelard, we are better disposed to accede to your request than such humble entreaty would seem to anticipate. It is thought convenient that his trial should proceed, and by the result, our mercy, if it be needed, shall be fully granted.

Emboldened, by this assurance, he ventured to reply with renewed entreaty, beseeching her Majesty, if the matter were so determined, to allay the agitation of Adelaide by extending the indulgence at once.

What the Abbot of Kilwinning urged upon that point had not been lost on the Queen; on the contrary, she saw in the formality of a trial, the result of which it was predetermined should not be carried into effect, only a solemn mockery of justice, and, in consequence, the supplication of Chatelard produced a commnesurate impression.

"In truth, Livingstone," said her Majesty, turning towards that young lady, "there is something too fine in this policy of a trial as a preliminary to a pardon. I have thought much of it all night; and my thoughts incline, for that and for many other reasons, to order the pardon to go forth at once.

Chatelard on hearing this re-urged his suit with redoubled zeal, and Mary, a little tired with his importunity, in the weariness of her spirit, said—"It shall be so." And, as was customary on conceding a grace, she presented him her hand to kiss, and then suddenly moved on without speaking until she was some ten or twelve paces away, when she said—

"Livingstone, this must be ended. That young man regards me too much as a woman, and forgets the humility due to my station ; let him not be permitted to come to us in the evening, nor until I shall have had time to consider of him."

Mary Livingstone smiled, and said,

" If he is in love, I'll wager my best earrings, and they are those your Majesty gave me, that it is with one that may not be named."

" Thou art too pert," said the Queen, " I prithee sheathe that sharp tongue of thine. I like its glitter, but its edge is dangerous."

Chatelard, exulting at the ready compliance with his solicitation, immediately left the garden ; for, although he conceived his success to be entirely the effect of the Queen's partiality, he yet imagined that she did not choose to evince it, and that her tacit reproof was not incurred by his presumption, but was only a sacrifice to decorum.

In leaving the garden he met Adelaide advancing to join her Majesty, and with great warmth of satisfaction, congratulated her on the merciful determination of the Queen. At this juncture the Prior of St. Andrew's accidentally joined them ; but he partook not of their pleasure, when informed of Chatelard's success. On the contrary he appeared much discomposed, and moved with rapid steps towards the parterre in which the Queen was walking. Suddenly, however, he checked his speed; and returned ; while Adelaide, full of gratitude and rejoicing, hastened to join the Queen. He had not, however, come many paces back, when he was met by the Earl of Morton, who had just parted from Rizzio.

" He is a deevilish clever hempy, that Dauvit Ritchie, or Rizzio, as we must name him amang the foreigners. The fellow has the e'e of a hawk, and a tongue that would wile the bird frae the tree. I'm thinking if we kent a thought more about him, and he would cast off his papistry, we might make something of him."

"If," replied the Protestant Prior, " you make it his interest, his papistry would soon be doffed. It's a loose cloak and sits easy on him."

" Say ye sae, James. Aye, ye're gayen auld farrent yourself; for I think wi' you that Dauvit's no very strait-laced. I would make his plack a bawbee, to hae servitude wi' his gudewill. He would make a capital tool in any bit plottie that the need of the times may oblige us to get up for the gude of the realm."

" Take care," replied the Prior, " that, in making him your tool, you don't find that he makes himself your master."

"Eh! James, but for an honest lad ye hae ill thoughts of other folk. I tell you that Dauvit is a very kind-hearted tod in his way, and I'm sure would do meikle for gratitude. The Queen has not amang a' her red-legged aliens a leiler servant."

"I hope he will prove so, my Lord," replied the Prior; "but I have got grievous tidings just now. Come with me, and I will tell you," and with this they quitted the garden together.

CHAPTER LVI.

"What is station high?
'Tis a proud mendicant; it boasts and begs:
It begs an alms of homage from the throng,
And oft the throng denies its charity."

OTHELLO.

THE determination of the Queen to pardon Knockwhinnic was soon generally known, and excited very little attention; for it had been expected by many as almost a necessary consequence of Adelaide being her favourite attendant. Southennan, before the news had reached him, went early to the Palace, where he found the Count Dufroy alone in the gallery, and in evident agitation, not on account of the pardon, but the manner in which it had been granted on the solicitation of Chatelard.

"I shall not long remain in Scotland," said the Count; Adelaide will soon be under the protection of her father, and my advice is no longer likely to be useful to the Queen. And were it as acceptable as I once flattered myself it was, your Scottish nobles are too apt to resent the interference of a foreigner in their national concerns, to make the condition of his service honourable. He must submit to suffer and endure, which does not well accord with the humour of my temper."

Southennan, with unaffected regret, lamented the decision of the Count. Having acquired some knowledge both of France and England, he was sensible of defects in the manners of his countrymen, and was of the number of those who considered the intercourse with the former, which had been rendered so free while her Majesty resided there, as a public benefit. The arrival, with the Queen, of so many accomplished adherents and members of her French Court, he also regarded as calculated to continue that desirable intimacy.

"Perhaps," said Dufroy, "had I still enjoyed the confidence of the Queen, the roughness of the nobles might not have so soon hastened my determination : but that being no longer allowed, my occupation is gone. To her, as the widow of France, my homage and service were due, and they were loyally performed ; but I have no right nor claim to meddle in your troubled politics, nor motive to remain where I can only expect mortifications."

Southennan, not being yet aware that the pardon of Knockwhinnie had been granted upon the solicitation of Chatelard, or, at least, was so believed, expressed some degree of surprise at hearing the Count thus open in his dissatisfaction, and said—

"It gives me pain to think worth like yours should be so little esteemed here, that the apprehension of neglect moves you to leave us."

"Not the apprehension only, but the experience. Know you not that the Queen has pardoned Knockwhinnie?"

"I have heard it rumoured that she was likely to do so," replied our hero ; "but I did not fear it would have been felt by you so much as an injury, though acquainted with your sentiments respecting the nature of his offence."

"Then you cannot have heard in what manner it has been granted?"

"I have been just told that it was suspected : nor has it surprised me; so much has her Majesty been urged to it ; last night she almost conceded as much to the Abbot of Kilwinning."

"Had she done it then," replied the Count, "and on the solicitation of one so valued, I might have been at question with myself on the propriety of the grace ; but to refuse so good and great a man—a dignitary both of the church and realm—and yield on the first asking to one scarce better than a menial ! Oh, shame!"

"Was it to Chatelard?"

"Would it were in my power, Southennan," cried the Count, with irrepressible emotion, "to give you a rude answer, for imputing the possibility of such weakness to her who, till this fatal morning, hath ever been untarnished as the pearl that can receive no stain. Alas! 'tis even as you have said."

"It grieves me exceedingly," replied our hero, "to see how deeply this matter affects you. I am in part to blame, having been the first to entreat the mediation of Chatelard?"

"Why did you that? What suggestion moved you to think his mediation might be of any efficacy?"

The Count, in asking these two simple questions, appeared alarmed, and suddenly thrown off his guard, which Southennan observing, became confused; for he could not well answer either, without explaining his suspicions of Chatelard's attachment to the Queen.

"Have you noticed aught particular in her conduct towards him?" resumed Dufroy eagerly, without waiting for an answer.

"Not in hers," replied Southennan.

"But in his towards her? Is it so?" exclaimed the high-minded Frenchman; and he added, in a tone of affecting compassion, "Truly, it must be so. The destiny of her family hath overtaken her: but it mitigates the misfortune that he had not dared of his own presumption to be so bold."

While they were thus speaking Rizzio happened to pass across the gallery, and Dufroy beckoned him to draw near.

"Can you, Rizzio," said he, as the Italian approached, "tell us how this miracle came to pass?"

"What miracle! of what do you speak, my Lord?"

"How! have you not heard that the Queen, upon the intercession of Chatelard, has ordered a pardon to Knockwhinnie?"

"Impossible!" exclaimed Rizzio. "Presumptuous as he is, he durst not venture on so bold a suit."

"Had he not been sure of success," rejoined the Count, with a sigh.

Rizzio, however, remarked that he might have been incited by his declared admiration of Adelaide.

"Yes," interposed Southennan: "it must be as you say." And he recapitulated what had passed when he spoke with Chatelard on the subject.

But the Count gave little heed to what he said, which Rizzio observing, rejoined—

"Might it not have happened from the importunity with which her Majesty has been so beset? She may have granted the pardon from annoyance, being unable to resist farther solicitation."

"It is well and loyally said," rejoined the Count, "but how came he to have been so bold as to interfere at all. It is, in its complexion, an adventure not reconcileable to common causes."

Rizzio, conscious of the subtle part he had himself played

in the business, was visibly disturbed by this remark—so much so as to attract the attention of Southennan, who, in ignorance of the cause, said respectfully—

"May it not be, my Lord, that this whole affair is too largely estimated? To you the rashness of Knockwhinnie must be a thing of serious recollection; but the world, which has no special interest to remember it, will set little account on the pardon."

The Count looked at him gravely, and then added, with a steadily-sustained voice, approaching to severity,

"Think you it is the pardon that molests me; or that I can repine because the Queen has exercised the fairest attribute of royalty? No, Southennan; I am grieved only because she has conceded to Chatelard a favour refused to better men, and that too, in opposition to the wisdom of her Chancellor. It is a thing in itself, perhaps, of small importance; but, by the manner in which it has been done, it may be made serious. I pray to Heaven that evil may not come of it."

All this anxiety appeared to our hero disproportioned to the cause. He thought there was, perhaps, something of envy in the tone with which Dufroy expressed himself concerning Chatelard, especially as he was persuaded that some lurking resentment still affected his disposition towards Knockwhinnie. But the alteration in the countenance of Rizzio, when the Count remarked that the proceeding of Chatelard was not to be accounted for by ordinary causes, haunted his imagination; and he suspected the Italian of being in some way a party to it. He, however, said nothing, deeming it prudent, in the dissatisfied mood of the Count, to refrain from any question or observation which might have the effect of exciting it still more. Dufroy himself was not inclined to continue the conversation.

The more the Count reflected on the transaction, he became the less content with his information. He discerned, by his innate perspicacity, that some peculiar instigation had influenced the conduct of Chatelard; and he was convinced it could not be the effect of that attachment only which he professed to cherish for Adelaide: for he was in common with many of the Court doubtful of its sincerity. In fine, he could not but entertain a derogatory suspicion of the Queen; and he resolved, in consequence, out of the true and dignified loyalty with which he was actuated, to avail himself once more of the freedom she had allowed to him on all occasions, to point out the hazard she ran of incurring the forfeiture of those golden opinions which her people seemed then so willing to treasure up for her.

CHAPTER LVII.

"Officious fool! that must needs meddling be
In business that concerns not thee."
COWLEY

SOUTHENNAN parted from Rizzio at the same time that the Count Dufroy retired. He was too well satisfied that Knockwhinnie had received a pardon, to feel any particular interest in the means by which it had been obtained. It seemed to him, however, that Rizzio had been in some way accessary to the application of Chatelard, although he evidently wished not to be known in the transaction. These reflections passed through his mind as he was retiring, and some degree of curiosity was in consequence excited. He was too ingenuous himself to suspect others of sinister intentions, nor could he account for the embarrassment which the Italian appeared to suffer, as if an act of benevolence had been one of shame.

As he went out at the portal of the Palace he met Chatelard in a state of flushed exultation; his countenance was elated, and a vibratory emotion visibly affected his whole frame; his eyes were eager and unsteady, insomuch that he could neither look another firmly in the face, nor bear the inquisition of any eye bent upon his own. There was moreover an increased style of courtesy, bland and patronizing, in his manners, and an altogetherness of grace and condescension in his air and deportment which, to our hero, seemed incomprehensibly disproportioned to his circumstances. Their reciprocal salutations were stiff in their mode; with more, however, of an apparently assumed restraint on both sides, than of any actual diminution of intimacy.

Southennan congratulated him on the success of his application to the Queen, and cordially thanked him from himself for the favour he had been the means of procuring for his friend Knockwhinnie, adding, however, in a tone tinged as it were with irony,

"This cannot fail to secure your triumph with Adelaide.

It must have been to you delightful to tell her how you had succeeded."

"I have scarcely seen her since," replied Chatelard.

"Was it not in her name you applied to her Majesty?"

Chatelard seemed a little confused at this question, but evidently gratified; for he answered in a simpering, half earnest, half jocular voice, that it was almost by an accident he had succeeded; and he then described how he had met the Queen and Lady Mary Livingstone in the garden.

"But how came you to think of applying at all, every other application having failed?"

"Of my own modesty," replied the Frenchman with a laugh, at the same time blushing, "I should not have undertaken the adventure; but Rizzio encouraged me."

"Indeed! to help your suite with Adelaide!" said Southennan. "But I must carry the glad news to her father," and with these words he wished Chatelard good morning.

He was not surprised to hear that Rizzio, who had so recently affected to know nothing of the pardon, had really been at the bottom of the whole affair: and he could only account for his equivocation, by supposing that he was afraid lest his interference might be resented by the Count Dufroy. It seemed a strange business: and yet there was nothing in the incidents of it which ought to have surprised him, farther than that Chatelard should have dared to approach the Queen after so great a dignitary as the Abbot of Kilwinning had been obliged to retire unsatisfied.

These thoughts passed rapidly through his mind, as he slowly ascended the Canongate. In the midst of them a hand was familiarly laid on his shoulder, and, on turning round, he found Rizzio at his side in a state of inward enjoyment, with that expression in his countenance of crafty gratification which is always the consequent and disagreeable index of triumphing cunning. Our hero on seeing him also smiled, and inquired, why it was that he had pretended to Dufroy ignorance of Chatelard's proceeding, when in fact he was the father of it.

Rizzio was, as the sailors say, taken aback by this sudden question, not being aware that Southennan had met with Chatelard; but he was ever too much the master of himself to be long disconcerted, and accordingly with his wonted readiness he replied,

"In sooth, Southennan, it seems but a thankless service to do you any good. You know that Chatelard's passion for

Adelaide is but mere painting—a semblance without substance—a glow without fire or flame; while yours is all fire, and yet shows no gleam which she regards. Now what if I thought it would help your cause, to show her to what aim his wishes were bent? Might it not have the effect to turn her eyes in some measure from him to you, by making the Queen's true sentiments visible?"

This was said in so artificial a manner, that Southennan was convinced of its insincerity, and felt as if there were something in the very nature of Rizzio to be distrusted; he made no answer farther than by remarking, in a jocular manner, at the same time looking impressively at the Italian,

You are too shrewd: such management as love seems to require at Court, would frighten simple country folks to fly from it. It is enough to make the snared bird struggle until it has snapped the springs."

Rizzio, however, had by this time fully recovered his self-possession, and contrived, as they walked up the street together, plausibly almost to persuade Southennan that he had been animated, in the incitement of Chatelard, entirely by a wish to serve him.

"In truth, my friend," said he, "let us look at this affair reasonably, as we should do. The fellow has talked so much of his wonderful heart, and ardent passion for Adelaide, that no one believes a word he says about it; and you and I have not been unobservant spectators of who is the true loadstone of his affections; and, therefore, so that her Majesty be not offended, all stratagems are fair to get him out of your way."

By this time they had come near the entrance to the Unicorn, at the door of which Balwham was accidentally looking out. Rizzio, being bound to the house, walked at once in, and Southennan would have proceeded up the street, but Balwham came hastily to him, and said,

"A word wi' you, Southennan!" who accordingly turned, and went with him into his private room.

"Oh dear," cried Balwham, as soon as they were in and the door shut; "Isna' this a dreadfu' concern; a' the town's in a hobbleshaw; the Provost is louping about the Council-room like a frightened water-wag-tail in a cage, and the Bailies and a' the Counsellors are sitting in a consternation, like puddocks on the lip o' a well."

Our hero's thoughts running on Knockwhinnie's pardon, attributed this alarming state of the magistracy to something unpopular which had resulted from it; whereas, the worthy host was speaking of the amazement which the discovery of Auchenbrae's escape, and the substitution of Cornylees had occasioned. Under this misconception, Southennan replied,

"I hope the agitation will soon subside, and that the people will incline to the side of mercy."

"I would fain houp sae too; but I am just terrified out o' my seven senses, for they say that the instigators, and a' that were art and part in it, are to be brought to condign punishment."

"Oh! you don't say so. Is it already come to that?"

"Na, for any thing I ken to the contrary, Thomas Noose, the hangman, may hae gotten his commands; for Johnnie Gaff is dismissed. Puir creature! he was here telling me o' the interlocutor, and was in sic a panic that he would hae dwamed had I no gi'en him a tass o' Lode-vie."

"You astonish me."

"'Deed, I 'm astonished mysel', for he counselled me to tak leg bail."

"You!" exclaimed Southennan, "what had you to do with it?"

"Me! I'm an honest man, Southennan, a lang-respected member o' the Vintners' Company: what I did was for the best, and scaith was as far frae my thoughts as frae the brain's that's unborn."

"But, in the name of all that is wonderful, how came you to be, in any way whatever, connected with Monsieur Chatelard?"

"Eh! preserve me, is he in the frying-pan too? What's his transgression, and how cam' he to be conjunc' wi' us?"

"With us—with you," cried Southennan; what is that you say?"

"Hae ye no heard that the Tolbooth had been broken, and Auchenbrae aff and awa', leaving Cornylees, your ain friend, for a nest-egg to cleck mischief out o'? I thought the whole town kent this, and I was just keeking out at the door to see if there was a crowd coming to take me up, for flee the country I winna'. I hae a conscience void o' offence, baith to man and beast. And what would come o' the Unicorn and a' the gentlemen? It's fash enough, wi' a' my forethought, o get their dinner as it is!"

Southennan perceived that they had been at cross purposes, but without explaining the source of his own misconception, he inquired into the particulars of Balwham's story, and immediately after quickened his steps towards the Tolbooth.

CHAPTER LVIII.

"I am undone; there is no living, none,
If Bertram be away!"
SHAKSPEARE.

In the mean time the Count Dufroy had requested an audience of the Queen; which her Majesty, unconcious of having done any thing equivocal, was surprised at. It had been the custom of the Count, at all hours after she had come for the day into the presence-chamber, to obtain admission without the formality of asking leave. She was still more surprised when on his entrance she saw by his countenance that something had occurred to disturb him; and there was a thoughtful sadness in his eye which made her feel as if she had given occasion for some remonstrance or exhortation. In consequence, she stood waiting until he should address her. A reception so reserved and so unusual was attributed by him to the consciousness of error; and he spoke to her with an unwonted degree of solemnity:

"Madam, I have just been informed that your Majesty has been pleased to extend your royal mercy to Knockwhinnie."

The Queen with a pensive smile replied that it was so.

"But," said she, "I cannot hope that your stern justice will applaud the deed!"

"It is not to the clemency by which your Majesty's benevolence has been gratified, that I would present to object; But I would be assured that it has not been granted in the manner I have been informed."

The Queen smiled, and said, with her usual affability, "And what is the contingency if it has been so?"

The Count paused to meditate his answer, and then said, with profoundest respect, "I shall return to France."

The Queen looked in the utmost amazement, and then said, struggling with emotion,

"Can I have done any thing to cause me to forfeit such estimable service? Count Dufroy, I have here few friends; there may be around me honest men, but I know not yet which to trust; and therefore, I beseech—I would almost say command, you—to stifle that intention, granting that I have erred. But in what consists my error?"

Dufroy paused again before he replied, and then said,

" In conceding to the young man Chatelard the pardon of Knockwhinnie, in opposition to higher and graver advice; and after your Majesty had deemed it expedient to refuse the application of the Abbot of Kilwinning."

A blush overspread the Queen's countenance. She discerned at once his whole mind, and saw the construction of which her compliance was susceptible; but she added firmly,

" How know you that the pardon was granted at the request of Chatelard?"

" It is so stated: if it be not true, none of all your Majesty's faithfulest subjects will more rejoice than myself."

" Is there, then," exclaimed the Queen, in evident alarm, " so much importance fastened to my consenting that the pardon should go forth, merely because Chatelard was made the agent of my intention."

" It is to be deplored that your Majesty had not consented to the solicitation of the Abbot of Kilwinning, or to any other of your Court, rather than to that presumptuous young man."

" Heavens!" cried the Queen, with increasing alarm, and resuming her seat, " What do your words portend? What is said of me, that you, from that true loyalty which I have ever experienced, should deem it needful to speak so plainly? Tell me, what is it that you think? As for the babbling gossip of the Court, I account it but as the east wind."

" And that is blighting," replied the Count; and advancing towards her, he knelt, and she extended to him her hand to kiss. " Pardon my boldness! In these times and in this country I fear your Majesty may not lightly consider the mildew of such detraction; there are many of high power and great influence in the kingdom, who look upon your Majesty's religion as an obstacle to the ascendency they covet in the state. I grieve, more than words can express, that Chatelard is so honoured by your Majesty."

The Queen started up, her eyes flashing with indignation, and after hastily moving across the room, said,

" My Lord—no, let me rather say my friend—speak with your wonted candour! I will not disguise that I am now well aware of all you think; but on what show of evidence or of conjecture dare any one suspect, that in this grace I was infected with any unbecoming motive?"

It was impossible for the Count not to feel the sincerity of this impassioned address; and he immediately replied, with his old accustomed freedom, that of her Majesty nothing derogatory had ever been insinuated till this unfortunate occurrence; and he added more sedately, that the ill-placed attachment of Chatelard was evident to the whole Court.

"Has it, indeed, been so observed?"

"Then," said the Count, dryly, "your Majesty knows it, and yet encouraged his presumption, by granting to him a request denied to others?"

"Encouraged! Can the Count Dufroy say so?" And she burst into a passion of tears, exclaiming, "Yes, I have done wrong; but it was not from any estimation of him: my spirit was worn out by the importunities I have endured: his application was but the atom that turned the scale. Do with him, Count, as you deem most accordant with my honour; let him be instantly sent forth the kingdom."

The Count stood for some time viewing her with compassion, as she walked across the room, abandoned to grief, and indulging her tears. In the midst of this agitation, she suddenly halted, and, turning towards him, said,

"I see, in doing that, we shall only give warranty to the venom of slanderous tongues; and yet what else can be done?"

Dufroy attempted to console her, by assuring her of his conviction, that as there had been no oblivion of her own dignity, the story might pass away, when Chatelard should be sent home to France.

"But," said the Queen, "how can he remain here without some change being shown to him in my demeanour. Will not that be observed? and how can I stoop to dissimulation with his audacity? No, Count, there is no other course; send him forth the kingdom!"

"I fear there is none other," added the Count. "I did think a middle course might have been steered; but your Majesty's condition forbids all expediency."

"Then let him be at once informed his service is dispensed with, and that he come no more to this house. I can make sacrifices of things dear to me when need requires; but this is none. I did not suspect that this measureless arrogance had been so noted by others!"

Adelaide entering at this moment, the Count retired, and the Queen, bending upon her shoulder, again wept bitterly.

"Alas, Madam, is he still so ruthless?" said Adelaide; "while all the Court rejoice in your Majesty's clemency?"

The Queen, instead of replying to this appeal, abruptly inquired,

"Have you observed in Chatelard aught towards me to justify the malice of evil tongues. Answer me plainly, for you can have been no negligent observer of him. You do not answer. It is enough, and I forgive you. But tell me sincerely, have ever I, by accident or inadvertency, showed him any particular favour?"

"I have not myself," replied Adelaide, with diffidence and gentleness: "but I have been told, that on more than one occasion your Majesty has been too gracious to him."

"Who dare say so?" cried the indignant Queen. "It is some idle fancy of the ante-chamber. Twice he touched my hand with too much of fellowship; and I made him conscious he was too bold. But such foolery cannot be again: he is dismissed my service; and by the first vessel and favouring wind he goes to France."

This sudden intelligence smote the enthralled heart of Adelaide; she became pale, and, almost swooning, sank into a seat.

"Why, thou weak girl, what hath overcome thee? Verily, thou art more forwards in thy love than accords with modesty. I take blame upon myself for not reproving thy too-well seen affection before. He is not worthy of it; nor doth it much enhance thy discretion, to have made such a choice, when one so far surpassing him in all manly and mannerly excellence is pining unrequited. Think no more of him; and give such heed to young Southennan as in time may draw that cherished folly from thy breast. But I will urge thee no farther at this time, than that thou should prepare to meet thy father with happy looks; for doubtless he will presently be in quest of thee here. Go then, and set thy countenance in better plight. It would argue little for thy good-nature, which has hitherto been all gentleness, to meet thy father with a visage so wobegone. Go at once, and send in Livingstone. Verily, she is a better companion for one who hath discarded a suitor, than the hapless nymph who long in hopelessness hath loved too well!"

CHAPTER LIX.

> ———" With what greediness
> Do I hug my afflictions! there is no mirth
> Which is not truly seasoned with some madness."
>
> FORD.

KNOCKWHINNIE, from the time of his incarceration, had suffered much in his mind. He did not greatly dread the ignominy, nor the result of his trial, being persuaded that as his offence had not proved fatal, the indictment would be restricted to an arbitrary punishment, according to a prerogative which the public prosecutor of Scotland, the Lord Advocate, has long exercised; but still his anxieties were sharp and manifold.

He had been now for a long period of years absent from his lands and castle, which, in the interval, had fallen into decay. He thought the Lord Kilburnie, his father-in-law, had acted towards him with a rigour that could only be justified by some great wrong, and he was unconscious of having committed any towards him. He considered him as the spring of all his domestic misfortunes, by having, as he supposed, influenced the Lady Ellenor to remain in Scotland when she was so earnestly entreated to come to France. His heart was also troubled on his daughter's account, both with respect to the state of her affections, and the relationship in which she stood to the Count Dufroy by the adoption; for habitual reflection, even after he had ascertained the innocence of that high-minded nobleman, made him still think of him with something of the heat and irritation of an enemy. But the chiefest source of his annoyance arose from the confinement.

Accustomed to the freedom, activity, and adventure of an outlaw, he felt as if his spirit were girded within a hoop, and he moved in agitation through his gloomy chamber, like a wild bird when first imprisoned. This physical suffering, however, for it was of that nature, though arising from the ineffectual struggles of his mind, subsided in the course of the first night, and by the time Southennan was admitted to him, a gloomy melancholy had succeeded to the vivid emotions and sudden fluctuation with which he was at first so violently affected. In its calm, however, there was no peace. It was like the unwholesome fen, which in its sullen silence breathes forth infection. He became afflicted with misanthropical antipathies; his reminiscences were sour and indigestible; and his spirit, sickened with the nausea of self-dissatisfaction, revolted against the world for the sufferings he endured, unjustly disproportioned, as he thought them, to the extent of his errors.

When Southennan entered he was standing near the grated aperture of his dungeon, into which a dim reflection of the sun from the glass of an opposite window shone with a dull and sallow lustre upon the ruins of his tall and manly form; his arms were folded on his breast, and his head was slightly bent in rumination.

On hearing the door opened he turned round his eyes without changing his position, and on observing that it was not the jailer who entered, he assumed a proud attitude until his visiter had come into the light.

Our hero advanced with cheerfulness; and, animated with the news he had to tell, held out to him both his hands. Knockwhinnie coldly acknowledged the warmth of his friendly eagerness, and with a seeming reluctance touched only one of them.

Southennan, though sensible of this ungracious return, suppressed his feelings, and joyously told him that the Queen had consented to his immediate pardon, and that he might expect his release in the course of the day.

At this important information the mood and temper of the prisoner underwent no immediate change. He heard it with apparent indifference, and only inquired for his daughter.

"How is this Knockwhinnie?" said Southennan; "you hear me as if I were the bearer of some household errand."

"'Tis even so, and I am grieved at being unable to return your zeal and ardour with but the words of thankfulness. This dark, damp, narrow chamber, and the prohibited door, have chilled my heart with a morose torpidity. I am a thing dischaged of its uses—of a humour to be pleased with a sight of miseries."

Southennan remonstrated with him on the indulgence of such unprofitable fancies, and endeavoured to dispel his dejection; but until the officer with the pardon had been admitted, all argument was unavailing. His countenance, however, then brightened, and when he reached the open street, he fetched a long deep breath, as if he drank a refreshing draught, and said,

"How delicious is the free air—how wide the path of liberty!"

They had proceeded together to Knockwhinnie's lodgings, where he dressed himself for the palace, being eager to visit his daughter, before Southennan recollected what the host of the Unicorn had told him of Cornylees's confinement. This induced them to separate; for our hero was constrained by his humanity to hasten back to the Tolbooth.

Knockwhinnie had not proceeded many steps down the street, when suddenly recollecting that he had neglected to inquire to whose mediation he was indebted for his pardon, he hastily turned back, and overtaking our hero, begged to be informed as to this.

The question was discordant to Southennan's feelings. It implied a sense of obligation on the part of Knockwhinnie: but he, however, disdained to conceal that his gratitude was due to Chatelard.

"Say you it was the young Frenchman!" exclaimed Knockwhinnie, "he who professes such affection for my daughter?"

Our hero felt, as it were, the chill shadow of a cloud overcome his spirit, and he replied in a marked and emphatic manner,

"The same. He does indeed openly profess the most inextinguishable love—too openly."

He would have added more, but was restrained by motives of delicacy. He knew that the gossip of the Court would soon set the professions of Chatelard in their proper light; and he therefore rejected the suggestion as mean, which prompted himself, though but for an instant, to think of deteriorating the grateful sensibility by which Knockwhinnie was then animated. But his fears were awakened; for by this time he had learned enough of Court practices to think it not beyond the scope of probability, that Chatelard would accept the hand of Adelaide, to disguise the daring and ambitious passion which he had cherished for the Queen, and which he so sedulously but insufficiently endeavoured to conceal.

END OF VOLUME I.

STEREOTYPE WORKS

RECENTLY PUBLISHED BY J. & J. HARPER.

COOPER'S SURGICAL DICTIONARY. 8vo.
MOORE'S LIFE OF BYRON. 2 vols. 8vo.
ROBERTSON'S WORKS. 3 vols. 8vo.
GIBBON'S ROME. 4 vols. 8vo. With Plates.
HOOPER'S MEDICAL DICTIONARY. 8vo.
CRABB'S ENGLISH SYNONYMES. 8vo.
BROWN'S CONCORDANCE. 32mo.
MILMAN'S HISTORY OF THE JEWS. 3v.18mo.
LOCKHART'S NAPOLEON. 2 vols. 18mo.
SOUTHEY'S LIFE OF NELSON. 18mo.
LIFE OF ALEXANDER THE GREAT. 18mo.
NATURAL HISTORY OF INSECTS. 18mo.
HOUSEKEEPER'S MANUAL. 12mo.
PARKES'S DOMESTIC DUTIES. 12mo.
PELHAM; THE DISOWNED; DEVEREUX; PAUL CLIFFORD; and FALKLAND. 9 vols.

Stereotyping, and nearly ready,

RUSSELL'S MODERN EUROPE. 3 vols. 8vo.
GOOD'S BOOK OF NATURE. Improved. 8vo.
HOSACK'S LIFE OF CLINTON. 18mo.
COLDEN'S LIFE OF FULTON. 18mo.
BUSH'S LIFE OF MOHAMMED. 18mo.
PAINTERS AND SCULPTORS. 18mo.

New-York, October, 1830.

SD - #0049 - 020625 - C0 - 229/152/12 - PB - 9780259432005 - Gloss Lamination

1,000,000 Books

are available to read at

Forgotten Books

www.ForgottenBooks.com

Read online
Download PDF
Purchase in print

ISBN 978-0-259-43200-5
PIBN 10816693

This book is a reproduction of an important historical work. Forgotten Books uses state-of-the-art technology to digitally reconstruct the work, preserving the original format whilst repairing imperfections present in the aged copy. In rare cases, an imperfection in the original, such as a blemish or missing page, may be replicated in our edition. We do, however, repair the vast majority of imperfections successfully; any imperfections that remain are intentionally left to preserve the state of such historical works.

Forgotten Books is a registered trademark of FB &c Ltd.
Copyright © 2018 FB &c Ltd.
FB &c Ltd, Dalton House, 60 Windsor Avenue, London, SW19 2RR.
Company number 08720141. Registered in England and Wales.

For support please visit www.forgottenbooks.com